TAINTED BLOOD

Enyo screamed in agony and rolled over, staining the snow scarlet with his blood and feeling his broken bones grind together. Sobbing in agony and sudden terror, he stared up through the one eye left to him as a horrible apparition of a female Vampyre, dressed all in white, snarled at him through dripping fangs. Her lips curled back in a savage grin as she raised a sword in her hands and swung it down at him like a baseball bat. Enyo put up a bloody, broken arm to fend off the blow, but the razor-sharp *katana* sliced through the arm and then his neck like a hot knife through butter. Enyo's head catapulted through the air, staring back down at his ruined body lying shattered and bloody in the snow. It was the last thing he saw before the darkness opened up and swallowed him.

TAINTED BLOOD

JAMES M. THOMPSON

PINNACLE BOOKS
Kensington Publishing Corp.
http://www.kensingtonbooks.com

PINNACLE BOOKS are published by

Kensington Publishing Corp.
850 Third Avenue
New York, NY 10022

All Kensington Titles, Imprints, and Distributed Lines are
available at special quantity discounts for bulk purchases for
sales promotions, premiums, fund-raising, and educational
or institutional use. Special book excerpts or customized
printings can also be created to fit specific needs. For details,
write or phone the office of the Kensington special sales
manager: Kensington Publishing Corp., 850 Third Avenue,
New York, NY 10022, attn: Special Sales Department, Phone:
1-800-221-2647.

Pinnacle and the P logo Reg. U.S. Pat. & TM Off.

First Pinnacle Books Printing: August 2004

10 9 8 7 6 5 4 3 2 1

Printed in the United States of America

The great questions of the day will not be settled by means of speeches and majority decisions . . . but by iron and blood.

Otto Von Bismarck (1876)

Prologue

The Assault

The Vampyre assault force gathered in the darkness around their leader, softly stamping their feet and flapping their arms to ward off the frigid Canadian chill.

As the lightly falling snow gathered on their shoulders, Michael Morpheus whispered in a voice harsh and gruff with suppressed bloodlust, "They probably won't be expecting us, but just in case, go in fast and hard and take them out!" He hesitated, and then he added through clenched teeth, "And if it's possible, save the redheaded one for me. I have a special treat in store for her and I don't want her to die too easily." This last comment brought a knowing smile to the lips of Morpheus's second in command, Theo Thantos.

As they began to move up the road, the human shapes began to melt and coalesce and morph into their Vampyre forms. They were all clutching swords, axes, and guns in their claws as they loped through the frigid darkness in knee-deep snow, growling softly at the thought of the fresh blood awaiting them ahead.

Theo put his hand on Christina Alario's arm and slowed her down until they were bringing up the rear of the column of Vampyres when the group reached the road leading toward the cabin. The rough-hewn log structure was barely visible through the falling snow, but they could all clearly smell the odor of the wood fire going inside. The added aroma of the Normals' warm blood in the building caused their mouths to water in anticipation of the feast that was to come.

Morpheus, confident of the element of surprise, took the driveway, Marya Zaleska at his side, and waved the others into the dense forest that surrounded the cabin. "Spread out and approach the cabin from different directions," he urged in a low voice.

Gerald Enyo and Louis Frene circled off to the left and jumped over a dry creek bed, crouching low. They'd moved only thirty yards when a bright light came on in a tree just ahead of them, blinding them with its glare.

"What the hell?" Enyo said, taking another step forward and tripping the black wire strung between two trees. A tremendous explosion from five feet in front of him sent a huge cloud of smoke and dirt into the air, along with several hundred four-inch nails.

The dense cloud of nails blew Enyo and Frene off their feet, shredding and flaying their skin and tearing their arms and legs to ribbons.

Enyo screamed in agony and rolled over, staining the snow scarlet with his blood and feeling his broken bones grind together. Sobbing in agony and sudden terror, he stared up through the one eye left to him as a horrible apparition of a female Vampyre, dressed all in white, snarled at him through dripping fangs. Her lips curled back in a savage grin as she raised a sword in her hands and swung it down at him like a baseball bat. Enyo put up a bloody, broken arm to fend off the blow, but the razor-sharp *katana* sliced through the arm and then his neck like a hot knife through butter. Enyo's head catapulted through the air, staring back down at his ruined body lying shattered and bloody in the snow. It was the last thing he saw before the darkness opened up and swallowed him.

Louis Frene, who took the brunt of the explosion and most of the nails, couldn't see anything as he opened his mouth and screamed for help, for both of his eyes were ripped from his skull by the force of the explosion. He didn't even see the blade of TJ's *katana* as it whistled through the air and tore his head off clean at the neck. He was dead before his screams quit echoing through the forest.

Jean Horla and Peter Vardalack, walking next to each other in the deep woods on the opposite side of the trail, jumped and stared as lights began to come on all around them and Frene's and Enyo's screams came on the heels of a tremendous explosion off to their left.

"What the fuck was that?" Horla asked, just as a white demon rose out of the snow between them, a silver blade flashing in the light as he swung it at Horla's head. Horla ducked and managed to get his own blade up in time to partially deflect the blow, causing it to glance off and embed itself in his left shoulder down to the bone.

"Peter," he screamed, his voice rising in pitch as the waves of pain seared through his brain and blood spurted from his shoulder as from a fountain. "Help!"

Peter Vardalack took one look into the demon's red-rimmed, hate-filled eyes and he dropped his sword and began to sprint for the cabin just ahead, thinking if he could just make it to the door and inside he might be safe.

Horla shook his head and fought off the pain long enough to swing his sword one-handed at Pike, who couldn't seem to get his machete loose from Horla's shoulder. Pike stuck his left arm up and caught the sword on it, wincing at the sound of the bones in the arm breaking and the lightning jolt of white-hot pain it sent up into his shoulder.

Pike let go of his machete and grabbed a handful of Horla's hair in his right hand, jerking backward to bring his chin up and expose his neck.

He leaned forward before Horla could strike again and ripped Horla's throat out with his fangs, jerking his head from side to side like a dog worrying a bone. Finally, the vertebrae in the neck gave way with a crunching sound and the head came loose in his hand. Horla's body crumpled to the ground with Pike's sword still embedded in the shoulder.

Vardalack made it to within fifteen yards of the cabin, running and looking back over his shoulder, panting more from fear than from fatigue. "Oh Jesus . . . oh Jesus!" he chanted, praying to a God he'd forsaken dozens of years before.

From in front of him there came a loud double-explosion, and he felt as if he'd been kicked in the head by a mule. The force of the twin loads of 00-buckshot took the top of his head off along with the left half of his face and one ear. His body spun half around, hit the snow, and flopped like a fish, his screams of pain and fear sounding only as gurgles through his shattered mouth and throat.

Screeching like a rabbit caught in a wire snare, he reached up and sleeved the blood and tissue from his good eye just in time to see a Normal bending over him, a grimace of distaste on his face.

"Please," Vardalack croaked through broken stubs of teeth, spraying blood onto the night air. "Help me."

"I'll help you straight to hell, you bastard!" Shooter said, reaching down to grab bloody hair in one hand while with the other he sliced through the neck of the monster in front of him.

Vardalack died without his customary grin, for he had no lips left to smile with.

As the explosions and bright lights and screams pierced the night, Theo Thantos and Christina Alario slowed even more, letting Morpheus and Marya and John Ashby pull ahead of them on the road to the cabin.

He put his hand on her arm and whispered in her ear, "I think from the sound of things, we ought to get the hell out of here."

She snarled and bared her fangs as the smell of burning flesh and fresh blood wafted toward them on the night breeze, making her own blood boil and her mouth water. She shook her head and tried to pull her arm away. "Blood!" she growled, red drool running down her lips.

Theo tightened his grip on her arm and shook it. "Don't be a fool, Christina," he said urgently, trying to keep his voice low so Morpheus wouldn't hear. "They're ready and waiting for us. It's a trap and we're all going to die here if we don't leave!"

After a moment, Christina's eyes cleared and she forced the bloodlust aside and nodded her head. "As much as I hate to leave a good fight, I think you're right," she growled.

They turned and loped back down the road toward their car as fast as they could, still holding hands, their claws intertwined.

Marya Zaleska heard them leave and she touched Morpheus on the arm and pointed at their departing forms. He growled low in his throat. "Let the cowards go. I'll deal with them later."

As Morpheus and Marya continued up the road toward the cabin, with John Ashby a few steps behind, a Normal man in a white suit stepped out of the darkness, a shotgun cradled in his arms.

"Morpheus, you sick bastard!" Matt yelled at him, recognizing the beast that had tried to take Sam from him.

Morpheus grinned and crouched, his sword swinging in a slow arc in his right hand. "You fool," he snarled through fangs dripping scarlet drool, moving toward Matt and bringing the sword up while Marya circled to the other side. "Don't you know guns can't kill us!"

"No," Matt said though clenched teeth as he brought the barrel of the shotgun up, "but they can certainly fuck up your entire night!"

Morpheus rushed him, standing up straight just as Matt fired so the buckshot took him in the chest and arm instead of the head, blowing the sword out of his hand and stopping him in his tracks as if he'd run into a brick wall.

Morpheus staggered under the blow and twisted to the

side, leaking blood all over the snow. He glanced down at the gaping hole in his chest and the mangled claws on his right arm and he screamed in fury. He bared his fangs and sprinted forward, ignoring the burning agony in his chest until he was right in front of Matt. He swung his left hand, claws extended, with all his might and swiped Matt across the chest and shoulder, laying him open and knocking him to the ground.

"Now you die, you fucking Normal!" Morpheus growled, baring his fangs and leaning over a helpless Matt.

"No-o-o!" screamed Sam, racing out of the woods next to the road and leaping onto Morpheus's back, tearing at his eyes and face with her claws before he could get to Matt.

Marya snarled and raised her sword, looking for an opening to take Sam's head off, when Pike ran out of the darkness, his right arm hanging bent and useless, his machete in his left hand.

Finally, Marya saw her chance, and she swung at Sam's exposed neck, but Pike lunged forward and parried the blow with his weaker left hand. Marya's sword knocked Pike's lighter machete from his grip, and she spun around and jerked her own sword backhand and slashed Pike across his left arm, cutting it to the bone.

Pike grunted in pain and stepped between her and Sam, who was still clinging to Morpheus's back. He growled and bared his fangs in hate with both his bloodied arms hanging useless at his side, defenseless against her. As he snarled his defiance in the face of certain death, Marya grinned and slashed sideways with her sword, cutting the tendons to his right leg, causing him to topple to the ground next to Matt.

Pike rolled to cover Matt with his body, trying to protect him as Marya screamed in fury and raised the sword for the final killing blow.

Before she could strike, a shotgun exploded from behind her, the buckshot catching her in the back and blowing her forward onto her knees.

Ed Slonaker ran up the road, his still-smoking shotgun in

one hand, and his K-Bar Assault knife in the other. As he ran toward her, knife extended, she lashed out one-handed with her sword and caught Ed in the thighs just above his knees, doubling him over and knocking him to the ground.

Marya climbed slowly to her feet, blood pouring from dozens of wounds in her back and again raised her sword with both hands, this time aiming at Ed.

Kim Slonaker, a few yards behind Ed, dove headlong into Marya's body, both of them rolling over several times until Marya came up on top, her sword point at Kim's neck, her fangs dripping crimson drool as she snarled and growled, her eyes wild and crazed.

John Ashby, who'd stood by, transfixed by the drama until now, stepped quickly forward and grabbed Marya's wrist, stilling her deathblow to Kim. "Marya, that's enough!" he growled, jerking her to her feet.

"But . . ." she yelled, rage filling her eyes as she jerked her hand, trying to escape his grip.

"I said," John said firmly, snatching her sword from her. "There's been enough killing tonight. Let it go!"

Marya glared at him for a moment, her fondness for him warring with the bloodlust in her veins, until finally she ducked her head in submission and put her arms around his neck, collapsing into his arms, feeling for the first time the pain in her back.

John looked over her shoulder at Kim and Ed lying next to each other and smiled. "That was for old times' sake, and for friendship," he said, picking Marya up in his arms and loping down the road out of sight.

Sam and Morpheus continued their death struggle, rolling around in the snow among the bodies lying on all sides of them. Their claws were locked on each other's throats, their fangs snapping and biting and tearing at their flesh, seeking a killing wound.

Morpheus, weakened by the gunshot wound to his chest and unable to fully use his right arm, jerked his head forward and snapped, his fangs tearing a deep chunk of flesh from Sam's right cheek. She howled in pain and brought her right knee up as hard as she could between Morpheus's legs. Morpheus screamed in agony and doubled over, letting go of Sam's neck with one hand as he grabbed his crushed genitals.

That was all the opening Sam needed; she dipped her head and turned it sideways and sank her fangs as deep as they would go into the soft flesh of Morpheus's neck, screaming with anger as she ripped out his trachea and esophagus and tore the major arteries to his brain in two.

As he crumpled to his knees and stared up at her, his eyes beseeching her to let him live while he tried vainly to stem the pulsating jets of blood from his neck with his left hand, Sam calmly reached behind her, picked up the sword Marya had dropped, and in one lightning blow cut his head off.

Without another look, she dropped the sword and turned and ran to take Matt's bleeding body in her arms, pressing on the gashes in his skin to stop their bleeding, telling him over and over how much she loved him and that she'd never forgive him if he died on her.

As John Ashby loped through the knee-deep snow of the Canadian forest, he glanced down at Marya. She'd fainted from the intense pain of the 00-buckshot slugs in her back and chest and had reverted back to her human form as her Vampyre blood tried to heal itself. Even now, with all that had happened over the past hour, he felt a stirring in his loins at the sight of her helpless in his arms. She was so beautiful, with her long, flowing blood-red hair and pale skin, her cheeks and nose dusted with faint freckles that only served to accentuate her emerald-green eyes.

He shook his head to clear it of his building lust. He had to be careful—they might still try and follow him to finish it all once and for all.

He got to where they'd left the cars just as Theo Thantos and Christina Alario were getting into one of the big, black

Explorers. They too had already changed back into their human forms.

"Hey, guys," Ashby called, moving swiftly toward them, "wait up."

Christina glanced over her shoulder and looked at them over the roof of the car. "Aw, shit," she said under her breath. "That bitch and her boyfriend survived."

Thantos looked across the car at her and grinned evilly. "That's okay, Chris, maybe we can use them."

She ducked her head and got in the front seat with him. "If you say so, but I swear . . . some day I'm going to tear that bitch's throat out."

She closed her mouth and stared straight ahead out the windshield as Ashby jerked the rear door open and slipped inside with Marya still unconscious in his arms. "You mind giving us a lift back to town?" he asked, pulling Marya close to him to keep her warm as he reverted to being human. "I don't think I can drive with Marya like this."

Thantos glanced at Christina and smirked as he replied, "Sure, Johnny, no problem."

He jerked the wheel to the side and made a wide U-turn in the road, spewing clouds of snow to the side as he raced back down the road toward the main highway.

Christina turned in her seat and looked back at John and Marya. "Is she hurt bad?" she asked, trying to keep her hatred for the other woman out of her voice.

Ashby pulled his hand away from Marya's back and saw it was covered with blood. "Yeah, she took a pretty good hit with a shotgun. She's gonna need some time to heal."

"That could be a problem, Johnny," Thantos called back over his shoulder. "That other Mountie friend of yours is gonna be calling the troops out to look for us, so we're gonna have to make ourselves scarce in a hurry."

Ashby shook his head. "Uh-uh. Marya won't be able to travel for a couple of weeks at least, and besides, Ed won't be organizing a search for us. It'd be far too dangerous to bring any attention to what happened out at the cabin, so all we have to do is go to ground somewhere out of sight for a while until Ed gets tired of looking on his own."

"He's probably right, Theo," Christina agreed, turning back around to face forward. "The Mountie is going to be too busy trying to cover all this up to worry about who might have escaped."

Thantos grunted. "By the way, Johnny, did anybody else make it out alive?"

Ashby shook his head. "Not as far as I could see. I think we're the only ones."

"How about Morpheus? Did he manage to kill any of the others?"

Ashby snorted. "Not hardly. The last I saw one of the females was separating him from his head with a sword."

"Then our quest to stop the Vampyre vaccine from production has failed?" Christina asked.

"Only for the time being," Thantos answered grimly, "but I'm not through with them yet—not by a long shot!"

Chapter 1

Elijah Pike stood at the window in the loft of his cabin near North Waterford, Maine, and stared at the loons floating serenely on Jewett Pond just beyond his backyard. He sighed. Lately, there had been too much going on to allow him many moments like this—quiet contemplation of the beauties of his home state.

It'd only been a few weeks since the battle in Canada, where he and his friends had defeated Michael Morpheus and his band of killers in their quest to keep the Vampyre vaccine from being produced.

As one of the baby loons paddled up to its mother and climbed up on her back to nestle down between her wings and garner a free ride, Elijah smiled and turned back to his desk. His leather-bound journal lay on the blotter, still open to the spot where he'd quit reading the night before. He'd carried the journal with him for over two hundred years and it chronicled his life as a Vampyre.

He took a deep swig of his coffee and sat down, idly thumbing through the pages, his mind elsewhere. When he got to the beginning of the book, where he described how he'd been transformed into a Vampyre while trapped overnight in a blizzard not too far from this very cabin over two hundred years before, the words written in India ink on pale, yellowed parchment caught his eye: "My name is Elijah Pike," the book began, "and the story I am about to put down is strange and incredible, but true nevertheless."

Pike chuckled as he read the words. It was still strange to be once again using his real name. When he'd found out what kind of monster he'd become those two hundred plus years ago, that he'd have to kill for the blood he needed to survive, he'd left his wife and family behind and had gone on the run, crossing the nation while leaving a trail of dead bodies behind him.

In order to survive without being apprehended, he'd begun using aliases and had carefully documented and arranged dozens of false identities. He only recently had gone back to his true name and it was still taking some getting used to.

I changed back to my own name, he thought, when I decided to never again kill an innocent Normal to satisfy my hunger. Only when I pledged to never again dishonor the Pike name did I feel justified in using it again.

He glanced back down at the journal and thumbed ahead to the pages he written when he'd finally discovered how he'd been transformed; how by drinking the blood of another Vampyre creature, one could be infected with a mutated virus carried by bacteriophages that would change one's own DNA and forever make him a monster. The infection with bacteriophages brought on an illness that would cause the never-ending hunger for human blood, the extreme sensitivity to sunlight, the body's amazing ability to heal itself of almost any wound, the psychic abilities, and last, but certainly not least, the virtual immortality that was oftentimes more a curse than a blessing.

He snorted. The unwanted but permanent infection was responsible for the creation of another race, one whose members often considered themselves to be superior to the Normals on whom they fed.

An infection, furthermore, that up until now had neither cure nor any amelioration other than death by beheading— something not many Vampyres would willingly endure to rid themselves of the curse.

There had been no cure for thousands of years, that is, until he and his friends had come upon some new research by Dr. Bartholomew Wingate at McGill University in Canada that offered, if not a cure, at least a chance to cause the sickness to go into hibernation, to stop the hunger and keep it hidden—to prevent the need to kill in order to survive.

In sudden anger, Pike slammed the journal shut and gnawed on a thumbnail as he stared unseeingly out the window, his mind a jumble of thoughts. How could he have been so blind as to believe that all other Vampyres felt as he did—full of self-loathing at their murderous thirst for blood? Why hadn't he realized that some members of his race actually relished their bloodlust, in fact even living for the thrill of the hunt, the quick satisfaction of the kill?

He'd naively offered up his serum, his "cure" that would enable all Vampyres to once again lead normal lives, though not actually become normal again. He'd told them joyfully that they would never have to be at war with the Normals again, would never have to hunt and kill, to rend and tear and suck the life out of innocents ever again.

He tasted the coppery saltiness of blood and took his finger out of his mouth without looking at it. He should have known there'd be those like Michael Morpheus and his cohorts: Animals who relished their superiority over Normals, who considered humans to be their rightful prey, monsters who could never allow his vaccine to become available—at least not without a fight.

Thus, the first battle in what Pike had come to call the Vampyre Wars had been fought in a snow-covered forest in Canada a couple of weeks ago. The first battle had been won, but the war was just beginning and Pike knew it was going to be a long and bloody one, for there were many of his race who feared the vaccine would be the end of their race as well as their way of life.

He leaned back in his chair and thought about his friends who'd given up their professions and their own way of life to help him in his quest to make the vaccine available to all who wanted it. They were the only allies he had to fight the Vampyre army, and he wondered if they were enough:

TJ O'Reilly was short, standing only about five-feet-two-inches, and had tousled black hair that was usually covering half her face. The beautiful and brilliant internal medicine doctor had been in her third year of residency when Pike, going by the name Roger Niemann then, kidnapped her and began to transform her into a Vampyre, intending to make her his mate for life.

Samantha Scott, a doctor of pathology, was TJ's best friend and roommate. She was five and a half feet tall, with reddish brown hair, freckles, and emerald-green eyes. She was on the fast track to become the youngest head of a department at Baylor College of Medicine when Pike came into her life.

Matt Carter stood five-feet-eight-inches tall and had an average build and a pleasant though not handsome face. He'd been an emergency room physician and assistant professor of emergency medicine when he and Sam had been drawn into Pike's web of killings back when he was still living off the blood of Normals. In his defense, Pike had even then tried to take only the lowest dregs of society—criminals, prostitutes, and those he determined deserved to die.

Shooter Kowolski, Matt's best friend and a homicide detective on the Houston police force at the time, had joined in the hunt for Pike after he'd kidnapped TJ. Shooter was twenty-five at the time, dark-skinned with a perpetual five o'clock shadow, and was of medium height and build. His dark, curly hair and blue eyes made TJ think he looks like a young Tony Curtis.

As it turned out, Pike remembered, with an involuntary shiver, they'd found him living on his boat, the *Night Runner* and had almost succeeded in killing him as they rescued TJ from his lair.

He shook his head ruefully. The experience had changed Pike's life. He decided to never again allow himself to kill for his food, electing instead to put all of his energies into discovering some way, some magic potion or elixir that would allow him to conquer the hunger that invaded his every waking moment.

Now, here they all were. In a strange twist of fate, the doctors and the cop had come to be friends with Pike and to sympathize with his desire to help other Vampyres to stop having to kill to survive. The doctors had given up their practices and Shooter his career in law enforcement to help Elijah make his vaccine available to all who needed and wanted it.

In so doing, they'd crossed paths with Michael Morpheus, who in his insane desire to stop the vaccine's production, had kidnapped Sam and managed to transform her into a Vampyre like Elijah and TJ before she was rescued.

Pike's lips pressed tight as he thought about the sacrifices his friends had made to help him on his quest. They were very special people indeed.

Downstairs, Samantha Scott was leaning over, stirring the coals in the fireplace with a poker, when a pair of hands caressed her hips.

"You know you shouldn't bend over like that in front of me," Matt Carter said from behind her, his voice husky with lust.

A light laughter from the kitchen door on the other side of the room caused Matt's face to blush furiously. TJ O'Reilly just shook her head as she laughed and tried to cover her mouth.

"Jesus," she said between chuckles, "I thought Shooter was the only one who went berserk at the sight of a woman's butt."

Trying to regain his dignity, Matt glanced over at her and said, his voice dripping with disdain, "I wasn't berserk, I was only . . . uh . . . mildly stimulated."

Sam straightened up and turned, her hands on her hips and her right eyebrow cocked as she stared at her lover. "Only mildly stimulated, huh?" she said, her voice rising to that dangerous pitch where a man knows he'd better tread lightly or risk losing an important part of his anatomy.

Just then, Shooter Kowolski came out of the bathroom door, wearing sweatpants and a towel draped over his shoulders. His dark, curly hair was still damp from the shower. "Uh-oh, Matt," he called, winking at TJ, "Sounds like you've dug yourself another hole, podnah."

In spite of himself, Matt laughed. "Oh, and I guess you'd know, Shooter, since you're the resident expert on putting your foot in your mouth."

Unfazed, Shooter ambled over to put his arm around TJ's shoulders. "Yeah, but I'm cute enough to get away with it, Matt my boy. You're not."

Sam's face softened and she let her eyes drift down to the front of Matt's pants. "Oh, I don't know, Shooter," she said, not looking up. "He is sort of cute, standing there, all mildly stimulated."

At that, Matt crossed his hands in front of his lap and all four friends broke out laughing. After a minute, TJ managed to say, "I've got hot cocoa in the kitchen, if anyone's interested."

Shooter, who'd never been known to pass up a chance to eat, said, "Hell, yes, I'm interested," and started toward the kitchen, followed by the others who were still laughing together.

Chapter 2

John Ashby sat at a table in a dark corner in a small bar on the outskirts of Banff. Other than the fact that he was almost six-feet-four-inches in height, John looked perfectly ordinary. His hair was brown and slightly thinning on top and he had broad shoulders and a thick chest, but he wasn't so big that people took notice. In fact, he had the ability to completely blend in with his surroundings, a feat he'd used to his advantage many times in his previous occupation as a member of the Royal Canadian Mounted Police Force.

He took an occasional sip of a whiskey and soda as cover while he watched the other patrons closely. He had come to his particular bar because he wasn't known here, and he was looking for a special couple—the kind of people who did frequent this particular establishment.

He wanted a young couple that did drugs for a couple of reasons. First, their abrupt absence wouldn't be too unusual in those circles, and if they were eventually missed or their bodies were somehow found, their deaths would just be put down as a hazard of their living on the edges of society in the Canadian drug culture. Druggies in Canada weren't known for their long life expectancy.

He narrowed his eyes to concentrate and cast out with his mind, searching for just the right people in the crowd on the dance floor. There were no shortage of drug users among the patrons, in fact, the majority of people in the bar fit that description; but he needed some who were in need of a fix, some who wouldn't look a gift horse who offered them one in the mouth.

Suddenly, he found them. Both the man and the woman dancing off in a corner by themselves were bored and slightly anxious from not having scored any dope yet this evening. They were already starting to feel the first twangs of withdrawal as their habit made itself known. John could smell the woman's anxiety sweat from across the room and the man's fidgety movements and darting eyes gave his need away as clearly as if he'd worn a sign saying, "Will work for dope."

John's mouth watered as his habit also made itself known. The hunger was getting insistent and needed to be assuaged sooner rather than later. He needed some blood and he needed it now!

He pulled a small pad out of his jacket pocket, wrote a few words on it, and got up from his table. As he walked to the door, he brushed past the couple and pressed the note into the man's hand so no one could see.

John proceeded out into the parking lot, walking slowly toward the car he'd parked in the far corner, away from all the other automobiles.

He could hear the couple's footsteps crunching on the gravel parking lot as they followed him, and he smiled to himself. He'd written on the note that he had some good shit out in his car if they wanted to party with him. He could sense the man's excitement and hostility building behind him and smiled again. Perfect. The couple was planning on ripping him off and stealing his dope. Good, he thought. The little shits would deserve what they were about to get.

John fancied himself a good and honorable man and always tried to take prey that were somewhat bent, that he could at least pretend deserved what he was about to do to them. It was a matter of pride with him that innocents had nothing to fear from him, only those with larceny, or worse, in their hearts would ever be his victims.

John had his hand on his car door when the man behind him stuck a gun in his ear.

"Hold it right there, you son of a bitch!" the man growled, easing back the hammer on the small revolver to punctuate his demand.

John put a worried look on his face, raised his hands and turned around to face the couple.

"Hey, what is this?" he asked, pretending to be frightened. "I just asked if you wanted to party," he added. "Didn't mean to piss you off or anything."

The girl grabbed the man's left arm and snuggled up tight against him. "Hurry up, baby," she whined. "Make him give it to us. I'm startin' to hurt really bad."

"Give us your shit, asshole, or I'll blow you head off!" the man said in a harsh voice, the barrel of the gun shaking as if the man had a chill. He was sweating and the acrid smell of his need surrounded him like a fog.

John had to force himself not to smile at the man's tough-guy act. He could read the man's fear in his mind as clear as if he'd spoken it out loud.

"Sure, sure mister," John said. He turned his head. "I've got it in my trunk."

"Well then, hurry up and open it," the punk ordered, pointing toward the rear of the car with the pistol.

"Okay," John said and he pulled out his keys and moved to the rear of the car. "Are you sure you want to do this?" he asked. "After all, I didn't do anything to you."

"Make him hurry baby," the girl whined. Her nose was beginning to run and she sleeved it off on her arm. "I need a hit real bad." She was almost jumping up and down in anticipation of a needle to quench her pain.

As the trunk lid popped open, the man shoved John out of

the way and bent over to look inside. He straightened up and whirled around aiming the gun at John's stomach. "Hey, what is this?" he almost screamed. "There's nothing there!"

John smiled and shrugged as he glanced around the lot to make sure no one was watching. "Sorry, buddy," he said in a friendly voice. "I lied. I don't have any drugs."

"You son of a . . ." the man started to say, his finger tightening on the trigger.

Quick as a rattlesnake striking, John snatched the pistol from the man's hand and whipped it backhanded across his face, slashing his cheek and knocking him to his knees. John sighed and raised the pistol and brought it down hard on the top of the man's head.

The man dropped like a stone. The terrified girl put her hands to her mouth and started to scream. John grabbed her throat in his left hand and squeezed just hard enough to cut off the blood supply to her head but not hard enough to crush her larynx and kill her. She made a few gurgled cries, and her legs flopped around as John held her up off of the ground, and then her eyes rolled back and she fainted.

John hurriedly stuffed them both into his trunk and shut the lid. He climbed behind the wheel of the car he'd stolen just for this occasion in case someone managed to get a license plate number and he pulled slowly out of the lot. It would have been easier to kill the couple, but he wanted them both alive. It would be much more fun that way.

John drove for several miles, turning off the highway just before he reached the city limits of Banff. He followed a dirt road still covered with eight inches of snow for almost a quarter of a mile until he came to the log cabin nestled on the edge of the National Park just outside Banff.

The cabin was a rental, but since it was used mainly in the spring and summer, John hadn't bothered registering as a guest. He'd simply broken the lock and moved in when Marya had been wounded in the fight several weeks before.

She'd needed a place to rest and let herself heal, and the place had to be remote so they could feed without being bothered by any nosy neighbors.

The female Vampyre and current love of John's life, who had given herself the name Marya Zaleska after Dracula's daughter, was standing in the doorway waiting for John. She was dressed in a flimsy, white nightgown and her voluptuous figure could plainly be seen through the transparent cloth.

John killed the engine and stepped from the car, his lust already starting to build when he spied his mate waiting for him. Her bright red hair, pale skin covered with freckles, and brilliant green eyes made his knees weak whenever he saw her.

"Do you need any help?" she called.

"No, I can handle them," he replied, his voice growing husky with desire at the thought of a night of feeding and sex with Marya.

She smiled and brushed her long hair from her face with a casual swipe of her hand. "Good." She turned and started to walk away, glancing back over her shoulder with a sultry smile as she added, "I'll be waiting in the bedroom for you, lover."

Twenty minutes later, the unconscious couple were lying side by side on the double king-size bed in the master bedroom of the cabin.

John had stripped to his briefs and Marya was still wearing the nightgown as they stood at the foot of the bed and stared down at their guests.

"Should we do one now and save the other for later or do them both together?" John asked.

"Hmmm, I think both together, darling," Marya replied.

"It's been a long time since we had a double." She hesitated and then turned to him and gave him a long, slow kiss as she fondled his groin. "And I do so love to watch you work," she mumbled against his lips as he grew hard under her touch.

They separated and each moved to opposite sides of the bed and lay down, John next to the female and Marya next to the male. They each began to caress their partners awake, using their mind-control powers to quiet any fears or misgivings their guests might have.

As the young man lying next to Marya awakened and glanced at her with wide eyes, she pursed her lips and kissed him on the cheek as she snuggled closer to him, pressing her breasts against his chest. "Hi," she said sweetly. "What's your name, sugar?"

"Uh . . . Jerry," the boy answered, looking around at his still-unconscious girlfriend lying next to him being caressed by John. "What's going on here?" he asked, jumping a little as Marya's hand moved down his stomach to his lap and began to gently knead his genitals.

"Why, my friend told me he asked you and your lady friend if you'd like to party," Marya said innocently. "Would you like to party with me, Jerry?" she asked, slipping her hand inside his trousers to take hold of his penis.

As his penis grew hard, Jerry nodded vigorously and reached over with his hand to grab Marya's right breast roughly. "Hell yes!" he answered, his need for a fix of dope temporarily forgotten.

"Easy, boy," Marya said as she began to take his clothes off. "That's not a football you're holding," she said glancing at his hand on her breast. "Be gentle."

Within minutes she had him completely naked. She gently disengaged his hand from her breast and moved on the bed until she lay on top of him with her legs straddling his head and his face buried between her thighs. She held his penis in her hand and slowly licked the head as she stared across the bed at John, her eyes full of lust and desire.

John's partner was just coming awake, her face screwing up in terror at the sight of John lying next to her. "Easy, easy," he said in a low voice, calming her fears with his mind and his hand's gentle touch as he caressed her breasts. "We're just going to have a little party, and then I'll give you your fix."

Her face relaxed a little and she glanced at Jerry next to her going after Marya for all he was worth.

"What's your name, little one?" John asked, trying to get her attention off what was going on next to them.

"Maggie," she replied, rolling over to face John, her eyes still worried.

He slowly unbuttoned her blouse and pulled it open to reveal her braless breasts. He lowered his head and took a nipple in his mouth and began to suck on it while he undid her jeans and slipped them off. Soon she was lying naked next to him, moaning as he kissed and sucked her breasts and caressed her between her legs with his hand.

After a moment, she pushed him back and leaned over him, jerking his briefs off and taking him quickly in her mouth. She began to pump her head up and down furiously until John used his hands to slow her motion, saying, "Easy, Maggie. We've got all night. There's no need to hurry."

She slowed and began to kiss and lick and suck more gently, still moaning deep in her throat when John lowered his head and returned the favor by putting his mouth on her sex and doing some kissing and licking of his own.

This went on for a short while, John and Marya staring into each other's eyes as they made love to Jerry and Maggie.

Then, just as Marya began to shudder in the first throes of an orgasm, she nodded at John and she pushed Jerry back down on his back and straddled him, using her hand to guide his penis deep inside her.

John did the same thing, lying Maggie back down on her back and climbing between her legs, impaling himself within her with one quick thrust.

As the two couples bucked and thrust and made furious love, Marya leaned to the side and gave John a deep kiss, and then both of them began to change into their Vampyre forms.

Jerry and Maggie didn't notice anything at first, until Maggie felt the size of John's penis begin to grow inside her. It felt good initially, but soon the enormous size began to cause her pain and she opened her eyes to see what was happening.

When she saw the monster lying between her legs, his fangs dripping red saliva, his bloodshot eyes staring at her with bloodlust, she opened her mouth to scream.

Before she could make a sound, John lowered his head and fastened his fangs on her neck, rending and tearing as the coppery sweetness of her life's blood spurted into his mouth. His hips kept pumping until he exploded, emptying his semen into her as he drank her life down in great gulps.

Next to them, Jerry opened his eyes when he felt the pain of Marya's claws digging into his shoulders. He was already in the throes of his orgasm, spurting into her as she laid her head on his neck and ripped her fangs into his carotid artery.

He moaned one final time, whether in agony or in ecstasy was unknown, and then he died as Marya drained him dry.

When they were both satiated and their victims were empty, John and Marya tossed the dead bodies aside and grabbed each other in a wild, erotic embrace. They came together and made love as if they'd never stop, their blood-soaked mouths clamped together in raw, animal lust, unmindful of the lifeless husks slowly cooling on either side of them.

Chapter 3

John and Marya had just fallen into an exhausted slumber when a loud pounding sounded from their front door.

John sat up and glanced at the dead bodies lying on either side of the bed, wondering who could be visiting at this hour. Marya rolled over and sat up also. She put a hand on his shoulder and narrowed her eyes as she cast her mind out to see who was calling at this late hour.

The stiffness went out of her neck and she relaxed, grimacing in disgust. "It's only Theo Thantos and Christina Alario," she said, leaning back against her pillow and closing her eyes, as if by shutting them she could make the unwelcome visitors disappear.

John moaned and climbed out of bed. He grabbed a pair of pants and pulled them on as he moved slowly toward the living room, stifling a wide yawn and pulling the bedroom door shut behind him.

When John pulled the front door open, Theo ran his eyes up and down, taking in the crusted clots of dried blood on John's body and the heavy, musky scent of sex that still clung to him like a shroud.

"So, you had a party and didn't invite Christina and me,

huh?" Theo asked, his thin lips curling in his characteristic smirk.

John forced a smile and motioned the pair inside. "There was only enough food for two," he said wryly.

Christina moved past him, her eyes both sexy and mocking as she looked at him hungrily. She pressed her body against his and slowly put a finger to his cheek and then put it in her mouth, sucking off the dried blood with a feral glint in her eyes. "Still, it would have been nice to be asked," she said, staring at him intently. It was no secret that whatever Marya had, Christina wanted, if only to cause Marya pain. The two women had hated one another since Christina had been in love with Michael Morpheus and realized he preferred Marya to her. The fact that Marya detested Morpheus and had never given him the slightest encouragement in his affections seemed only to make Christina's hatred more intense.

As far as Marya was concerned, she felt Christina was a vain, stupid gold digger who'd never had an original thought in her empty head.

"And where is the lovely Marya tonight?" Theo asked, brushing past them and ignoring the sharp look his comment earned him from Christina as his eyes searched the small cabin's living room.

"I'm right here, Theo," Marya said, walking out of the bedroom and yawning and stretching. Her movements caused the sheer white nightgown to tighten over her voluptuous breasts. Her nipples were hard as rocks and strained against the thin fabric, catching Theo's eye as she knew it would.

"Fucking whore," Christina murmured as she left John's side and moved quickly to take Theo's arm and reestablish her claim to him.

Theo shook her off and moved over to Marya, putting out his hand and brushing it across her breast where it was stained with blood.

"I didn't realize you were such a sloppy eater," Theo said,

his eyes fastened on her bloodstained nipple as he spoke to her.

Marya moved back out of his reach and walked toward a couch in the center of the room in front of the fireplace. "I'm not usually, but Johnny and I were having such a good time it seemed a shame to worry about a few drops of spilled blood."

John looked at Christina's flashing eyes and smiled to himself. He knew Marya was flirting with Theo to get Christina's goat, and as usual it was working. She certainly knew how to push Christina's buttons.

He figured he'd better intervene before the two women came to blows. "Can I offer you some wine, or something stronger?" he said to Christina, taking her arm and ushering her to a large stuffed chair next to the couch.

As they moved across the room, Christina let her hand drop to "accidentally" brush against John's groin, a move not unnoticed by Marya, who frowned slightly. It seems, John thought, that Christina could do some button pushing of her own.

"Sure," said Theo as he took a seat across from Marya so he could stare at her without being too obvious. "How about some wine?"

John glanced at Christina, who nodded and looked around the room, unwilling to even glance Marya's way.

"I think I'll have a glass too, darling," Marya said, arching her back slightly for Theo's benefit when she noticed him still staring at her. Her move caused his tongue to peek out of his lips and quickly lick his lips.

"Jesus," Christina said disgustedly. "Why don't you put a robe on or something?"

"Oh," Marya asked innocently, glancing down at her semi-transparent gown. "Am I embarrassing you two? If so, I'll gladly go put on something more . . . demure."

"No, no," Theo said hurriedly, glancing irritably at Christina, "not at all. In fact, I think you look quite charming, Marya."

John tried to hide his smile as he handed out glasses of wine to everyone and took a seat next to Marya on the couch.

"So," he said after they'd all took a sip, "to what do we owe this visit?"

Theo drained his glass in one long swallow and leaned forward, his elbows on his knees. His eyes seemed unable to turn away from the sight of Marya's breasts as he spoke. "Christina and I went back to the cabin where the fight took place this afternoon. We wanted to see if Pike and his friends were still there."

Marya put her hand on John's thigh and moved it in slow circles as she smiled sweetly at Theo. "And I'll bet you found they were long gone."

"Yeah, but how did you know?" Theo asked.

Marya finished her wine and said, "Elijah Pike is no dummy, Theo. After all, he was ready and waiting for us when we attacked him and practically destroyed us with none of his people getting killed or even seriously hurt. To me, that means he's much too smart to hang around waiting for us to mount another attack."

"Well, you're right about him not hanging around," Theo said. "Now we just have to figure out where they've gone and how we can best get to them."

"That's easy," John said, slowly swirling the wine around in his glass without drinking it. "They've gone back to the States."

"How do you know that, Johnny?" Christina asked, almost batting her eyes at him as she tried to stir his interest in her.

" 'Cause Canada's too provincial for a group of Americans to set up in without the locals noticing . . . and what the locals notice, they talk about." He shook his head. "No, I think Pike knows they'd be too easy to spot if they stayed here and tried to set up a place where they could distribute their vaccine to others of our race. He's going to need a country with porous borders, and a good transportation and communication system. That leaves the United States as his logical choice."

"One thing, Theo," Marya said. "Why do you care where Pike and his bunch went? Are you still planning to try and stop the vaccine distribution?"

"If you are, it's a bad idea, Theo," John added. "Like my old friend, Ed Slonaker said to me before the big fight, you can't put a genie back in a bottle. Once the vaccine's been discovered and the formula shared, someone's going to make use of it no matter how hard we try to stop them."

Christina grinned and went to sit on the arm of Theo's chair, putting her arm around his shoulders and kneading his neck. "Theo's thinking is much bigger than that, Johnny," she said, pride evident in her voice.

"Oh?" John asked.

Theo held up his glass. "Why don't you get us another glass of wine and I'll tell you what I've been planning for the past couple of weeks?"

"Planning to do what?" John asked as he rose and took Theo's glass.

"Why, my plan for us Vampyres to take over the world," Theo answered simply, a sly grin on his face.

Elijah Pike took a last sip of his coffee, closed his journal, and went downstairs to see his friends.

"Hey, Elijah," TJ called from the breakfast table where they were all munching on donuts and drinking hot cocoa, "come on in and have a bite with us."

"Uh, not a propitious choice of words, my dear," Shooter said, raising an eyebrow at Pike as his lips curled in his trademark boyish grin.

In spite of himself, Pike laughed out loud. "Now Shooter,"

he said as he took a donut from the package on the table. "You know I've sworn to give up my previous nefarious ways and tread the straight and narrow."

"Yeah," Shooter said with a smirk, "and I swore to give up cigarettes, and you all know how well that's going."

Pike looked down at the pastry in his hand. "Hey, this is really good."

"It's from Tut's," Sam said, speaking of the small grocery cum restaurant about two miles from the cabin. "TJ got up early this morning and ran down to get 'em fresh."

"It's not Tut's anymore," TJ said around a mouthful of donut. "They've renamed the place Melby's."

Pike shook his head. "There's just no respect for tradition anymore," he said. "It was Tut's when I grew up here and Tut's it shall remain to me."

"Speaking of your growing up," Matt interjected, "we have some questions for you."

Pike poured himself a cup of cocoa and took a seat at the table. "Fire away," he said as he reached for another pastry.

"The girls have offered Shooter and I the chance to become transformed into Vampyres like them," Matt said, cutting his eyes toward Sam.

"I know," Pike replied. "It was my idea, so that the four of you would age . . . or rather, not age, together."

"Well, we'd like a little more information about just what it is we're getting ourselves into," Shooter said. "We've all picked up tidbits of information about the history of Vampyrism and some knowledge about the infection that causes it, but Matt and I would like a few more details before we do something that is irreversible."

"That's completely understandable," Pike replied, swallowing the last bite of his donut and settling back in his chair as he began to talk. "As I don't know exactly how much the two of you have learned about my race, I'll just give you the long version and you'll have to forgive me if I repeat something you already know."

When the boys both nodded, he continued, "Since the dawn of time," he began, his eyes on the ceiling as he concentrated on the facts he'd learned over years of investigation and research, "another race has coexisted alongside man. Members of this race call themselves Vampyri. They are descended from a small group of gypsies from the Carpathian mountain region of Europe, inbred for untold generations due to their physical and social isolation. Many hundreds of years ago, a mutant gene arose in this group, causing a disease known today as *Erythropoetic haemolytica,* or simply porphyria. Symptoms of this genetic birth defect are pale, white skin that blisters and burns on exposure to sunlight, phosphorescent teeth that glow in the dark due to abnormal accumulations of phosphorus in their enamel, and a congenital hemolysis or rupture of red blood cells, causing red, blood-stained eyes and tears, and a progressive anemia leading to death at an early age."

He paused to take a drink of cocoa, and went on to say, "Sorry if this is too technical for you Shooter, but I'll try and tell it so you don't have to be a doctor to understand it."

When Shooter and the others nodded, he continued. "With time and experimental diets, the villagers learned to control the anemia by feeding their infants whole blood mixed with milk. Over time, due to inbreeding of this reclusive group, the genetic defect became very widespread throughout all of the gypsy villages in the area. Other genetic traits, at first rare among the gypsies, also became potentiated by their sexual inbreeding. Known for years for their 'second-sight,' precognition, and mind-reading abilities, the gypsies slowly by natural selection increased both the prevalence and the strength of these valuable psychic powers. Another trait of the mountain people, also potentiated by their inbreeding, was their tendency toward extremely long lives. In fact, the average life expectancy of the affected villagers rose from fifty to over one hundred and fifty years in the space of just a few generations, and continues to rise with every generation of Vampyres that is produced.

"Eventually, after many hundreds of generations, an infection of bacteriophage infested the race that was already becoming known in that part of the world as Vampyri. This microscopic viruslike particle had the capability of transferring genetic material from one cell to another. By chance, it latched on to the chromosome carrying the porphyria gene, the genes for psychic ability, and the genetic code for long life, and absorbed them into its own genetic makeup. Thus, the sickness and the abilities were passed from one person to another by the sharing of blood rather than just by genetic chance in their offspring.

"The practices of mixing blood and milk became a standard part of the Vampyri culture, for both ceremonial and quasi-religious reasons, and soon entire villages were infected with the Vampyre bacteriophage and the race expanded throughout the Carpathian mountain region. As they became more successful due to their mental powers and long lives, they began to move beyond their mountain valleys and to mix with other people throughout Europe. As you can guess, it didn't take long for the Vampyri to become envied at first and then hated for their long lives and other abilities, and feared when it became common knowledge they drank blood. Soon there was an undeclared but nevertheless vicious war between the Vampyri and the so-called Normals. Over time, the Vampyri were hunted down and slaughtered until they were driven underground and forced to go into hiding and conceal their identities. But the war had another consequence. So many of the Vampyri suffered egregious wounds, that once again by natural selection, those that had the ability to quickly heal themselves became the majority of the race. After many years, only members who were virtually impervious to injury were left to survive and procreate."

Pike sat back in his chair and spread his arms. "Have I left anything out?"

"So, since your condition is due to an infection by an organism that carries the same genetic material as all the other Vampyres, you're all pretty much equal in your abilities?" Matt asked.

Pike smiled and shook his head. "No, Matt, not at all. Just as two geniuses may mate and have several kids, some extremely smart and some just average, all Vampyres are not equal. We have some that are very smart and others that are dumb as posts, some that are exceptionally strong and others just about the same as Normals. Also some have more or less psychic ability than others, due to a variety of factors I haven't fully worked out yet."

"So, what's the bottom line?" Shooter asked. "What do you recommend we do?"

Pike shook his head. "I can't make that decision for you, boys. I cannot tell you exactly how the Transformation will affect you or how you'll handle the changes to your body and mind. In fact, all I can tell you is that if you don't do it, you two will continue to age and grow old and will finally die while your sweethearts remain as you see them now. You still have a choice, and it's one only you can make."

"The good news," Sam said, reaching across the table to cover Matt's hand with hers, "is that with the vaccine you won't be consumed with a horrible hunger for blood like most of the rest of the race."

Pike held up his hand, "But you will still have the occasional urges," he said. "It will just be up to you to control them, just as you do any other appetites you may have."

Matt glanced over at his lover, Sam's hand still in his. "I think we need to talk about this privately," he said.

Shooter nodded and took TJ's hand in his. "Us too, sweet-heart," he said.

Elijah looked at them, wondering what he would have done if he'd been given a choice about his own transformation. He knew for a fact that without the vaccine and the possibility to live a relatively normal life and to exist without the necessity of killing innocents, his answer would have been a resounding no. He sighed. The presence of his vaccine changed everything, and he only hoped it was for the better.

Chapter 4

At first, John Ashby grinned when Theo Thantos said his plan was for the Vampyre race to take over the world, but his smile faltered when he saw Theo was dead serious.

In his job as a Mountie stationed in the city of Banff but having responsibility for hundreds of thousands of acres of wilderness, Ashby had seen his share of kooks and nutcases, and he had to admit that in all of his previous dealings with Theo he hadn't seen any evidence of schizophrenia or paranoia or any other type of mental disorder manifest itself in the man—but this was craziness. True, the man was an egotist and had a rather exaggerated sense of his own importance, but Ashby knew that most of the other Vampyres he'd met suffered from those maladies.

Hell, Ashby thought as he refilled their glasses with wine, the entire number of Vampyres worldwide can't be over a few hundred thousand. How can Theo possibly think we could prevail in a fight against the Normals?

As John handed Theo his wine, Theo's lips curled in a smile, and for a moment the cruelty that was always present behind his eyes disappeared and his face was almost handsome. "I can see the wheels turning, Johnny boy," Theo said lightly. "Is old Theo crazy or what?"

John laughed nervously and handed Christina and Marya their glasses. "You're right, Theo. I was just figuring the odds against us must be on the order of several million to one."

He took a sip of his wine. "And those are tough odds to overcome in a war," he added, watching Theo over the rim of his glass as he drank. He tried a tentative mental thrust at Theo to see if the man had any doubts, but he found only a supreme self-confidence. Strangely, this alarmed Ashby more than the finding of some doubts would have. At least then he'd have known that Thantos was fully aware of the magnitude of the task he was advocating they undertake.

Theo raised his eyebrows and shrugged. "Well, Johnny, I guess it depends on the type of war doesn't it?" he asked, not really answering Ashby's question.

"What do you mean?"

"You're absolutely correct that in the old style in-your-face type of war, troop numbers matter a great deal, but in a guerrilla war, the smaller numbers actually work to our advantage."

"Guerrilla warfare?" John asked doubtfully. "You mean like blowing up bridges and assassinating troops—that kind of thing?"

Theo smiled again and shook his head. "Oh, Johnny, I thought you had more imagination than that," he said, almost sadly. He leaned forward, speaking earnestly with his elbows on his thighs. "No, I don't mean blowing up bridges and stuff like that. What I mean by guerrilla is that our enemy is big and powerful, but that also makes him slow to react. We on the other hand are small in number, which makes us able to react quickly and to hit and run with impunity."

He paused and took a sip of his wine before continuing his lecture. "Think about the unique position we're in, Johnny. Number one, our enemy doesn't know we exist and has absolutely no idea of our many strengths. And when you factor in our immortality and virtual indestructibility, it allows for us to make plans that work over many years."

"Okay, so we're stronger and live a lot longer than the Normals," John conceded. "But, our very strengths you tout also have kept us undercover for our entire history. There is not a single Vampyre in a position of political or military authority in the entire world. There can't be 'cause we have always had to remain hidden under the radar of public awareness precisely because of our long lives and failure to age."

"You are correct, Johnny, and that is one of our weaknesses that I plan to correct. In fact, you've picked the very first step in my campaign for us to rise to our rightful place as the leaders of the world and to our eventual domination of the inferior beings we call Normals."

John leaned back and crossed his legs, staring at Theo. The man did seem to have actually thought about this, at least enough to have formulated a plan. "All right, you've got my interest. Tell me how you plan to go about engineering this takeover of the world."

"First," Theo said, draining the last of his wine, "let me tell you another of our strengths—the one that is going to make all this possible."

John nodded. "Go on."

"We have the ability, by the Rite of Transformation, to not only increase our numbers rapidly, but to actually turn any of our enemies into one of us." Theo grinned and spread his arms wide. "Just think about it, Johnny. In all of history, in all of the thousands of wars that have occurred since the dawn of time, never has one army been able to cause the other's soldiers to change their allegiance, to make them change sides and become allies almost overnight."

John laughed. "Don't tell me you intend for us to go on a Transformation binge and change millions of citizens into Vampyres so they can help us win the war do you?"

Theo frowned at the tone of derision in John's voice. "No, you're thinking too small, John," he said sternly. "It is only the leaders of the Normals that we need to change to give us the power to prevail. Think about it, boy! All we need to do is transform a few dozen men and women into Vampyres and then let them do the same to their essential underlings, and we can seize control of the government and, if we're very careful, no one will even know!"

John was becoming intrigued now. He turned Theo's arguments over in his mind. Theo had a point. "I see what you mean," he said. "If we could get the president and the Joint Chiefs of Staff of the military, so to speak, and maybe the speaker of the house and the majority leader of the senate . . ."

Theo waved a dismissive hand. "Forget the president. He's much too closely guarded to gain the necessary access to transform him. Remember, it takes several days for the sickness to go away, days in which several blood feedings are necessary."

"Oh," John said, deflated. He had forgotten for a moment just how little privacy the president had in his daily life.

"But, you're on the right track, Johnny. The vice president isn't nearly so well guarded, and his children are even less watched. Suppose we could get his wife or one of his older children transformed? They would have intimate access and could probably do the rest for us right under the noses of the Secret Service."

"Of course," John said. "And once we had the vice-president, it would be easy enough to get rid of the president, putting our man in power where he could go right down the chain of command transforming those he needed to do our bidding."

As Theo leaned back, smiling, John looked down at his hands, which were trembling with the knowledge that it could in fact be done. The revolution would take some years, but hell, they had plenty of those to spare.

He took a deep breath. Yeah, it could be done, but *should* it be done—that was the question John had to face. Theo obviously thought so, but John wasn't so sure. He didn't know if he was ready to face a world controlled by men, or rather by creatures like Theo Thantos. Hell, in John's previous experience with members of his own race, he'd found few he liked, and even fewer that he truly respected. Ed and Kim Slonaker were just about the extent of his experience with Vampyres, and he knew that neither of them would ever go for a scheme like this one.

As he thought about it, he kept his mind carefully shielded. He knew that if Thantos even suspected he had any doubts, the man would kill him without a second's hesitation. He chuckled to himself. Such were the people he was allying himself with.

Elijah Pike stood up and stared into Matt and Shooter's faces, meeting their eyes. "I think I've answered most of your questions, and as for any others like how does it feel and so forth, the women can handle those. Now, I'm going to go over to the Wal-Mart in Norway and get some supplies while you four talk it over."

After he left, Shooter shook his head, a worried expression on his face. "I don't know, guys. You are all doctors, and you're used to dealing with infections and viruses and bacteriophages or whatever they are. Me, I'm just a flatfoot cop who doesn't know from nothin' about that kind of stuff. This is all way over my head."

Matt glanced over at Sam and smiled. "The way I see it, there are pros and cons to be considered, just as in any major decision." Now he looked at Shooter. "The pros are we get to stay with the women we love for a hell of a long time, and in addition we'll be free from disease and will be able to heal from almost any injury that befalls us. We'll also get some sort of psychic ability, though we won't know how much until after it's over."

"Yeah," Shooter said, his face somber. "And the cons are we'll be changed forever with no chance of undoing what we've done, and we'll be dependent on a vaccine to keep us from becoming . . ." he hesitated, blushing as he looked at TJ.

TJ laughed and rubbed the back of his neck with her hand. "Go on and say it, Shooter, it's all right. You're afraid of becoming blood-sucking monsters like Sam and me, right?"

He gave her his lopsided grin. "Darlin' I wouldn't exactly put it that way, but yeah, kind'a. After all, I've seen what you and Sam can turn into if you stop the medicine, and it ain't exactly pretty." He took a deep breath. "In fact, it's downright scary."

"Is that what's bothering you, Shooter?" Matt asked. "Are you afraid you might be forced to kill innocent people for their blood?"

Shooter's grin faded. "Yeah. What if for some reason, the vaccine stops working, if we build up a tolerance for it after a few years or something?"

Matt shrugged. "Then, we still have a choice about how we get the blood we need," he said. "That doesn't mean we'll go around killing people to feed on. Look at Elijah. Once he decided he wasn't going to do it any more, he just took blood from his patients and used that without harming anyone."

"I think what Shooter's afraid of is that he might revert to some sort of killing machine, like Michael Morpheus," TJ said. "That he might in fact find that he likes to kill and suck other people's blood. Right, sugar?"

Shooter hung his head as he nodded. "You guys are all doctors who love humanity and have taken oaths to protect and help people. Me, I'm just a cop who for the past ten years has had to deal with the dregs of society." He looked around, "In fact, present company excluded, I don't particularly like people very much. I'm just afraid if I had the power and the vaccine didn't work, I wouldn't be all that particular where I got the blood I needed."

Sam put her hand on Matt's shoulder and made a gesture with her head toward their bedroom. "I think we should all go to our rooms and talk about it with our mates in private," she said. "The decision doesn't have to be made right now. We've got some time to make up our minds about what to do."

"Come on, baby," TJ said, pulling Shooter to his feet. "Let's go discuss it in our room."

As they walked away, Matt and Sam could hear Shooter whispering to TJ, "You're not gonna hold that blood-sucking monster thing against me, are you sweetheart?"

TJ gave him a stern look. "Who knows? I might have to take you over my knee and give you a spanking."

Shooter laughed as they disappeared into their room, but his words were plainly audible. "A spanking? Now that's something we haven't done yet!"

Chapter 5

As soon as they were in their room, TJ grabbed Shooter by the shoulders and turned him to face her. She ran one hand lightly through his curly black hair and looked up into his sky-blue eyes. His five-foot-ten-inch frame towered over her by eight inches and she was so close she had to tilt her head to look up at him.

"Don't you dare doubt yourself, Shooter," she whispered. "You are one of the kindest and most gentle men I've ever known, and no amount of Vampyre bugs in your blood could ever change that, vaccine or no vaccine. You could no more harm an innocent person than you could hurt me."

Shooter grinned and put his arms around TJ and pulled her toward him until they both tumbled down on the bed.

"I thought we were going to talk about your feelings about this possible transformation," TJ said, a smile on her lips and a familiar glint in her eye.

"Oh, we'll talk *first*," Shooter said, his lips against her neck and his hand cupping her breast.

"Not if you keep that up," TJ said, pulling back and rolling off him to lie next to him on the bed. "Now, I know you've got some questions, so ask me."

Shooter put his hands behind his head and stared up at the ceiling, trying to ignore the warmth and heaviness in his groin touching her had caused. "Okay, what does it feel like to be a Vampyre?"

TJ rolled on her side and gently caressed his stomach with her right hand as she spoke. "For the most part, it feels wonderful. The every day aches and pains and discomforts we deal with as humans are gone. Every sense is magnified a thousand times. I can taste and smell and hear and feel things like I could only imagine before. And my mind is so clear and focused that I can almost read your thoughts before you're even aware of them."

Shooter grinned. "That could be dangerous. What if I thought about another girl?"

TJ moved her hand down to his groin and cupped his genitals, giving them a slight warning squeeze. "You're right, pal, that could be dangerous," she said ominously. "So, you'd better just be sure to think only of me."

"Seriously," Shooter said, turning his head to look at her. "Isn't it a problem for all of you to know what the others are thinking? It's like you have no privacy."

TJ smiled. "No, not at all, babe. With the power to read others' thoughts and emotions, comes the ability to shield your own. That way, unless you want them to, no one can read your thoughts."

"Oh," Shooter said, an expression of relief on his face.

"As a matter of fact, most of us go around with our minds at least partly shielded for that very reason. Of course, if someone is vastly more powerful psychically than you are, they can probably break down your shield and get some sense of your thoughts and emotions, but you're going to know they're doing it. Any thing else?" TJ asked.

"With your heightened senses," he asked, blushing slightly, "is making love better than it was before?"

"Not necessarily better, but a thousand times more intense," she answered. "Now when you open you mind to me and we make love, I not only feel what you're doing to me, but I can also share what you feel when I do things to you." She grinned. "It's like that old song, a 'double shot of my baby's love.' I can enjoy it from both aspects and the feeling is so good it is absolutely scary."

He shook his head. "I don't know, babe," he said. "As good as you make me feel now, if it were any better I don't know if I could stand it."

"Trust me," TJ whispered, leaning over to put her lips on his, her breath warm against him. "You'll love it."

As he opened his lips to her thrusting tongue, she slipped her hand inside his jeans and wrapped her fingers around him, causing him to become immediately hard.

"I thought you wanted to talk," he said, gasping at her touch and pushing his pelvis against her hand.

"I did, but now the talking is over," she replied breathlessly as she moved her hand on him.

They both groaned as they rapidly tore their clothes off and came together naked in the middle of the bed.

Her breasts were on fire as he caressed them and she grabbed his buttocks and pulled him tight against her, until she could feel his hardness pressing against her pubic bone.

"Now!" she whispered urgently and moved her hips until he slipped inside her wetness.

He moaned and thrust against her as their lips locked and she pressed her breasts tight against his chest, riding him like a stallion.

Matt and Sam were having a similar conversation in their room next door. Since the rooms were small and had little furniture in them other than a bed and small chest of drawers, they too were lying on their bed at they talked.

Matt was on his right side, looking into Sam's face. "I know what Elijah said just now," he began, "but I want to know how you feel about having gone through the transformation, especially since it was against your will."

She pursed her lips as she thought about the question. "Obviously, if I had my choice, I'd wish none of this had happened to us and that we were still living our lives in blissful unawareness of the whole Vampyre mess."

Matt grinned. "I sense a 'but' in there."

She returned his smile. "Yeah, but since it did happen and since we are all intimately involved, I'm kind'a glad I was changed."

"Why specifically?"

"Many reasons. For one, it allows me to look at the big picture of things, knowing that baring something unforeseen I'll live another few hundred years instead of just fifty or so. It sort'a frees up the mind to think about the consequences of our actions that would normally only occur long after we were dead."

"Okay, what else?"

"Physically, it's been amazing," she said, her eyes lighting up. "I'm able to experience things—feelings, tastes, smells, thoughts, that I'd only been able to imagine before, and I'm strong as an ox to boot!"

"I can attest to that," Matt agreed, thinking of how she'd torn into Michael Morpheus during their fight awhile back. "But, now, tell me the downsides to this new you."

Her face sobered. "The obvious one is my desire for and need for frequent feedings of blood, though the vaccine makes it much more bearable than it was before."

"Uh-huh."

"Another not so obvious one is the danger I . . . that is, all of us Vampyres face by drinking human blood."

"You mean, the danger of catching diseases?"

"Yeah. The most serious is spongiform encephalopathy, or Mad Cow Disease. According to Elijah, he's had to kill several of his kind that caught the disease. Evidently, it cannot kill us but it drives us insane and we live out our lives as blithering idiots."

"What about the other blood diseases, like AIDS or hepatitis?"

She shrugged. "Elijah says they aren't really threats, that with our heightened immune systems we can usually handle those without any problem unless we suffer an overwhelming infective dose."

"So," Matt said hesitantly, "you think all things considered, it's a positive experience?"

She grinned wryly. "I wouldn't go quite that far, lover, but it's certainly not all bad. And the real upside is that you and I will have hundreds of years together instead of just a few dozen."

"But, what if you get tired of me, or we fall out of love?" he asked, his eyes worried.

She patted his arm. "Not to worry, Matt. If the time does come in some distant future when either of us wants to separate, then we'll do it and hopefully remain friends. I don't think either one of us is the type to try and keep the other prisoner."

"There's another thing," he added, his eyes not quite looking at her.

"Yes?"

"I remember Elijah saying once that Vampyres don't look at sex the same way us Normals do, that for you guys it's often a part of the feeding process and is considered more . . . uh, recreational than a binding emotional response signifying love or commitment."

His eyes found hers and bored in. "Is that how you feel now, Sam?"

"If you mean could I have sex with another man, or another Vampyre and not feel guilty about it, the answer is yes, dear."

She hurriedly added when she saw his face fall, "But, that does not mean that sex between us would be any less special, or that the sex I had with someone else would mean as much to me as it does with you. Sex between Vampyre mates is very special indeed, Matt, for it includes the bonding of minds and souls on a much deeper level than is possible for two Normals, but probably due to their long lives and the very real part sex plays in feeding, Vampyres do not consider sex with persons other than their mates to be a betrayal. They look at it like you said, as a mere recreational experience to be enjoyed and then forgotten."

Matt shook his head, his lips curled in a slight smile. "I don't know, Sam. That sounds sort of like a teenage fantasy—endless sex without responsibility."

She shrugged and reached out to caress his cheek with her palm. "Yes it does, and it is, sort of, Matt. Sex without love is just physical enjoyment, and as such harms no one assuming both parties agree to the ground rules, but sex with love, as between two mates, is glorious indeed, as I hope you have the chance to find out."

He leaned over and put his lips against hers, whispering, "Well, now that you mention it . . ."

She moved her hand from his cheek to his belt and tugged on it. "Maybe we should get out of these clothes before we go any further," she said breathlessly.

"Good idea," he replied, moving as fast as he could to do just that.

Chapter 6

"I need to know whether you're with us on this," Theo Thantos said, breaking into John Ashby's thoughts.

John looked up into Thantos's eyes, which though fevered still showed no signs of insanity. "Why do you care, one way or the other," John asked. "I'm sure you'll find plenty of converts to your cause, Vampyres who've been chafing under the rule of the Normals for hundreds of years."

Thantos glanced at his mate, Christina, and then back at John. "I was hoping you'd be my point man in Canada. I don't know any of the local Vampyre groups up here and if we're going to succeed in this upcoming war, we're going to have to plan to simultaneously hit the Canadian government to keep them out of our hair in the States."

John thought about what Thantos was saying for a moment, and then he shook his head. "I don't think so, at least not at first, Theo."

"Why not?" Thantos asked in an accusing tone of voice, as if John were somehow conspiring against his grand scheme.

"Because the Canadian prime minister is just a figure head when it comes to running the country," John explained. "Each province is pretty much autonomous, much more so than the individual states are in the lower fifty." John hesitated, and then he added, "And what's more, they're proud of their independence and would not take kindly to interference from any titular head of the government you might convert. No"—he said, shaking his head again—"It just won't work that easily up here."

Thantos pursed his lips. "Then, what you're saying is that to be effective, we'd have to hit the leaders of every province in Canada at the same time?"

"Yeah, so if you're asking my advice, it would be to take care of business in the States first, and once you've got your leaders there in our camp, then we can start to operate up here to do the same thing."

Thantos smiled. "You said 'our camp.' Does that mean you'll join me in my quest to make the world safe for our kind?"

John shot a glance at Marya and then wagged his head. "I don't know yet, Theo. I'll talk it over with Marya and let you know later—but no matter what I decide, I won't do anything to go against your plan."

Christina growled, her hateful gaze on Marya, "You'd better not, either one of you!"

Marya stared back at her and grinned insolently. "Better put this bitch on a leash, Theo," she said, "before she gives someone rabies." She paused before adding, "Or before I put her down like the mad dog she is."

Thantos got hurriedly to his feet, glancing at Christina with worried eyes, as if she might attack Marya before he could get them out of the cabin.

"All right, John. I'll take your word on it that you won't try and interfere if you decide not to join us." He pulled a small notebook from his jacket pocket and wrote something on it with a gold Cross pen. "Here is the name of the hotel we'll be staying at in Washington until I can find us an out-of-the-way house to rent."

John's eyebrows went up when he took the paper. "The Ritz Carlton, huh? Pretty fancy digs."

Thantos shrugged. "Might as well travel first class I always say."

"Except for the company you keep," Marya murmured, her voice almost too low to be heard.

Ed and Kim Slonaker clinked glasses as they lay next to each other in their bed. "To us," Ed said, staring into Kim's eyes. "To us," she replied, and then they each drained their glasses of thick, red liquid.

Ed took Kim's glass and put them both on his bedside table and turned out the light. As he turned back to Kim and put his arm around her to pull her toward him, she put a hand against his chest and leaned her head back, looking up at his face in the gloomy half-light.

"It's not quite the same is it?" she asked, a wistful note in her voice.

"You mean drinking prepared blood-bank blood from a glass instead of ripping it from some poor innocent's body?" he asked, an angry edge in his voice.

"Don't be angry, darling," she said, caressing his cheek with her hand. "I didn't mean it that way. I only meant that this is not nearly as exciting, as sensual as the way we used to do it." She lowered her hand and her eyes. "This is too clinical, too clean. It's like the difference between fast food at a burger joint and a real steak served on linen in a restaurant with a glass of wine. Both meals satisfy your hunger in a basic sort of way, but one is much preferable over the other."

Ed sighed and reached over to turn the light back on. He fluffed up his pillow against the headboard and moved to a semi-sitting position. He'd known this talk was coming for some time, better to get it over with.

"Yes, you're right, sweetheart," he agreed. "Taking the vaccine has calmed the hunger and made it manageable so that we only have to feed every few weeks, but the process is not nearly as exciting as the old days when we hunted our prey and then consumed them in an orgy of sex and feasting."

She shook her head. "I can't even remember the last time we changed into our Vampyre bodies," she complained. As she looked back at him, she added, "I'm sorry, Ed, but I miss those days. I can't help it. The anticipation beforehand, the excitement of the hunt, and then the actual kill and blood-feast that followed it . . ." Her voice trailed off and her eyes became distant and hooded in memory.

He reached out and pulled her to him, the feel of her naked breasts against his chest arousing him in spite of what she'd said about the dry, clinical nature of their feeding. "I have to admit that I miss them too, Kim darling, but I don't miss the guilt and self-recriminations we always had afterward."

She let her hand drift down across his stomach to his hardening groin. "I know it sounds like I want it both ways," she said, her lips against his chest. "And I guess it's true. I want the fun and excitement and sex, but not the guilt and sadness over having to kill to get it."

She lowered her head to his lap and kissed him with soft lips. "It's not that this isn't good, because it is," she added, flicking the head of his penis with her tongue and then rolling onto her back on his thighs and pulling his hand to her breast. "But try and remember what it was like before, sweetheart. It was mind-numbing, wild, glorious animal sex that left us both exhausted and satiated for days."

Ed felt his penis throb and jump at the memories of how they used to rut and feed before the days of Elijah Pike's vaccine.

He dug his fingers into her breast, squeezing the nipple until she moaned. "Do you want to stop taking the vaccine and go back to those days?" he asked, more than a little afraid she'd say yes. He knew he loved her enough to do it for her, but he didn't want to unless she forced him to even though he missed those days almost as much as she did.

She moved under his hand. "Not entirely, Ed, but why can't we continue to take the vaccine and still, when it comes time to feed, go after some people that don't deserve to live?"

"You mean try and find criminals to feed on?"

She sat up and put her arms around his neck. "Sure, why not? The only thing that kept us from doing that before was that we needed to feed so often you couldn't find enough bad people to satisfy the hunger. Now, with the vaccine, we'll have plenty of time to pick and choose our victims, making sure that we don't kill anyone who doesn't deserve it."

He grinned. It might just work, and he had to admit, she was right about one thing. It was better the old way.

"All right," he said. "When I get to the office tomorrow, I'll go through the files and see who I can find in the area that might be suitable candidates for our next . . . party."

"Oh, darling," she cried, pressing herself against him. "Just think how much fun we'll have—first picking the victims, and then stalking them and finally taking them and devouring them in an orgy of bloodlust." She grinned up at him with sparkling, excited eyes. "I love you!"

In answer, he threw her across the bed to land on her back and began to change into his Vampyre body, snarling and drooling as her eyes widened in delight and she began to change with him.

He sat there, stroking himself and growling softly until her change was complete, and then he launched himself at her. He fastened his fangs on her left breast as his claws dug into her buttocks and lifted her off the bed.

She howled and bit his neck and sank her claws into his back while she spread her legs and wrapped them around him.

He snarled in pain and desire, jerking her downward until he impaled her on his penis.

He humped and thrust and sucked blood from her breast as she drank from his neck, their minds intertwining and mingling until they were one organism with only one goal in mind—sweet release.

Seconds later, they howled in unison and collapsed in each other's arms, panting and gasping as they slowly changed back to their human forms.

"Wonderful," he gasped against her cheek.

"Delightful," she replied, cuddling against him, "but nothing compared to what we'll do next time, when we have company."

Ed was drifting off into an exhausted sleep when the phone next to the bed began to ring.

"Oh, shit!" he groused and rolled over reaching for it.

"This better be important!" he growled into the phone.

"Is a call from an old friend important enough?" John Ashby's voice said softly.

"John?" Ed asked, coming instantly and fully awake. He hadn't heard a word from John since the fight at Elijah Pike's cabin several months before. His friend had dropped out of sight as if he'd never existed.

"In the flesh," John replied.

Ed took a deep breath and eased out of bed and carried the phone into the living room so he could talk without waking Kim up. "How . . . how are you?" Ed asked, wondering why John was calling.

John chuckled. "How about we skip the small talk, Ed. We've been friends for much too long for that."

"Okay. What do you want? Is that direct enough?" Ed answered, his voice colder than he intended.

"Hmmm, I sense hostility," John said, "Are you still pissed at me about the Pike thing?"

"Why would you think that?" Ed replied. "Just because

you betrayed our friendship and worked behind my back and almost got Kim and me killed?"

"Hey, we ended up on different sides in a war, old friend. It happens."

Ed sighed. John was right, and he *had* saved his and Kim's lives in the end. "Okay, old buddy, I can see your point. Truce, okay?"

"Truce," John said, his voice sounding relieved. He counted Ed and Kim as almost the only true friends he had in the world, other than Marya.

"Now, why did you call me in the middle of the night?" Ed asked. "I'm sure it wasn't just to make up."

John laughed. "Same old Ed. Right to the point."

"Uh-huh, and same old Johnny, always dancing around without saying what's really on your mind."

"Okay, okay," John said. "I'm thinking about heading down to the States for a while, with my new . . . uh, lady friend, and I need to know what you've told them at Mountie headquarters about my sudden absence."

"You mean you want to know is there any heat on you and is it safe for you to travel under your own name?" Ed asked, a hint of humor in his voice.

"That's about it."

"Don't worry, John. I just told them you'd suddenly fallen in love with an American tourist and you'd decided to follow her back to the United States when she left. I even faked a notice of resignation so your pension will still be there for you if you ever need it."

There was silence on the phone for a few moments, and then John's voice sounded very sober. "You're a good friend, Ed, the best."

"Correction, Johnny. *We* are good friends and have been since we were both transformed. A little difference of opinion about our species' rightful place in the world is not going to change that."

"Uh, what if I told you our rightful place in the world was going to change soon, would you be interested?" John asked.

Ed sighed. "Johnny, if you're still mixed up with those crazy zealots you put in with before, no I wouldn't be interested. I've told you I believe in Pike's vaccine as the best way for us to get along in this world without having to kill innocent beings to live. I haven't changed my mind about that since the last time we had this conversation."

Ed could hear John laughing over the phone. "Same old Ed, stubborn as a mule," John said. "And twice as ornery."

Ed chuckled too. "Yep, still as stubborn as ever, Johnny, but I still wish you the best, that is unless you're going down there to cause trouble for Pike or any of his group. They're friends of mine, Johnny, so anything you do against them is the same as doing it against me. I wouldn't want you to forget that again."

There was silence for a moment, and then John's familiar chuckle sounded. "I will give you a promise, Ed. I have no intention of seeing, contacting, or in any other way causing harm to Pike or any of his associates, and as far as I know, neither does Theo Thantos or any of his people. Does that satisfy you, my friend?"

Ed felt relief wash over him. "Yeah, Johnny. You've never lied to me before, so I'll take your word for it. Now, you be careful down in the lower fifty, you know those Americans are crazy."

John laughed, remembering Ed was a transplanted American who'd come to live in Canada after falling in love with Kim, who was a Canadian native.

"Take care, old pal. Maybe I'll see you again some day."

"Yeah, you too, Johnny." Ed hesitated for a second, and then he added, "Oh, and Johnny . . ."

"Yeah?"

"This bunch you're running with, they seem to be pretty bad guys from what Pike told me, and I'd hate to think you'd ever trust them enough to turn your back on them. I want you to remember, whatever they're into, it's for their good, not necessarily yours. So, if things get hairy down there and you need someone to cover your back, like the good old days, just give me a ring and Kim and I'll come running."

"Thanks, pal," John said sincerely. "I'll keep that in mind."

Chapter 7

Elijah Pike was in the loft of his cabin going over some of his research notes when his cell phone rang.

"Hello," he said, carefully not giving his name until he found out who was calling. Though only a few trusted friends had this number, he hadn't survived this long by being careless in his security.

"Elijah, this is Ed Slonaker, up in Canada," the remembered voice said.

"Hey, Ed," Pike answered warmly. "How are you doing? And how is your lovely wife, Kim?"

"We're doing great, Elijah. I just called to run a few things by you, to get your input."

Pike frowned. "It's not the vaccine is it? It's still working for you isn't it?"

"Oh, yeah, don't worry about that. It's doing exactly what it's supposed to—it lowers the intensity of the hunger so we can go several weeks without feeding, and then we can get by with the canned blood like you recommended."

"Good!" Pike said, relieved about the vaccine. So far, of the dozen or so people he'd given it to, there had been no failures he was aware of. "All right then, if it's not the vaccine, Ed, what can I do for you?"

"Well," Ed said hesitantly, "I wanted to warn you that I heard from John Ashby last night."

"Your Mountie friend and ex-partner?"

"Yeah. He called to tell me he's headed down to the States with his lady friend, and I kind'a got the idea that he's still involved with that group of crazies that attacked us when you were up here."

"Did he say they were still going to try and stop the production or the distribution of the vaccine?" Pike asked with a feeling of dread. He'd hoped the Vampyre wars were finished with the death of Michael Morpheus.

"No, as a matter of fact he promised me that the group was through with you, and he hinted they were working on some other stuff."

Elijah caught something in Ed's voice, some wariness or subliminal warning. "Other stuff, Ed?"

Ed went on to tell Elijah what John Ashby had told him, that Thantos and his friends were going to try and put Vampyres in power over Normals.

"That's stupid, Ed," Elijah said when he'd heard what John Ashby had said. "There is simply no way that a few hundred thousand of us could ever defeat several billion Normals, no matter how superior to them Thantos and his zealots think we are. Hell, right now we're in the catbird's seat—they don't even know we exist."

Ed chuckled. "You know that and I know that, Elijah, but remember crazy people don't always think straight, and that goes for Vampyres as well as for Normals."

"Yeah, ain't that the truth?" Pike said, chuckling himself. "Well, I guess there's not much we can do about whatever crazy plan they're working on, except to wait and see if it brings grief down on all our heads someday."

When Ed remained silent, Pike suspected there was something else on his mind. "Uh, is there something else you wanted to talk to me about, Ed?"

"Yes, but now that I'm actually talking to you, I feel kind'a silly bringing it up."

"Come on, Ed. We've spilt blood fighting together and I count you as one of my closest friends, so what could there be we can't talk about?"

"Okay, Elijah. Kim and I've been on the vaccine since you left here, and like I said before, it's working great." He hesitated, and when Pike didn't interrupt, he went on. "But, Kim and I both feel there's something missing since we've been on the medicine. The blood bank blood satisfies our hunger, but drinking it is just not the same as taking it from prey that we've hunted down and shared."

Pike sighed. He knew what Ed was talking about, for he had much the same feelings about his diet while on the vaccine. "I know what you mean, Ed. All of us that are taking the vaccine feel the same way, and it's just something we all have to deal with in our own ways."

"Well, Kim and I've decided that at least once in a while, we're going to go back to the old way, only we're only gonna take as prey people that deserve to die. What do you think of that? You think we're fooling ourselves and just trying to justify what we want to do?"

Elijah wasn't about to rain on Ed's parade by judging him or Kim, especially since he knew exactly what they were going through. "No, Ed, I don't. In fact, I've done much the same thing over the years, even before the vaccine was perfected. At least with the vaccine, you'll have the self-restraint to wait until you can find a suitable candidate that meets your requirements of being deserving of death."

"So, you don't think too badly of us for what we're thinking of doing?"

Pike laughed. "Of course not. I've spent too many years on that same path to ever think badly of someone else who's walking down it too."

"Good," Ed said, "And I know Kim will be relieved. She thinks an awful lot of you, Elijah, and it would really hurt her to think we'd disappointed you in any way."

"Not at all, Ed," Pike replied. "I know it's different with a mate, and that feeding together is very much a part of the intimacy you both need. Hell, if I had a mate right now, I'd probably be doing the same thing."

"Speaking of that, do you have any suitable candidates in mind?" Ed asked.

Pike laughed again. "No," he said, a picture of TJ forcing itself into his mind until he pushed it away. "Right now I'm much too busy working on this vaccine and another new project to think about that."

"Another new project?" Ed asked.

"Yeah, and it's one I may ask you and Kim to help me with when the time comes."

"Whatever you need, pal. What's it about?"

"We're fixing to perform the Rite of Transformation on a couple of men down here . . ."

"Those two who fought with us up here against Morpheus? Matt and Shooter?"

"Yes, at least they're considering it as we speak."

"So, what's the project have to do with that?"

"I've got a theory, Ed. If during the Transformation, we introduce the blood of several different Vampyres to the men simultaneously, it may just be that the transferees absorb the best parts of each of the donors. If that's the case, then we might be able to form a new breed of Vampyre, one that is as superior to us as we are to the Normals."

Ed was silent for a moment, and then he said, "You mean like if they took both my blood and Kim's blood, they'd get my superior strength and her superior psychic ability?"

"Something like that, Ed, only multiply it by dozens of different traits, from intelligence to speed to precognition to telepathy to God knows what. In fact, just about everything that is passed on by genes could be affected."

"That sounds interesting, Elijah. What do you want us to do, send you some blood?"

Pike sighed. "I'm afraid that won't do, Ed. The chemicals we need to mix with the blood to keep it from clotting in the tube might interfere with the genetic materials carried by the bacteriophages in our blood that give us our particular Vampyre traits. I'm afraid the only way to have an effective test of my theory is if you and Kim come down here and give the blood directly to the boys during their initiation rites."

"Whoa, that gets complicated, Elijah. You know that sharing blood is a very intimate experience, one that usually involves sex and only occurs between mates."

"I know, Ed. In fact, that's probably why no one in our race has ever thought about this possibility before. The very idea of multiple donors in a Rite of Transformation goes against just about everything we've ever been taught."

He paused. "That's why I'm giving you time to talk it over with Kim before you have to make up your minds. I realize it's a lot to ask, but I think the possibilities are worth the intrusion on your privacy. Think it over, discuss it, and let me know by next week. And Ed, it won't affect our friendship no matter what you and Kim decide."

"Thanks for that, Elijah," Ed said, thinking to himself that Kim would almost certainly veto any such suggestion. As wild as she was with him in bed and when hunting down prey, she was still very much a traditional sort of gal. "I'll get back to you as soon as I can with our answer."

When Ed got off the phone, he went into their bedroom and found Kim sitting in front of her dresser brushing out her hair. He moved up behind her and placed his hands on her shoulders and began to give her a soft rubdown.

Kim put her brush down and leaned her head back against him. She could feel his erection through his pants and was glad of his response to touching her, just as he noticed her nipples becoming hard and poking out against the thin layers of her nightgown.

"Ummm, that feels good," she murmured, moving her head a bit back and forth to further stimulate him.

"Kim," Ed said, "I've got a question for you."

"Go ahead," she replied sleepily, drowsy from the effects of his massage.

"Elijah is planning on performing the Rite of Transformation on Shooter and Matt, the two men who were up here with he and the girls."

"Uh-huh," she said, her eyes still closed.

"Well, he's got this theory, this idea that if multiple Vampyres donate blood to the transformees during the ceremony, the best traits of all the donors will be passed on to them and they'll become sort of super Vampyres."

Her eyes opened. She had been with Ed so long she didn't need her psychic abilities to see where he was going with this. She straightened in her chair and turned to face him, putting her arms around his waist and staring up into his eyes. "I guess he's aware of the nature of the interplay between the donors and the transformees during the sharing of blood?"

Ed nodded.

"And he's asked us to come and be a part of the ceremony, hasn't he?"

Ed nodded again.

She smiled, shaking her head. "And what did you tell Elijah Pike when he asked?"

"Uh, I told him I'd check with you, but that I was pretty sure you'd . . . uh . . . decline to participate."

"Oh, you did, did you?" she teased.

He stuttered and stammered for a moment before she let him off the hook. "Oh, come on, Ed. Don't be such a stick in the mud. You and I both have had sex with countless victims before, and most of the time right in front of each other. Why would you think I'd not want to help Elijah in his research?"

"Well," he began.

"Especially with such handsome young men," she teased him again.

"So that's it, you horny broad," he said mock sternly. "You just want to have sex with those young hunks, huh?"

She grinned up at him and kissed the front of his pants lightly. "Sure, but remember big guy, those two hotties they're in love with will be participating also."

He grinned back at her. "Say, you're right. That means we can both have some fun and do some good for Elijah at the same time."

She took the tab to his zipper between her teeth and inclined her head, pulling the zipper down. "My thoughts exactly," she said, taking his erection between her lips when it sprang from his trousers.

Chapter 8

Theo Thantos, unlike most others of his race, didn't believe in hiding out in out-of-the-way houses so his nocturnal feeds wouldn't be discovered. On the contrary, he craved action and crowds like an addict craves morphine, and so he and Christina had elected to stay in the Banff Springs Hotel, paying fourteen hundred dollars a night for a rather ordinary room. The hotel itself was extraordinarily beautiful, with elaborately carved balustrades, ancient oil paintings lining the halls, and best of all, from Thantos's viewpoint, hundreds of nooks and crannies where inconvenient objects could be stashed with little fear they'd be found in the near future.

This latter feature was important to Thantos because he also wasn't the type to be particularly careful to hide the bodies of his prey after he was done with them. Of course, he also usually frequented large cities in the States and moved around frequently so that he didn't leave too much evidence of his feeding in any one place.

In large cities with hundreds upon hundreds of dreadful murders to try and investigate every year, the occasional body drained of blood with extensive neck wounds just didn't rate very high on the cops' radar, especially if the victims were from the seamier side of life.

When they'd first arrived in Canada, Michael Morpheus had warned Theo and his other compatriots to dispose of the bodies carefully, since the population of Banff was relatively small and the Mounties were known to get very excited about homicides in their districts—most especially those of an exotic or nonroutine manner. Most Canadians were an unimaginative lot when it came to murder: guns, knives, and the occasional blunt object were the norm. Corpses with their throats ripped out would garner all too much attention, at least so Morpheus had said.

Theo went along with this as long as Morpheus was alive and in charge, but now that he was on his own, he said to hell with it. He and Christina weren't going to be around this place much longer so he decided to have some fun before leaving town, and by the time the Mounties discovered his leavings, they'd be sipping martinis in Washington, D.C.

Christina came out of their shower, toweling her hair dry, and found Theo standing in front of the large mirror over their dresser. He was dressed in traditional Vampyre hunting clothes—black jeans, a dark turtleneck shirt, and black tennis shoes. His hair, which he typically wore long and almost to his shoulders, was tied back in a ponytail.

Christina narrowed her eyes and stood there, naked, the towel draped over her shoulders. "Are you going out, Theo?" she asked, her voice low and dangerous.

He glanced at her in the mirror and smiled. She was getting tiresome, he thought to himself but didn't say out loud. For some reason, she'd seemed much more desirable to him when she was Michael Morpheus's girlfriend and he was trying to steal her away. But, now that he had her . . . ah well, he thought, carefully masking his thoughts from her prying mind, c'est la vie.

"Yes, Christina, I'm getting a mite restless and thought

perhaps it was time for a little hunting party before we leave town."

One corner of her lips turned up in a half-smirk and she moved over to stand in front of him, pressing her naked breasts against his chest. "You were going to invite me, weren't you, baby?" she asked.

He sighed as he felt himself becoming aroused in spite of her churlish manner. She was still a very beautiful woman, and if she could just manage to keep her sarcastic comments to herself, she'd be very desirable. Oh well, might as well make the best of it, he thought. There'd be plenty of time for him to find someone new when they got back to the States if she didn't change her ways and start treating him right.

He put his hands on her shoulders and massaged the muscles there. "Of course, darling. I was just waiting for you to finish your shower."

"Ummm," she moaned, looking up at his ponytail and giving it a small tweak with her fingertips. "I like your hair like that."

He stiffened. "Because it's like Michael used to wear his?" he asked testily.

"No, no, baby," she said, blushing slightly at the mention of her old boyfriend. "I just think it makes you look . . . cool and sophisticated."

He forced a smile, easing her away from him. "Okay. Now, why don't you get dressed and we'll go cruising for something good to eat?"

Becky Robertson was angry and getting angrier by the second. Here it was her nineteenth birthday, and her boyfriend Billy was out on the floor dancing with one of her girlfriends instead of her. He didn't think she could see the way he was grinding his pelvis against Sue Anne's crotch. She sniffed. And Sue Anne, that bitch! She was pushing right back and it looked like she was trying to shove her pointy breasts right through Billy's chest.

Becky glanced around the club to see if there was anyone else there that she knew so she could use them to make Billy jealous.

As she turned in her seat and looked around the crowd, her eyes met those of an older man who seemed to be staring at her. He looked to be about thirty years old and was sitting at a table over in the corner with one of the most beautiful women Becky had ever seen. They must be tourists, 'cause she would sure as hell have remembered them if she'd ever seen them before.

She shook her head and let her eyes rove over the rest of the crowd. Just like a man, she thought bitterly. There he is with a real knockout and he's still scoping out other women.

Out of the corner of her eye, Becky saw the pretty lady get up and head toward the restroom.

The man immediately stood up and moved toward her table. She quickly averted her eyes, though the man was much more handsome than Billy.

"Good evening," he said, standing before her smiling.

"Hello," Becky said, keeping her voice cold. She didn't want to encourage him.

"I noticed that you haven't been dancing much, and I wondered if you might like to dance with me?" he asked, leaning forward with his hands on the back of Billy's empty chair.

Becky cut her eyes toward the restroom. "Won't that make your girlfriend mad?"

Theo followed her gaze and chuckled. "Oh, that's not my girlfriend," he replied, "She's my sister."

"Oh," Becky said, thawing a little. Maybe he wasn't such a lout after all. Any man who'd take his sister out dancing couldn't be all bad.

She glanced at the dance floor and saw Billy wrap his arms around Sue Anne Carver and pull her close as the music changed to a slow dance. The bastard didn't even have the grace to look and see if she was watching his flirtations.

Becky forced a smile and stood up, smoothing back her hair. "Sure, I'd love to dance with you," she said, unable to keep from glancing at Billy again as she secretly unbuttoned the top button of her blouse to reveal a healthy cleavage. Sue Anne wasn't the only one with tits around here, she thought bitterly as she felt the man move up against her. The warmth of his body made her shiver.

Theo put his arm around her shoulder and led her out onto the floor. "Don't worry about your boyfriend," he said softly as he took her in his arms and pulled her against him. "We'll make him good and jealous."

Becky laughed and glanced into his coal black eyes, shivering again because she had the sudden thought they were like dolls' eyes—flat and dead. "How'd you know that's what I was thinking?"

"When a young man treats a lovely young woman like you so bad, it would be the logical thing for you to think."

"Right on, mister," Becky said, ignoring her misgivings and pressing her chest against him and putting her right hand on the back of his neck, glancing over his shoulder to make sure Billy was watching.

Theo squeezing her back and murmured, "Ummm, your breasts feel good against my chest. Can you feel what they're doing to me?" he asked, pressing his erection against her pelvis as they danced.

Alarmed at his pass, Becky started to pull away, but suddenly a voice in her head said, Why not? Billy's been feeling that Sue Anne up all night so I'll just show him two can play that game.

She pressed her pelvis back against the hardness and blushed. This just wasn't like her. She hadn't remained a virgin for nineteen years by doing things like this, she tried to tell herself. But the voice in her head kept telling her it was all right, and it did feel good.

As they danced, the man's hands roamed around on her back and slowly dipped down to lightly caress her buttocks, moving in slow circles over their ripe swellings.

She started to protest, but her mouth just wouldn't form the words and she was starting to tingle and get wet between her legs from the constant rubbing of the man's penis against her pubic bone as they moved around the dance floor.

Wow, she thought, if he keeps this up much longer I'm going to come right here in public. She only hoped she could keep from screaming if it happened.

Just as the man's head dipped and he slowly licked her neck in a gentle kiss, a hand appeared on his shoulder and he was pulled around.

"What the hell do you think you're doing, Mister?" Billy demanded, his chest all puffed out and his face red and angry.

The stranger spread his arms out wide. "Why, I don't know what you mean, young man."

"What're you doing feeling up my girl?" Billy asked, his voice rising.

"Oh, this is your girl?" Theo asked innocently. "I never would have known it from the way you've been dancing with that other young lady all night."

Billy's face turned even redder. "That's none of your business," he blurted out, glancing nervously at Becky to see how she was taking all this.

Theo glanced around. Several couples nearby were watching them to see if their argument developed into a fight. "Come, let's not be angry," Theo said, his voice soft and reasonable. "Let my sister and I buy you two a round of drinks and we can forget all this unpleasantness."

"Well," Billy said, mollified somewhat that the man was trying to apologize, and he sure as hell didn't want him saying anything else to Becky about how he'd been dancing with Sue Anne all night.

"Oh, come on, Billy," Becky said, taking his arm and pulling him toward their table. "You have been acting like a jerk."

Theo waved his arm toward the table in the corner where Christina was sitting, watching them with a slight smile on her face. "Come on and join us. Our table's larger than yours and I'll get the waitress to bring us all fresh drinks."

After they'd all gotten seated and a round of drinks was ordered, Christina leaned toward Billy who was sitting on her left and said, "Hi. My name is Christina. What's yours?"

As Billy opened his mouth to speak, Christina slid her hand under the table and onto Billy's right thigh, letting her fingertips brush the bulge in the front of his jeans. Billy jumped, his eyes going immediately to Becky to see if she was watching, and then he swallowed as the bulge in his jeans got larger. "Uh, my name's Billy," he managed to croak.

"Oh," Christina whispered as Theo began talking to Becky across the table from them. "You're a very big boy, aren't you?" she asked as her fingers continued to caress him under the table.

Unable to help himself, Billy's hips began to give little tiny jerks as he tried to press himself tighter against her hand. He stared at Christina and almost moaned. Damn, she was the best looking woman he'd ever seen and she was making a pass at him. The boys at the shop were never going to believe this, he thought, already planning on how he could dump Becky and go home with this beauty.

Across the table, Theo was talking in a low voice to Becky while he moved his hand up her thigh and under the hem of her dress. While he talked, he slid his hand all the way up to her crotch, smiling when he felt how wet her panties were.

With a little twist of his wrist, he insinuated his finger under the edge of her panties and began to make small circles on her clitoris while watching her eyes half close and her lips open slightly.

When she was on the verge of an orgasm and was starting to take quick, short breaths, Theo moved his finger down to her vagina, surprised and delighted to find her hymen intact.

He hadn't had a virgin in, oh, more years than he cared to remember. Better to save her for later.

He removed his hand and turned his attention back to Christina and Billy. He almost laughed at the expression on Billy's face. The poor boy looked like he was about to cream in his pants, which he undoubtedly was, Theo thought.

Theo picked up his drink and held it aloft. "A toast to new friends," he said. Billy and Becky both seemed to suddenly come awake and picked up their drinks. Thantos winked at Christina as everyone drained their glasses.

He slammed his glass down and grinned. "Now," he said, "Christina and I have a suite of rooms at the Banff Springs Hotel. How about you two young people joining us there? They have a great bar on the second floor and I am on an unlimited expense account." He looked back and forth at Billy and Becky. "We can drink all the champagne you two can hold."

Becky looked at Billy, who just stared stupidly back at her as if his mind were a thousand miles away. Becky had lived in Banff all her life and had never even seen a room at the Banff Springs Hotel, much less attended a party there. These two people must be loaded to be staying there, she thought.

"Yeah, that'd be great," she said, gathering up her purse and getting to her feet.

Billy blushed and slowly got to his feet, turning to the side and putting his hand in his jeans pocket to hide his erection as he did so. "Sure, why not?" he said, still hoping to somehow manage to get the dark-haired beauty alone later.

Chapter 9

As they entered the massive doors to the Banff Springs Hotel, Becky shook herself. She didn't know why she'd ever consented to come here. After all, she didn't know these people, and as for Billy . . . well, he couldn't seem to keep his eyes off that Christina woman. Becky felt she might as well be invisible for all the attention he'd paid to her since they hooked up with this strange pair.

Her doubts were mollified somewhat when they entered the fancy lobby of the hotel, with its frescoed ceilings and elaborately carved woodwork on all of the walls. She had always wanted to see what the place was like, and if she had to spend some time with this older couple, well then so be it.

So far it was even better than she'd always thought. Most of the people in the lobby and on the grounds were dressed in coats and ties and elegant evening gowns. She felt absolutely shabby in her jeans and blouse. Even the fancy embroidered vest her mother had given her for her birthday looked downright dowdy in this crowd.

On the other hand, she thought shivering as Theo put his hand on her back to usher her into the elevator, every time this handsome stranger touched her, it was as if her skin was on fire and the fire was shooting straight through to her groin. She'd never met anyone who radiated sex like this man. Not that she intended to *have* sex with him, but it might be fun to string him along for a while and see how good he could make her feel short of going all the way.

It was a game she'd played for several years with the local studs in Banff, and she didn't see why it wouldn't work with this older guy. Men were so stupid when it came to sex. All you had to do was bat your eyes, let them see a little tit, and they'd practically drool all over you to give you what you want. And if you consented to give them a rub and a tug, then they were yours for life.

"Theo," Christina said from the back of the elevator where she stood with her taunt buttocks pressing into Billy's groin, "why don't we stop by our suite before we go to the bar? I need to freshen up a bit first."

"Fine with me," Theo said. He smiled down at Becky. "That way we can show Billy and Becky what the rooms look like, in case they're interested."

Becky glanced sideways at Billy, but his eyes were fixed on the back of Christina's neck, who was standing much closer to him than the space required.

"Sure, okay by me," Becky said, giving Billy a sharp nudge with her elbow to get his attention. "How about it, Billy?"

"All right," he replied, his eyes half-closed and his words slurred as if he'd had too much to drink and was slightly stoned.

He can't be drunk, Becky thought, he's only had three drinks or so. It usually takes him at least six or seven to get this blitzed. She glanced down and was astonished to see his groin pressed up against that woman's buttocks. The bastard, she thought.

Finally, the elevator opened on the top floor and Theo and Christina led them down the hall to one of the largest suites offered by the hotel. When he opened the door and stepped back, Becky's mouth dropped open and she walked in staring around at the opulence of the rooms.

As was usual for Theo, he was in the most expensive suite in the hotel. He always traveled first class, and even though he and Christina were sleeping in the same bed, the suite had two bedrooms, along with an elaborate sitting room and huge bathroom with an oversize tub fitted with jets for a Jacuzzi-like effect. It couldn't compare to the rooms at four-star hotels in the States, he thought, but it was pretty nice for a backwoods place like Banff.

Theo moved to a bar in the corner and made them all drinks. He handed them out and then said to Christina, "Why don't you show Billy the other bedroom, Christina, why I show Becky around the sitting room bath?"

"Love to," Christina said, hooking her arm in Billy's and leading him through the far door, kicking it shut behind her with her foot as she passed.

Becky was about to protest when Theo put his arm around her shoulders and gently led her into the sitting room. Her stomach quivered and jumped at his electric touch and she forgot what she'd been about to say. She took a quick sip of her drink to quiet her trembling nerves and get her mind off the heat that was smoldering between her legs as he showed her the exquisite antiques that made up the furniture in the room.

When they got to the bathroom, he set his drink down on the sink and put his palms on her cheeks. He bent down and gently kissed her on the lips, causing her to almost moan in delight as he caressed her face with his hands and licked her lips with his tongue.

After a moment he asked, "Would you like to try the hot tub out? It's most relaxing."

For some strange reason, Becky could see nothing out of the ordinary about the question, and she had been thinking about what it would be like to lay back in the tub and let the bubbles cascade over her naked breasts.

"Uh . . . sure," she answered in a somewhat dazed voice, wondering what he was going to be doing while she took a bath in the middle of a date.

"Excellent," he said, taking her drink from her hand. "I'll just go and freshen these up a bit while you get undressed and into the tub."

Before he left, he bent over and turned the water on and sprinkled some bath salts into the tub, causing waves of lilac-scented fumes to fill the room.

Without quite knowing how it happened, Becky found herself lying naked in the tub, her thoughts feeling as though they were wrapped in cotton. She reached over and turned the jets on and was rewarded with a gentle massage as if a thousand tiny fingers were touching her body. She rolled slightly to the side and let the bubbles caress her inner thighs, sighing as the warmth spread from her crotch up to her breasts, making her nipples as hard as rocks.

When the door opened, she turned her head and looked through clouds of billowing steam at Theo entering the room. He was completely naked and held a drink in each hand.

Becky gasped as her eyes naturally fell to his groin, where his enormous penis stood at full erection. It seemed to be pointing right at her. She tried to come awake and focus her thoughts, but it was if she'd been drugged. All she could think of was that she couldn't allow him to try and put that thing in her—it would split her in half.

Theo bent down and handed Becky her drink, letting his hand glide down across her breast to lightly tweak her nipple as she took it.

"You have lovely breasts, my dear," he said, his voice growing husky with lust.

Becky took a drink, more to have something to do than because she was thirsty. "Uh, where's Billy?" she managed to croak, her eyes darting around the room, looking at anything to keep them off his body.

He set his drink down on the edge of the tub and stepped into the bubbling water, easing her up to a sitting position and sliding down behind her. He wrapped his arms around her, his hands on her breasts, and pulled her back against him so she was sitting between his legs.

She could feel his erection poking against her backbone as he said, "Billy and Christina are busy in the other room, my dear. You don't have to worry about him interrupting us."

In spite of herself, Becky threw her head back and moaned when his left hand caressed her breast while his right hand dipped down and his fingers entered her wetness.

She could feel him throb against her as he moved his fingers in and out and she bucked her pelvis against his hand. She tried to say no, but the words wouldn't come and all she could do was pant and gasp at the feelings he was causing her to have. She forgot all about her vow not to let him have sex with her—in fact, she felt as if he didn't do something soon, she was going to scream in frustration.

Becky was just on the verge of an orgasm when his hands moved under her arms and he lifted her up without apparent effort. He positioned her over him and dropped her down onto his penis, pausing for a moment as it met her hymen.

"Please, don't," she gasped, summoning all of her will to try one last time to deny him. "I'm a virgin . . ."

"Not anymore, my dear," Theo growled, jerking her down and impaling her upon his staff.

He cut off her scream of pain by twisting her head around and covering her mouth with his as he pumped and pounded against her buttocks with his groin. The water in the tub turned scarlet as he ripped his way into her inner recesses.

She dug her fingernails into his thighs, trying to dislodge him, until after a moment her eyes glazed over and she began to push back against him as orgasm after orgasm shook her to her very core.

When she moaned, "Yes . . . yes," against his lips, he pulled his head back and put his lips against the warm, pulsating artery in her throat.

When his penis began to throb and spurt inside her, he let himself change and he sank his fangs into her neck, sucking her blood as he filled her with his essence.

Becky opened her eyes and tried to scream at the sight of the monster's face against her neck, but for some reason, her throat wouldn't work.

Theo's gleaming red eyes bored into hers as the light faded from them and she died.

He didn't stop pumping against her when she went limp, and he continued to feast on her for several minutes until she was drained and empty.

In the bedroom, Christina wasted no time. As soon as the door was shut, she turned to Billy and put her arms around his neck. "You don't mind if I change into something more comfortable, do you, dear?"

As she said this, Christina let her thigh push between Billy's legs until she could feel him responding.

"Uh, no," he managed to say, his eyes bulging out. "Go right ahead."

She turned her back to him and raised the hair off the back of her neck. "Would you mind undoing me?"

He reached up and with trembling fingers undid the clasp at the neck of her dress. His eyes bulged with disbelief as Christina let it fall to her hips. She wasn't wearing a bra and she backed into him and pulled his arms around her and placed his hands on her breasts. Damn! He thought. This was like something out of a movie. This just didn't happen to guys who worked at Al's Garage in Banff, Canada.

"Do you like that?" she whispered.

"Oh, yes!" he moaned, kneading and squeezing her breasts as hard as he could.

Christina frowned and turned to face him. "Easy, Billy, they're to play with, not break."

"Oh, I'm sorry," he said, blushing and jerking his hands off of her.

"Here, let me show you how to hold them," Christina said, reaching down and unzipping his jeans. She pulled his erection out and gently ran her hands up and down the shaft, making it jump and throb. Then she cupped his balls, being very gentle.

"See, easy does it big boy."

He almost fainted at the feeling as he pushed his penis against her hand and put his hands back on her breasts, more gently this time.

He bent down and put his lips on hers, groaning when she stuck her tongue in his mouth and pressed herself against him.

Seconds later, she reached up and ripped his shirt off, moaning "Hurry, hurry," under her breath.

When they were both completely naked, she put her hands against his chest and pushed him back on the bed, following him and straddling him.

As he clumsily pushed against her, trying to get inside, she laid out flat on his body and used her hands to help him. When he rammed his penis in her and began to buck and thrust as fast as he could, she reached down and cupped his balls in her hand again and squeezed.

He gasped and quit moving as he opened his mouth to yell in pain. "Not so fast, dear," Christina said, her voice hard. "This isn't a race, so slow down!"

His face burning in embarrassment, Billy nodded and began to move slowly in and out inside her.

"That's better, sweetie," Christina said, kissing him on the lips and putting his hands back on her breasts.

When he moaned and closed his eyes and it became evident he wasn't going to last much longer, Christina climbed off of him.

"No . . . no . . . don't stop!" he pleaded, trying to pull her back on top of him.

"Uh-uh, darling," she said. "Little Christina wants to enjoy this too, and you'll never last long enough this way."

She twisted on the bed and threw her right leg over his head and lowered herself down onto his face. "Now, you go to work up there," she said, lowering her head and kissing his penis, "And I'll go to work down here."

She teased him by slowing and stopping her kissing and sucking whenever he got close to climaxing, until finally she felt the beginnings of her own orgasm. As she pulsed and throbbed, she dipped her head and brought him to conclusion at the same time.

He was still groaning and spurting when she flipped around and let herself change. He opened his eyes in time to see her fangs glistening with red drool as they moved toward his neck.

"No-o-o-o!" he tried to scream, until she tore out his throat and drank his life away.

After she was finished with Billy, Christina rolled over onto her back and saw Theo standing in the doorway, naked and stroking himself as he'd watched her feed.

She grinned and held out her arms to him. He growled and leapt onto the bed, landing between her legs.

He raked his fangs against her neck and tore deep furrows along her back with his claws as he rammed himself into her.

She growled and snarled back, sinking her fangs into his shoulder as she bucked back against him until they both came together with muted howls of pleasure.

Chapter 10

Elijah Pike joined his four friends at breakfast. Though he was by nature a morning person and usually in a good mood when he came down to eat, a larger than usual smile was on his face this day.

"Whoa, look at the cat who looks like he just swallowed a canary," Shooter said as he slathered a huge amount of butter onto an English muffin.

"Yeah, what's going on, Elijah?" TJ asked as she took the muffin away from Shooter and took a large bite.

"I just got off the phone with Doctor Wingate at McGill University, and he told me the new batch of plasmids is about ready to ship to us."

Shooter made an attempt to grab his muffin back but TJ was too quick for him. With a mock scowl he took another from the basket in the middle of the table and began to butter it. "Hey, how about speaking English for those of us"— he paused, glancing around the table and smirking—"uh, those of us who aren't doctors."

"Let me explain it to him, Elijah," TJ said through a mouthful of muffin, "I'm used to forcing myself to come down to his level."

Shooter smirked again, his usual cocky smile back on his face. "Yeah, I remember how you had to *force* yourself last night, dear."

TJ blushed and gave him an elbow in the ribs. "Shooter, if you can get your dirty mind back to business, what Elijah was saying is that the ingredients for the new and improved vaccine are ready to be shipped to us."

"You mean those plasmid doohickeys he was talking about?"

"Shooter," Elijah said as he took a seat at the table and reached for the muffin basket himself, "Plasmids are like tiny little animals that love to eat bacteriophage, or at least grab onto them and keep them from reproducing, and as you remember, bacteriophages are the little, uh, doohickeys in our bloodstream that carry our Vampyre characteristics."

"Yeah, and the plasmids are pretty particular," Matt added. "Each species of plasmid will only attack certain species of bacteriophages, so Doc Wingate has been working to get a family of plasmids that will more specifically go after the type of bacteriophages that cause the Vampyre syndrome."

Shooter smiled and spread his arms, "Well, why didn't you just say that in the first place?"

Everyone laughed and dug into their eggs and bacon and sausage, until Elijah interrupted the meal again with a question. "That reminds me, Sam," he said, "how are you coming on the database of possible recipients?"

Sam, as the one of the group most accomplished with computer programming, had been assigned the task of taking all the names of Vampyres that Elijah had accumulated over his many years and finding out current addresses or phone numbers by using the Internet. These contact points were to be used to offer them the vaccine when it was ready.

She looked up. "I'm about ninety percent done, Elijah. Some of the names just don't show up anywhere on any of the search engines I've been using."

He nodded. "I'm surprised you found that many that did,"

he said. "Most of us value our privacy highly and are loath to let our names get out into the public domain."

"Well, most of the numbers I've gotten are cell phones, which as you know are pretty anonymous and won't really enable anyone to be found. Just like you, they get one with a nationwide plan and they can be thirty states away from where they purchased it and no one could tell."

"Yes, cellular phones and the Internet have made staying hidden much easier than it was in the old days," Elijah said, a wistful look in his eyes as he remembered some of the elaborate schemes he'd used over the years to cover his tracks.

"Of course, most of our eventual users are going to find out about the vaccine through word of mouth," TJ said as she took a final bite of Shooter's muffin.

"Which brings up another question," Shooter said. "Speaking as the member of this group in charge of security, exactly how are you going to set it up where we can administer the vaccine to the ones who want it without revealing our location to those who might want to use deadly force to stop us from giving it out?"

"That's easy," Elijah replied. "First off, any interested applicants will be given a cell phone number we'll purchase just for that purpose. Once they've been told the basics, we'll get an e-mail address and a post office box number for them and then, using our GhostSurf program to hide our location, Sam will email them explicit instructions and a list of side effects. If they're still interested, they'll e-mail us back and we will mail them a vial of the medicine large enough to last them for a year. Those that want to help, will be enlisted as distributors and before long we'll have dozens if not hundreds of Vampyres doing our work for us."

"How about the postmarks on the packages?" Shooter asked. "Couldn't a hostile check that to see where the packages were mailed from?"

"Sure," Elijah replied, "and that's where the most difficult part of this is going to come in. We're each going to have to fly periodically to other cities and mail the packages from there so as not to leave any traces of our home base."

"That sounds awfully expensive, pal," Shooter said, looking around at the group, "And since none of us are currently employed, how are we going to afford it? Are we going to charge for the vaccine, and if so, how will they get the money to us?"

Elijah smiled. "Not to worry, Shooter. In the first place, my net worth is something over four million dollars and it's earning five percent a year, which gives us about two hundred thousand dollars a year to spend on our little venture. And yes, I will ask those who want to if they will give a voluntary donation to help cover the costs of manufacture of the vaccine by Doctor Wingate, and the distribution by us. If they want to donate, they'll be given a number to a Swiss bank account which is identified only by another number, so it cannot be traced to us."

Shooter smiled wryly. "Looks like you've thought of every thing, pal."

"Years of practice, Shooter. After living as a hunted being for over two hundred years, you soon learn to cover all the possibilities or you don't survive."

He hesitated. "That brings up something else," he added. "I don't want to rush you, but I'm going to need your decision fairly soon on whether you two men want to be transformed. The process itself will take about a week or ten days for you to get through, and if you decide to do it, then the girls and I will have to go off the vaccine for at least a couple of weeks prior to . . . uh, donating our blood to you."

"What?" Sam said, a look of dismay on her face. "Wait a minute, Elijah. Why will we have to go off the vaccine before the Rite of Transformation?"

Elijah smiled sympathetically. "I know it's not something you want to do, Sam, to have to face the hunger again and not be able to satisfy it, but it's necessary. If we keep taking the vaccine, it will keep the level of bacteriophages in our systems at a very low level, perhaps too low to infect Matt and Shooter." He shook his head. "No, if we want this transformation to be successful, I'm afraid we're going to have to go back to being wild again, at least for a short while."

Matt, knowing how Sam dreaded the thought of having to endure the constant yearning to rend and tear and kill for blood the hunger would bring, put his hand on her arm. "I'm sorry, sweetheart," he said. "If it means putting you through that again, I'll just not go through with the process."

She glanced at him and smiled through scarlet-tinged tears. "No, Matt, that's unacceptable. I want you with me forever, and no price is too high to pay for that privilege. Besides, Elijah has plenty of blood bank blood on hand, and that will keep the hunger at bay until we can get back on the serum."

Elijah glanced at her out of the corner of his eyes. They both knew that wasn't true. The hunger, when it came, demanded far more than just blood meals. It demanded the hunt and the kill and the feasting and all that went with it, including blood rich with the adrenaline-taste of terror the kill engendered in the victims. He knew that Sam and TJ and he would all have to endure a craving far worse than that of the heroin addict in order to transform the men. He only hoped they were strong enough to fight the hunger off without giving in to it before the job was done.

"How about you, TJ?" Shooter asked, his eyes full of concern.

"Been there, done that," she answered shortly. "Remember, we went off the vaccine before when we had to go up against Morpheus."

"Yeah, but then you got to, uh, hunt and kill," Shooter replied. "It's gonna be much worse for you not to get to do that."

She put her hand over his on the table. "I'll be busy nursing you, big boy, and that will keep my mind off the hunger," she added, knowing what she was saying wasn't true. For nothing could keep a Vampyre's mind off the hunger once it set in—nothing except a fresh kill.

"So, we're all decided then?" Elijah asked, respecting the girls' desires to not let the men know what they were going to have to go through. "Both of you men want to go through the Rite of Transformation and all that it entails?"

All four at the table nodded.

"Good. Then we'll go off our vaccine as of today, and I'll give Ed and Kim a call asking them to do the same thing." He'd already explained to everyone his theory of multiple donors perhaps enhancing the attributes of the transformees.

Sam raised her glass of orange juice high. "A toast," she said, "to Matt and Shooter, soon to be with us forever."

Five glasses were raised and all drank, each of them wondering what they were letting themselves in for.

Of the five, three knew that the next few weeks were going to be a living nightmare of the agony of unfulfilled hunger. A mind numbing experience that all three hoped they could endure for as long as was necessary to transform the men into members of their race.

The other two, Matt and Shooter, knew only that they were embarking on a journey of no return—one that would keep them with the women they loved for hundreds of years. They both knew that was worth any sacrifice.

Chapter 11

It was about four days after Ed Slonaker had gotten the call from Elijah telling him that if he and Kim were going to participate in his experiment with the new transformation method, they were going to have to go off the vaccine, that his new number two man came running into his office at Mountie headquarters.

"Hey, Chief," Sonny Tedesco said, his voice high-pitched and breathless with excitement.

Ed sighed heavily. "Sonny, calm down before you have a stroke."

Sonny took a couple of deep breaths, and then he started off again, "Chief, they've found a couple of bodies over at the Banff Springs Hotel."

Ed cocked an eyebrow. Murder wasn't all that unusual in Banff, but it usually only claimed one victim at a time and he'd never had one at the Springs. "Yeah?" he asked, turning in his chair and leaning back. "Tell me about it."

Sonny consulted a small notebook in his hand, making Ed smile. He knew Sonny must have seen cops do that on the television, because it certainly wasn't something he'd learned in Mountie school. "Two young people, male and female in their early twenties or so, were found naked with their throats ripped out," he read. And then with eyes wide, he continued, "and get this, Chief, their bodies were stuffed in an air shaft in the ceiling on the top floor."

Ed felt his heart grow cold, for he knew what he was dealing with. Only one type of perp killed like this—Vampyres.

"You say they were young people?" he asked, turning to a folder on his desk.

"Yeah, Chief," Sonny said. He consulted his notebook again. "Look to be about nineteen or twenty or so."

Ed nodded, thumbing through the missing persons reports in the folder. After a moment, he pulled two sheets out and laid them face up on his desk. "A Miss Becky Robertson and one Billy Johnson were both reported missing three days ago," he read. He looked up at Sonny. "Seems Becky's mother said she and this Billy guy had gone out to celebrate Becky's nineteenth birthday and they never came back. She reported she thought they'd probably run off together. Said Becky was kind'a boy crazy and it was something she might have done." He looked up at Sonny. "Guess she was wrong, huh?"

Nineteen years old, he thought, his stomach churning. What a waste. He stood up and pulled his belt and holster off a nearby coat rack and belted it on. Taking his hat, he ushered Sonny toward the door. "You got the crime scene cordoned off?"

"Yes, sir!" Sonny replied as he led the way out the door toward their patrol car. "That was the first thing I did. I got the manager standing by making sure nobody messes with anything around the area."

Ed ducked under the yellow crime scene tape and looked at the bodies from a few feet away. The smell was strong enough to make his eyes water—old blood, excrement, and decaying flesh made quite a potent combination. The bodies of the young couple were lying in the middle of the top floor corridor where the workmen who'd pulled them from the air-shaft had laid them. Bloody sheets were crumpled around them and two piles of what appeared to be vomit were on the floor nearby.

Ed raised his eyebrows at Sonny and pointed to the vomit. "Yeah, the two men who pulled 'em out of the shaft puked when they uncovered the bodies and saw what'd been done to 'em," the deputy explained.

"Medical examiner on his way?" Ed asked.

"Yes, sir. He was in the middle of surgery but he said he'd be here in 'bout thirty minutes or so."

Like most towns in Canada, the medical examiner was a surgeon who also had other duties besides examining bodies at crime scenes.

Ed took a couple of steps closer to the bodies and squatted down, his gaze fixed on the open wounds around the necks of the victims. "Find out an approximate time of death and then get the manager to give us a list of all the people registered in the hotel from two days before to two days after the date of death, with special emphasis on those staying on the top floor," Ed dictated.

Sonny pulled out his small notepad and began to write Ed's instructions down. "Yes, sir."

"I imagine the time of death is gonna be about three days, around the time they disappeared," Ed said, still squatting down and letting his eyes roam over the bodies, searching for some clue as to who did this but knowing all he was going to find were two bodies completely drained of blood. "Soon as you get the list, call the airport and put the names on a watch list and tell the airport authorities not to let anyone on the list fly out until I've had a chance to talk to them."

"Okay, but don't you think they've already gone, sir?"

Ed nodded, sighing with frustration and anger. As much as he hated to, he was going to have to be very careful with this investigation. He couldn't afford to let it get out of his control and go in directions that would be dangerous for he and Kim. "Yeah, I don't think they'd have the balls to stay around and wait for the bodies to be discovered, but we've still got to cover all the bases."

"All right," Sonny said, getting a look from Ed that made him blush.

"Uh, I didn't mean to question your orders, sir," Sonny said contritely.

Ed chuckled and stood up. "Don't be silly, Sonny. The only way you're ever gonna learn to handle a crime scene on your own is to ask questions, so if you ever think I've missed something or you don't understand why I'm doing things a certain way, by all means ask."

"Yes, sir. Thank you sir."

"Now, while you get the CSI guys to lift any prints off the ceiling tiles they can find, I'll go on over to the office and log onto the VICAP computer site and see if there are any serial killers operating anywhere with a similar MO."

Sonny cut his eyes back to the bodies on the floor. "I . . . I've never seen nothing like that before, Chief," he said, swallowing audibly.

"Yeah," Ed said quietly, slipping his Mountie hat back on. "The perp is probably going to turn out to be some crazy American up here visiting." He shook his head. "If anyone in Canada was killing people like this I would have heard about it."

When Ed got back to his office, instead of logging onto his computer terminal to check the Violent Criminal Apprehension Profiles, he shut his door and dialed John Ashby's cell phone number. Though he had no idea where John went after their talk the previous week, he hoped he still had the same phone number and was carrying his phone with him.

After a few rings, he heard his old friend's voice answer cautiously, "Hello."

"Johnny, Ed here."

"Hey, Ed. What's up?" John asked, sounding surprised to hear from Ed.

"I got me a couple of bodies over at the Springs Hotel," Ed said slowly. "They've had their throats ripped out and I'm betting the ME's gonna find there ain't a whole lot of blood left in 'em."

John chuckled low in his throat. "And you called me up to see if your old friend Johnny had anything to do with their demise?"

"No, Johnny," Ed replied evenly. "I know you're too smart to shit in your own backyard, and I'd like to think you still think enough of our friendship not to leave a mess like this in my lap that's gonna raise a whole lot of questions I don't particularly want raised right now."

The humor disappeared from John's voice. "Well, you're right on both counts, old pal. I wouldn't do that to you and to Kim—not after all the years we were friends." He was silent for a moment. "I didn't have anything to do with those killings, but I think I know who did."

"Was it one of the men who came up here with Michael Morpheus looking for Elijah Pike? Was it the guy you mentioned the last time we talked—Thantos I think you called him?"

"Yeah, at least that's the only other one of our kind in the area that I know about. His full name's Theo Thantos, and he's traveling with a woman named Christina Alario, though I have no idea if those are the names they used to register at the Springs with."

Ed sighed. "I doubt it. Not if they planned on leaving a calling card like this behind them." He hesitated, and then he asked, "Why are you giving me their names so easily, John? Aren't they your new buddies?"

John waited a moment to answer. "In the first place, I know for a fact they're long gone, Ed, so I'm not hurting them by telling you who they are. In the second place, they're not my buddies as you call it. They just happen to be on the same side I'm on in our race's struggle for existence. It's like that old Japanese general wrote in *The Art of War*—the enemy of my enemy is my friend."

"I'm not sure that's where that quote originated," Ed said with a laugh, enjoying talking to the man who used to be his closest friend even though the circumstances of the talk were serious.

John returned the laugh. "Neither am I, but it sounded good, didn't it?"

"Yeah," Ed replied lightly, "You always could bullshit with the best of them, Johnny."

John's voice sobered. "Well, let me give you some advice that isn't bullshit, old pal."

"Yeah?"

"A while back, when this group I joined were preparing to go after Elijah Pike and his friends, we had eight or ten of our kind staying up here in the mountains around Banff for a couple of weeks."

"Uh-huh."

"Ed, I'm sure you realize they weren't on no diets while they were up here. I figure when the spring melt begins in a couple of months, you're gonna be up to your ass in bodies with suspicious neck wounds."

"Oh, shit," Ed said, realizing John was right. He had noticed a moderate increase in the number of missing persons reports over the past six months, but in the excitement of the fracas between Morpheus and Pike he'd not made the connection until now.

"Your only hope is that the animals will mess up the bodies enough that their causes of death won't be too apparent," John added, "or you're gonna have more brass from headquarters around here than a dog has fleas."

That's for sure, Ed thought. "Why are you telling me this, John?"

"In spite of all that's happened recently, with us being on

opposite sides in this war that's starting and all, you're still my best friend, Ed. I think maybe it's time for you to get the hell outta Dodge 'fore the shit hits the fan. Not even someone as good at acting like a Normal as you are is going to be able to cover this shit up when the bodies start piling up at the morgue."

"Thanks for the heads up, John," Ed said, and then he added thoughtfully, "You may just be right."

Chapter 12

In Washington, D.C., by the time the bodies they'd left behind had been found, Theo Thantos was bustling around his top floor suite at the Ritz Carleton Hotel like a nervous teenager before his first date.

Christina, who was sitting quietly on a sofa drinking a glass of champagne, just shook her head. "Theo, will you for God's sake please calm down? You're even making me nervous with all your prancing around."

He didn't look at her as he bent and straightened a plate of sandwiches and cookies on a sideboard that had been set up by the hotel staff.

"I told you, Christina, I need everything to be perfect for this meeting. These are very important people and I've got to convince them to join us under my leadership or my plan will never work."

She smirked. "If they're as smart and important as you think they are, Theo, then it's going to have to be your arguments that convince them to join us, not that pathetic plate of food."

He whirled on her, eyes blazing, just as the doorbell rang.

He took a deep breath, tried to calm himself, and went to answer it.

Within an hour, everyone he'd invited had arrived, been fed and given drinks, and Theo had the floor and their attention.

"I've asked you all to come here because of a dire threat to our race and our way of life," he began, striding back and forth in front of the men and women gathered around the suite.

A distinguished-looking man with salt-and-pepper gray hair combed straight back over patrician features held up a small envelope. "So you said, Theo, in this note you sent me," said Augustine Calmet, the night editor for the *Washington Post,* the city's leading newspaper. "But I'm due at two embassy parties tonight so would you please get to the point?"

Theo pursed his lips, wanting to rip the arrogant bastard's throat out—as if his parties were more important than the future of the race. With an effort he controlled his temper and continued. "All right, the short version then. A rogue among us named Elijah Pike has developed and almost perfected a serum, a vaccine that will enable any of our race to live as Normals again, without the necessity to feed on human blood."

The group looked at each other as excited murmuring spread throughout them.

"I'd heard rumors of such a vaccine," Gabrielle de Lavnay said from the sofa. She was a gray-haired woman who appeared to be in her sixties, though Theo knew for a fact she was only forty-two biological years old and used elaborate makeup to appear older. She was known around Washington as a wealthy recluse, who gave huge sums of money to both political parties to gain influential politicians' presence at her infrequent parties. "But I gave the rumors no credence. Do you mean to tell me there is such a vaccine?" she asked, her eyes narrowing as she stared at him.

He felt the familiar tickle of her attempting to read his thoughts and closed his mind against her. "Yes, Gabrielle, there is such a vaccine and it is my belief that it poses the most significant threat to our race that has occurred since the pogroms in the middle ages."

A man named Johannes Cuntius spoke up from where he stood leaning against a wall on the far side of the room, a drink in his hand. "But Thantos," he began, his voice bored, "how could such a vaccine, even supposing one really exists, be a threat to us? Surely, there will be a number of our kind who are tired of the life we are forced to live who might want to try this magic elixir, but so what? How can that harm the rest of us?" He glanced around the group with a supercilious smile on his face. "I think most of us feel as I do. I love my life and I don't intend to change the way I live in any way."

Theo knew him to be an executive with the local TV station, WXMB, who had something to do with producing the evening news, but Theo was unsure just what his actual job title was. "Let me answer your question this way, Johannes," Theo said, "and I'll try to be brief so Augustine can get to his parties. In my experience, there are two types of people within the Vampyre race—those who are proud of what we are, who love the thrill of the chase and the excitement of the kill, and who know in our hearts that we are the superior race and that the so-called Normals are here on earth to serve as our food stock."

He paused and glanced around the room, gauging the expressions he saw on their faces. He'd picked this group of people with care, for he knew they were not only very important in the tight-knit society of Washington, but that they were the type of Vampyres he'd just mentioned.

"And then," he continued, "there is the other type—the weak sisters who cringe at the thought that they need to kill to survive, who feel a profound guilt for their actions and a misguided sympathy for our natural enemies, the Normals. It is precisely these people who will line up to take the vaccine and try to become what they can never truly become, a Normal human being again."

"I say again," Johannes spoke up, "so what? I say good riddance to the bastards." He grinned savagely. "That just leaves more prey for the rest of us."

Theo noticed several members of his audience nodding their heads, so he held up his hands. "Oh, I don't bemoan the fact that they might choose to leave our race," Theo said, darting his eyes to each pair watching him, "what I do bemoan is the threat to our very existence that they represent."

"How so, Mr. Thantos?" Christabel Chordewa asked. Christabel and her mate, Brahma Parvsh owned and ran the city's largest limousine service.

"How long do you think it will be before one of these traitors to our race, once they feel that they themselves are back among the Normals, makes the fact of our existence public?" Theo asked. "Oh, they'll do it with the best of intentions, to force the rest of us to take their damned vaccine and become mindless sheep with the life expectancies of mayflies like them, but do it they shall!"

"Surely they wouldn't be so stupid," a man who used the single name Danag said. "They would be indicting themselves in the bargain."

Theo remembered the man was some sort of singer or entertainer as he gave an elaborate shrug. "We've all lived long enough to see the martyr syndrome in action," he said, looking around the room, "and does anyone here think that out of probably many thousands of this kind of weakling there won't be some who just can't wait to throw themselves on the mercy of the Normals, their new friends?"

"I can see your point, Theo," Augustine Calmet said. "I don't necessarily agree with it, but I can see the possibility of it happening. But, just what do you propose we do about it? Try to prevent the vaccine from being given out?"

Theo shook his head. "No, Augustine, it's much too late

for that. The formula is known to too many people and it would be impossible to silence all of them."

Calmet shrugged and spread his hands wide. "Then what are we to do, but hope what you fear won't come to pass?"

Now was Theo's chance to make his case. He took a deep breath and began. "We eliminate the threat by arising and finally taking our place as lords and masters of the Normals, as we were meant to be!" Theo said forcefully.

At first everyone just stared at him as if he'd lost his mind, then one by one the audience began to chuckle and finally to laugh out loud.

"Forgive me, Theo," Augustine said, wiping tears of laughter from his eyes, "but I hardly think a few hundred thousand of us would stand a chance of taking over the world from six billion Normals."

"Yes, Mr. Thantos," Brahma Parvsh said, a slight smile on his lips. "You are either making a bad joke or you are suffering from some mental malady to think such a thing is possible."

Theo held up his hands to get the attention of everyone. "Let me propose a way we might be able to accomplish just such a thing, gentlemen and ladies," he said.

Augustine smiled and glanced at his wristwatch. "I'll give you ten minutes, Theo, and then I'm leaving here and going back to the real world. As a news producer, I deal in facts, not wishful thinking."

"You're absolutely correct, Augustine, that we would not stand a chance if we went against the Normals face to face, but you are forgetting the tremendous advantages we have over our enemies: long lives, virtual immortality, psychic ability, and the most important of all, the ability through the Rite of Transformation to make any of our enemies into one of us."

The smile left Augustine's face as he thought about this while Theo continued earnestly. "I don't plan an armed insurrection to take over the world, my friends, but a much more subtle approach. Think about who runs the world we live in now: politicians and the media. The politicians make the rules everyone lives by, and the media is responsible for causing the people to accept the rules as good and normal."

Theo paced back and forth as he spoke, "Now, what if we began a covert campaign to transform the most influential politicians and the most important media figures and bring them into our race to work with us instead of against us? How long would it take for us to have, if not complete control, at least a strong say in what was going on in the world?"

"He makes a powerful point, Augustine," Brahma Parvsh said, his eyes thoughtful and speculative as he came over to Thantos's side. "And in addition to politicians and media moguls, we could target important federal and state judges, and perhaps even a Supreme Court justice or two." He smiled, but his eyes remained as dark as obsidian. "Then, if in the future, some misguided zealot tries to out our existence, we'd have the power to either squelch the accusations, or to have the authorities make the informer disappear before he could do any real damage."

"And due to our long lives, we could take many years to slowly invade and infiltrate the power structure across the world until at some point we could begin to work in the open, with laws to protect us and the media to paint us in a good light," Theo added.

Augustine got to his feet, a sly smile on his face. "I'm still not convinced this is necessary, or even the most prudent course to take, friends, but I do agree this is definitely worth consideration." He shrugged. "And if at some point in the future we decide not to go forward, then no harm has been done by transforming a few politicians and such into our kind. But, we must be very careful. Remember, this is a town that thrives on gossip and on conspiracy theories. It wouldn't do for us to be seen gathering together in one place, so we're going to have to be very careful as we make our plans and consider out options."

Gabrielle de Lavnay spoke up, "I have a summer house on the shores of the Delaware River. It's very isolated and I will send each of you directions on how to get there and we can have our meetings there without fear of being noticed."

"Excellent," Theo said, rubbing his hands together. "And at our next meeting, I would like everyone to bring a list of the first ones we should target, as well as some sort of plan on how we might get to them. Remember, the Rite of Transformation takes at least several days to a week or more to be done correctly, so the people we choose must be kept isolated for that long after we begin to change them."

"That's going to be very tricky, considering the importance and the public visibility of the people we need to get to," Christabel said.

"I agree, it won't be easy," Theo said, "but we are the greatest race in the history of mankind and we can do anything!"

Chapter 13

Elijah Pike smiled as he stood before the kitchen table in his cabin in Maine. "You boys need to lighten up a bit," he said, grinning at how frightened Matt and Shooter looked as they sat at the table with Sam and TJ.

Matt gamely tried to smile. "That's easy for you to say, Elijah, it's not you who's fixing to have some godawful hairy monsters nibbling at your neck."

Sam snorted and elbowed Matt in the ribs, an offended expression on her face. "You take that back, Matthew Carter. I am not hairy in my Vampyre form." She tried a seductive look, batting her eyes at him as she added, "In fact, I'm told I'm quite attractive."

Matt laughed at her attempt to relieve his worries.

"Of course you are dear," he said with more than a little sarcasm. "That's why Vampyres never seem to have any mirrors in their houses—the images of them are enough to scare the bejesus even out of themselves."

"I must interrupt," Elijah said, "even though I know you're kidding." He glanced from Sam to TJ and then back to Matt. "As a matter of fact, both Sam and TJ *are* very attractive Vampyres, at least they are to others of our species."

When Matt and Shooter both looked skeptical, he went on, "You see, boys, it's much like in the Normal world. What makes a female Normal attractive to others also does the same when she is transformed. So, a woman, or a man for that matter, who is attractive to their peers when in their Normal form, will also be attractive to their peers when in their Vampyre form."

Shooter leered at TJ and waggled his eyebrows. "So, male Vampyres like big breasts too?"

TJ shook her head. "Only bubba Vampyres, Shooter, so you should fit right in."

Matt laughed and held up his hand. "You're right, Elijah, I was just kidding. Sam is always beautiful to me, even when she's changed, though I must admit the first time I saw her like that it was quite startling."

Sam leaned over and kissed him on the cheek. "That's very sweet, darling, but you must learn never to tease someone who's about to, as you say, nibble on your neck."

"What about what Matt said, Elijah, about the mirrors and all?" Shooter asked. "I know you've told us that parts of the old legends arose in the Middle Ages when people actually believed in and knew about your race."

"That's correct, Shooter," Elijah explained. "You already know about the sunlight and how it affects our skin, especially in the days before sunscreen. I believe the myth that Vampyres cannot be seen in mirrors arose out of the fact that a lot of the old time Vampyres didn't keep mirrors in their houses because they suffered from extreme self-loathing about what they were and how they were forced to live—by killing others." He gave a low chuckle. "Even I myself was like that back in the days before I swore off innocent blood. None of my residences or ships had any mirrors in them."

"Must've been hell trying to shave without mirrors," Shooter said, eliciting a punch in the shoulder from TJ.

"What about some of the other parts of the legends, Elijah?" TJ asked.

He shrugged. "Actually, most were made up by fiction writers of the time, and enhanced and elaborated on by movie makers back in the thirties and forties." He grinned. "I've never felt the slightest urge to sleep in a coffin filled with the dirt of my homeland, or to run around wearing evening clothes with a cape."

As they all laughed, Elijah pointedly glanced at his wristwatch. "Well, I think it's about time we got started."

"What's the POA, Doc?" Shooter asked.

"POA?"

"Yeah, the plan of action," Shooter explained. "I mean, you said Matt and me were gonna get blood from all of you guys, so what's the order and exactly how do we go about it? Do you draw it up in a syringe and inject it or do we drink it or what?"

"Uh, Shooter, perhaps I should have explained the process a bit better. I don't know if the transformation would work that way or not. As far as I know, it's always been done in the traditional manner, which is by biting and sucking the blood from the neck or some other blood vessel in the transformer's body."

"But, why would that make a difference?" Shooter asked. "Blood is blood, isn't it?"

Elijah took a deep breath, trying to think of some way to explain the complexities of the Rite of Transformation to a Normal. "Not exactly, Shooter. You see, in the actual Rite of Transformation, there is quite a bit of emotional content to the act—sexual attraction, fear, anticipation, lust, hunger, excitement—and all of these emotions result in the release in both parties' bodies of hormones called pheromones. These hormones are not only in the bloodstream, but are also I suspect in both parties' saliva and maybe even in their sweat, so close personal contact may well be essential to the transformation's success."

Shooter looked worried. "Uh, Doc, forgive me, but the sexual part has me a little concerned. You see, I've always been enthusiastically heterosexual, and I just don't know about getting all worked up over another guy." He paused and cut his eyes at Sam, "Or even over my best friend's girl."

"Don't worry, Shooter, when I say sexual, I mean in the broadest sense of the word. If a person is heterosexual and drinks the blood of someone of the same sex, they feel an emotional connection naturally, but it's more like the deep liking and male bonding you'd feel for a best friend or a male relative—kind of like men hugging each other after a sports victory or some other shared endeavor."

"Yeah," said TJ, looking at Shooter and half-smiling, "like when you guys slap each other on the butt during a ballgame. What's up with that, anyway?"

"It's a guy thing," Matt said, "you women wouldn't understand. You're much more into hugging, but guys just can't do that."

"Why not?" Sam asked pointedly.

"Uh, well, it just wouldn't be manly," Matt answered lamely, his face flushing.

"Oh, you guys," TJ said disgustedly, "You're so damned afraid of being thought homosexual . . ."

Shooter looked at her and nodded, "Okay, I can see that, sort'a, and I've never had the slightest fear I was secretly homosexual so that kind of male affection won't bother me, but"—he looked over at Sam again—"what about with Sam? Hell, she's a beautiful woman and if I weren't in love with TJ and she wasn't with Matt, I have to admit I'd be attracted to her."

Sam laughed, shaking her head at his convoluted reasoning. "Thanks for the compliment, Shooter . . . I think."

He blushed, looking at TJ to make sure he wasn't in trouble. "Oh, heck, Sam. You know what I mean."

Elijah also laughed. "Yes, we know what you mean, Shooter, but here it's a bit more complicated. For a Vampyre, the act of feeding is always a sexual one, so in the vast majority of cases, male Vampyres target women and female Vampyres target men, unless they're hunting as a pair with their mate in which case the sex will usually be heterosexual between one of the pair and the victim and then with his or her mate."

Shooter again looked worried. "So, you're telling me that when Sam gives me blood, and TJ gives Matt blood, there's gonna be sex involved?"

Elijah held up his hand. "No, not necessarily, but it's likely there will be some sexual content to the feeding. Certainly, both parties will feel lust for the other and there will likely be sexual arousal." He hastened to add, "That doesn't necessarily mean there will be sexual intercourse engaged in. Sometimes it's just mutual caressing or kissing or holding." He shook his head. "It's hard to say, because in my experience, there has never been a Rite of Transformation performed except by two people who were going to be mates."

Shooter shook his head, his sad eyes on TJ. "I don't know if I like that, Doc." He sighed. "Even though in the past I've never been exactly . . . uh, monogamous with my girlfriends . . ."

"That's the understatement of the year," Matt said, laughing. "You were more like Don Juan."

Shooter drew himself up, "In spite of what my *friend* here says, it is different with TJ. Just the thought of her being with someone else, even my best friend Matt, makes me kind'a crazy."

"Trust me when I say that once you're transformed, it won't be a problem, Shooter," Elijah said, his face sympathetic. "Vampyres are able to distinguish between sex during feeding and the kind of sex one has with a mate. In a small way, it's kind of like a man on a business trip that has a one-night stand affair with a woman he meets in a bar. That act is one of sexual release only with no emotional content, and it doesn't mean he loves his partner back home any the less."

"Yeah," Shooter said ruefully, "but if his partner back home finds out she'll kill him."

"Not if she has the same attitude, Shooter," Elijah said. "The trick is to remember the difference between the sexual act, such as with feeding, and the loving sex between mates. It sounds like it is hard to do, but once you're transformed, you'll understand better and it won't be a problem."

He stood up and rubbed his hands together, looking at both couples. "Now, as for the order of giving blood, I think each of you should get your first . . . uh . . . taste from your mates, and we'll let their blood intermingle with yours overnight to give it a good foothold. Once you've shown signs of the infection, we'll switch around and you'll take blood from the others of us available."

As they got up from the table, Matt asked, "Are you going to observe the rite, Elijah?"

He shook his head. "No, the act is very private and is always done with the couple completely alone. You all go off to your rooms and I'll see you in the morning."

Matt and Sam were halfway to their bedroom when Matt stopped and turned around, a thoughtful look on his face. "Say, Elijah, you say that this getting blood from multiple other donors will increase our Vampyre abilities over getting it from just one donor?"

Elijah smiled and shrugged. "That's the theory, Matt. Why do you ask?"

"Well, if that's the case for transformees, why wouldn't the same thing apply to established Vampyres?"

"Well, because . . ." Elijah began, and then he stopped, a look of amazement on his face. "Why, damned if I know why it shouldn't, Matt. I've just never thought of it, since the only time Vampyres typically drink from other Vampyres is when they're with their mates, and of course that's not new blood to them." He stood there, stroking his chin for a moment and then he moved toward the stairway to his loft. "I'll have to give it some thought tonight," he said distractedly, his mind already on the problem.

"Way to go, Matt," Sam said, grinning, "now you've posed a problem to him that's going to keep him up all night."

"Hell, he wouldn't've been able to sleep anyway, darling, not with all the noise I plan to make tonight."

She laughed and slapped his bottom, "Well, in that case, we'd better get started, big boy."

By the time Matt got to the bed and turned around, his fingers on the buttons of his shirt, Sam was already naked and striding toward him, her body changing as she neared him.

In spite of himself, Matt felt a quick jolt of fear in the pit of his stomach at the sight of the magnificent creature she was becoming before his very eyes. He was more than a little surprised to find he'd been telling the honest truth earlier when he said even in her changed form Sam was beautiful to him. As a physician, he was analytical enough to realize that in any other person the changes to her body would be terrifying and horrible to behold, but on Sam the changes were like those of a magnificent animal—awe inspiring.

Seconds later, her change complete, she reached out to him with her claws and ripped his clothes off in a frenzy of lust. Picking him up in her arms as if he weighed nothing, she lowered him to the bed and climbed on top of him, straddling him with her muscular legs, her fangs dripping red-tinged drool onto his chest as she loomed over him.

He let his eyes roam over her body and admired the fine red fuzz that covered her and the rippling of her muscles. He put his hands on her breasts and smiled when she growled in pleasure and pressed her hips against his growing erection. He could feel her wetness already and knew she was ready for him.

He thrust as hard as he could with his hips and he groaned in ecstasy as he slipped inside her warmth. Reaching up he grabbed the back of her neck and pulled her face into his neck, matching her growl for growl and thrust for thrust as she sank her fangs into his carotid artery.

After a few seconds of incredibly building lust, she raised her head and stuck one of her claws into the side of her neck. As scarlet liquid pulsed out, she lowered her neck to his lips and he fed on her as they mated in wild abandon.

The coppery saltiness of the liquid tasted better than anything he'd ever consumed, and her hormones in the blood added to his and fed his lust like gasoline on a fire.

Down the hall, much the same thing was happening, except that Shooter was on top, and as he drove himself between TJ's widely spread thighs and into her inner core, he moaned and said softly, "I can't stand the thought of anyone else being like this with you."

She growled softly back at him as she smoothed his hair with her hand, carefully keeping her claws retracted, "Hush, hush, sweetheart. Soon it won't matter to you, for I shall never have another mate except you."

As they began to move together and she felt him throbbing inside her, she flicked a claw at her neck and pulled his lips to her wound. "Now, drink of me, my darling, so that we can be together forever," she said as her hips pumped against him and her breast swelled against his hand.

Shooter sucked and swallowed and tried to bury himself inside her as they moaned and groaned in mutual release.

After a moment, he forced his lips away from her neck and offered his own to her. She pulled him close and drank of him as he'd drank of her, until they were one.

Chapter 14

Allison Burton yawned as she answered the telephone next to her bed. She noticed it was not even seven o'clock in the morning yet so she was understandably grumpy when she said hello.

This did not deter the energetic voice on the other end from speaking rapidly in her ear, "Good morning! This is Ronnie Ranger of WBLM right here in Washington, D.C., on the line. To whom am I speaking?"

Allison's heart began to beat faster. She and all of her friends listened to WBLM all the time, and especially to the DJ known as Ronnie Ranger. He sounded like a hunk!

"This is Allison Burton," she replied, sitting up in bed and straightening up her hair, though of course he couldn't see her.

"Well, Allison, this is your lucky day," Ranger continued, " 'cause if you can answer the BLM question of the day, you and three of your best friends are going to be treated to a four-day stay at one of Virginia's most exclusive spas."

"Wow!" Allison shouted.

"Now, can you tell me the names of each and every one of the Beatles?"

I can't believe it's this easy, Allison thought excitedly. Was there anyone on the planet who didn't know the answer to that question?

"Sure, Ronnie. They were John, Paul, George, and Ringo."

She heard loud music and the banging of bells in the background as Ranger said, "Right you are, Allison. Now, you just hang on the line while I get back to you with the details of your prize."

Allison, who was just going on sixteen years of age and was the youngest daughter of Vice President Jonathon Burton, gasped and held the phone tightly to her ear, already planning on whom she would invite to go on the trip with her. She wondered if she would get to meet Ronnie Ranger and if he was as good looking and as sexy as he sounded on the radio.

Similar phone calls were being made to daughters and sons of three of the highest-ranking members of the Joint Chiefs of Staff as well as ten senators and fourteen representatives who chaired important committees in Congress.

Ronnie Ranger, who was a member of the Vampyre race, had readily agreed to the scheme, and the managers of the most exclusive spa in Virginia were even now being transformed so they could help with Theo Thantos's scheme to infiltrate the most important families in the country. To speed things along and to help divert suspicion, the young people's mothers and/or fathers would be invited along on the trips as chaperones. Of course, as important as the parents were, it was unlikely that they would attend, but the very fact that they were invited would help to alleviate suspicion.

The Rejuvenatrix Spa, located in an isolated area in the mountains of Virginia just south of Washington, would be an ideal place for a series of transformations that would give Thantos entry into the core families of the Washington elite, and these would then be able to spread out and infect their other friends until soon the leadership of America would be his.

He told Christina that within a year, he would be the de facto president of the United States. When he told her this, she gushed and drug him immediately off to bed. For her, power was almost as strong an aphrodisiac as fresh blood. He had also noticed that since he'd assumed leadership of his group of coconspirators, she was treating him with much more respect than she had previously.

So, with this new development, he decided not to dump her after all but to keep her around for a while. He was never one to deny his massive ego a supplicant's worship.

Besides, with all he had to do overseeing the plot to transform so many people, he didn't have time to search for a new mate.

The morning following their first meals of blood, both Shooter and Matt awoke to burning fever, headaches, and muscles that felt as if they'd been beaten with sticks.

Sam sat next to Matt on the bed and mopped the sweat off his brow with a cold cloth. "I know it's painful, Matt darling, but there is little we can do to ease the pain. Once the infection gets established, some of the aches and fever will diminish."

"How long will that take?" he croaked through dry, chapped lips, his muscles shaking and quivering with a sudden chill that left him feeling as weak as a baby.

She caressed his face and leaned down to kiss his lips lightly. "Soon, darling, soon. Tonight, TJ will visit you and you will feed again. Elijah thinks that multiple donors will speed the process along faster than is usually the case and shorten the length of time you're acutely ill."

He groaned and shivered again with fever. "Then send her in now," he pleaded, pulling his covers up to his neck.

She smiled. "Not yet, dear. The bacteriophages you got

from me last night must be allowed to take a good foothold before we allow any more into your bloodstream. Now you try to sleep and I'll be back in a little while."

Under the urging of her mind, he closed his eyes and was instantly asleep, though he continued to shiver and shake from the fever wracking his body.

She eased up off the bed and went into the living room, where she found Elijah talking on the phone.

"That's great news, Ed. I'll drive down to Portland and pick you and Kim up when your plane gets in."

He hung up the phone and looked at Sam with raised eyebrows.

She shrugged. "He's really hurting, Elijah," she said softly. "It's hard for me to see him like that."

He came over and put his arms around her and pulled her to him. "I know, Sam, but we have to keep thinking that it's for his own good. As a Normal, I don't believe he or Shooter would stand a chance of surviving this war we've found ourselves in with those opposed to our vaccine." He added, "Sooner or later they'll probably attack us again and we all need to be ready to fight."

"From the looks of Shooter," TJ said as she entered the room, closing their bedroom door behind her, "I don't know if they'll survive the transformation."

Elijah nodded. "I told you before we began that there is always that possibility," he said. "There have been rare cases where the transformees succumbed to the bacteriophage and died, probably from anaphylactic shock reactions or just overwhelming infection."

Sam stepped away from Elijah and went to hug TJ. "Don't worry, TJ, both the boys are strong. They'll make it through this just as we did."

"They'd better, 'cause I don't know how I'd live if something happened to Shooter," TJ said with red-tinged tears in her eyes.

Elijah, who'd performed the Rite of Transformation on TJ

the year before while intending for her to be his mate, turned away and went into the kitchen to hide his feelings for her, which were still very strong. He had to be on constant guard to keep his mind blocked so she or Sam couldn't read his love for her.

What he didn't know was that both of them had already realized it and had said nothing out of respect for his feelings and his privacy. In fact, TJ too still felt a strong attraction for Elijah, and had it not been for the depth of her love for Shooter, she would have been in his arms in an instant long before now.

"Hey, girls, how about some coffee?" he called, trying to make his voice sound normal.

"Sounds good," Sam said, feeling his lust for TJ and cutting her eyes at her friend, who just stared back and shrugged. There was nothing she could do about it—at least not at the present time.

"Sure," TJ echoed, and they joined him in the kitchen.

After he poured cups all around, he sat and joined them at the table. "Good news," he said. "Ed and Kim are flying down tomorrow from Canada to join us. They've both agreed to help with the boys' transformation, as well as with my experiment on established Vampyres trading blood."

"How's he getting away from his job?" Sam asked. "I know it's not time for another vacation."

"He's going to tell his superiors that he's got a serious illness in his family and take personal time off," Elijah said. He hesitated, and then he continued. "He said he needs to get away anyway, because when Michael Morpheus and his friends were up there trying to kill us, they left a slew of bodies lying around under the snow that will be turning up soon with the spring melt. He said he doesn't intend to be any part of that investigation."

"Do you think they'll suspect Vampyre involvement?" TJ asked.

Elijah shook his head. "Doubtful. Ed says the animals will probably ruin most of the forensic evidence and all the authorities will know is that there were a few more deaths than usual during the winter. In fact, he says they'll probably only find a few of the bodies involved, and the rest will be eaten or carried away by animals."

Sam nodded and picked up her cup, staring at Elijah over the rim as she drank. "So, tell us what you've come up with about Matt's suggestion that mature Vampyres could possibly benefit from sharing blood too."

"Just before Ed called, I was on the phone with Professor Wingate up at McGill," he replied. "He sees no reason why someone who is infected with a certain strain of bacteriophage wouldn't be susceptible to infection with a different, or competing strain."

"So the resident bacteriophage wouldn't fight off the invaders?" TJ asked.

"He says not," Elijah answered. "Evidently, bacteriophages don't work like that. In addition, since it's a chronic infection, the body evidently doesn't make antibodies against other bacteriophages so there should be no barrier to the new ones once they're introduced into the bloodstream."

"That means the new bacteriophage could bring in new DNA from another donor and possibly improve the host's condition," Sam said, her eyes thoughtful.

"Exactly," Elijah said with enthusiasm.

Before he could elaborate, TJ's hand started to shake and she dropped her coffee cup, uttering, "Damn!"

Elijah and Sam looked at her and she smiled sheepishly. "It's that damned hunger," she said. "Going off the vaccine is really hitting me hard."

"It's not easy on any of us, TJ," Elijah said, covering her shaking hand with his. "However, if you two want to be the first to try my new experiment, maybe our sharing blood will alleviate the symptoms of the hunger somewhat."

"You mean right now?" TJ asked, looking over her shoulder at her bedroom door.

Elijah shrugged. "Why not? The boys are going to sleep all afternoon, and we can't give them another feeding until tonight."

Sam and TJ glanced at one another and then back at Elijah. "Do you think we should try all three together, or just two at a time?" Sam asked.

Elijah blushed and smiled. "Well, since you and TJ need to share just as I need to share with each of you, all three at one time would be more efficient," he said.

TJ smiled and giggled. "Not to mention, a whole lot sexier."

Elijah stood up and held his arm out toward the stairs. "I wasn't thinking that at all, girls. This is strictly in the interest of science."

"Yeah, right!" TJ said sarcastically.

He grinned. "Well, it's at least partly in the interest of science, but I agree—it will be sexy as hell. Shall we adjourn to my loft?"

TJ and Sam held hands, as if to give each other courage, and then they led him up the stairs.

When they entered his bedroom, they turned to find Elijah was already out of his clothes and changing into his Vampyre form.

Sam let her eyes drift down to his groin. "It appears you're more than ready for us, Elijah," she said, smiling.

He took two quick steps to her and grabbed the back of her neck with his paws, claws retracted, and pulled her face to him, licking her lips with his tongue and growling deep in his throat.

"Oh, my!" TJ said, unbuttoning her blouse and shrugging out of it and her pants until she was naked. As she began to change, she moved up against Elijah and reached around him to take his erect penis in her hand while she nuzzled his neck, taking little nips with her fangs as she too began to change into her Vampyre form.

Elijah was busy, helping Sam out of her clothes, his eyes fixed on her naked breasts as her blouse fell to the floor.

"Hurry," he snarled, picking her up in his arms and moving over to his bed. He laid her on one side of him while TJ moved up against him on the other side.

He wrapped his arms around the girls, his hands on their breasts as they lowered their heads to his neck and began to feed on his blood.

While they fed, their faces close together, Sam and TJ stared into each other's eyes as they each reached down and fondled Elijah's genitals.

He moaned and pushed against their hands while he lowered his hands to their groins and into their wetness, teasing them with his fingers as they teased him with theirs.

After a few moments of this, fearing they would drink too much of his blood, Sam and TJ switched positions. Sam offered Elijah her neck while TJ lowered herself down on him and covered him with her mouth.

He groaned with pleasure against Sam's neck as he fed on her until moments later the girls switched again. Now it was TJ's neck against his lips and Sam's mouth on him.

Finally, unable to stand it any longer, Elijah forced TJ onto her back and pulled Sam up next to him. As he climbed between TJ's spread legs and entered her, Sam put her lips against TJ's neck and sucked from the same wound Elijah had used, her hands caressing TJ's breasts as she fed.

TJ almost screamed at the pleasure of being serviced by two of her kind at once. Her body was on fire and she could hardly stand the pleasure. She grabbed Sam and pulled her breasts against her own as Sam fed on her while Elijah pumped against her groin.

When she felt Elijah begin to throb, TJ pushed Sam off her and eased Elijah onto her friend. Sam licked the blood off her lips and spread her legs, pulling Elijah down onto and into her as TJ fastened her lips on Sam's neck and took Sam's hand and placed it between her thighs.

Elijah's hand went between TJ's legs to join Sam's and he had to bite back a scream as they all came together, clawing and biting and sucking until finally they lay panting in a heap with their limbs intertwined.

Chapter 15

Elijah Pike was a little surprised to discover that when he woke up from his post-feed nap, he was running a fever and every muscle in his body ached as if he had the flu—symptoms he hadn't felt since his own transformation over two hundred years before. It had been so long since he'd had any symptoms of illness he'd almost forgotten just how rotten fever and chills and aches made a person feel.

Well I'll be damned, he thought, stretching out his arms and grimacing at the pain the movement caused. I think it's going to work. He also vowed to be a bit more sympathetic with the boys now that he was reminded of just how bad they must be feeling.

He glanced at the women lying on either side of him, both still deep asleep from their exertions and the blood they'd consumed.

Sam was lying on her back, her arm thrown across her face, and her skin was pink and flushed as if she too had a fever. Elijah put a palm to her breast and sure enough, it felt hot as a griddle.

TJ, on the other side, was positioned on her stomach. Elijah ran a hand lightly over her buttocks and back and found them to be equally feverish.

He looked at the wooden clock hanging on his wall and saw that it was about time for the boys to get another feeding, though he didn't know if the girls were going to be up to it. Their blood supply was not going to be a problem, since they'd probably taken in more from him than they'd donated to him and the boys, but if they kept up the feedings, sooner or later they were going to have to come up with some alternate supplies of fresh blood. His test tube supply was running low, since he'd only intended it to be enough for him and with the girls taking increased shares since they'd been off the vaccine, it wasn't lasting nearly as long as he'd initially planned.

He leaned over and gave Sam a quick kiss on the lips, grinning at the surprise in her eyes at seeing his face leaning over her instead of Matt's. "Rise and shine, Sam, we've got work to do," he said, turning and giving TJ's shoulder a gentle shake. "You too, TJ. Time to get busy."

Sam sat up in bed, her arms instinctively moving to cover her naked breasts, and then she grimaced and moaned. "Oh, what hit me?" she asked.

"Ouch," TJ echoed as she rolled over and pulled herself to a sitting position on the edge of the bed. The sheet slipped down, exposing her breasts, but she made no effort to cover herself. "I feel like I've been rode hard and put up wet!" TJ complained, feeling her cheeks with her palms to gauge her fever.

Elijah scooted down between them and got up off the end of the bed, not bothering to cover his nakedness. "I think our experiment is proving to be successful," he said. "We've got all the symptoms of a fresh infection with each others' bacteriophages."

Sam shook her head and got to her feet, weaving a bit as a bout of dizziness hit her. She too was now comfortable in her nakedness and ignored it. "Wow, I'd forgotten just how bad the transformation made me feel." She looked over at Elijah and TJ and grinned. "I guess now I'll be a little more sympathetic to the boys."

At the mention of Matt and Shooter, TJ blushed and dropped her gaze. "Speaking of the boys," she said, looking back up and gesturing at their nakedness, "What are we going to tell them about this?"

Sam's face looked shocked, as if she'd put their episode of mutual feeding and lovemaking out of her mind.

Elijah smiled gently. "Not to worry, TJ. There's no need to mention it at all right now. By the time the boys are transformed and have acquired their psychic ability, they'll know what we've done and it won't bother them a bit at that point."

TJ shook her head. "You don't know Shooter, Elijah. He's pretty jealous."

"He won't be any longer, not after he's able to look deep into your mind and share your thoughts and see that you love only him," Elijah explained. "Jealousy comes from being insecure about our mates. Once we can know exactly how they feel, there's no longer any need to be suspicious."

"That's just it, Elijah," TJ said, her face flaming again. "I'm not exactly sure how I feel right now, about you I mean." She stared into his eyes. "I love Shooter just as much as I ever did, but after last night . . ."

Elijah moved over to her and put his hand on her shoulder. "TJ, don't be worried. It's natural to have strong feelings . . ." He hesitated, looking for the right words. After a moment, he continued, "To have feelings of friendship and even of a mild form of love after mutual feeding between Vampyres. After all, sharing your blood and your body is a very intimate thing to do. And remember, I'm the one who transformed you, so your hormones are getting a double whammy. Once you're back in Shooter's company, the feelings will fade until they're only a happy memory."

"I hope so, Elijah," she said, her voice miserable as her eyes drifted down to his naked groin. "Because right now, as horrible as the infection is making me feel, all I want to do is jump back into bed with you and do it again."

Sam noticed that Elijah's penis began to stir and thicken at TJ's words and so she quickly moved between them and put her arm around TJ's shoulders. "Come on, babe, let's get dressed and go down and see how our men are faring," she said, looking back over her shoulder at Elijah and winking.

He had the good grace to blush as he smiled back at her, for he knew that if he had the chance, he would have been back in bed with TJ in an instant. He still loved her as a mate—much more than the friendship feelings he had for Sam. It was something he was going to have to be very careful to conceal, especially after Matt and Shooter developed their psychic powers. He glanced down at his still erect penis. Now it was time for a cold shower and to get dressed.

Elizabeth Whitmire, manager of the Rejuvenatrix Spa, and her young assistant manager, Sammy Akins, were just about to lock the doors to their adjoining offices and leave for the day when a man and woman walked through the doors.

They were a very attractive couple and for a moment Elizabeth wondered what they were doing there. Neither of them looked to have an ounce of fat on their bodies nor did they appear to be dissipated from a surfeit of alcohol or drugs, unlike the usual spa customers.

She gave Sammy a look and shrugged minutely as she turned back to the couple. "Yes? Can we help you?" she asked, glancing at her watch to show them that the hour was late and they were keeping her from going home.

"Hello, Ma'am," John Ashby said, sticking out his hand to Elizabeth. "My name's Collins, Barnabas Collins."

"Good afternoon, Mr. Collins," Elizabeth said, her tone slightly frosty. She evidently did not make the connection of the name to the vampire character in the old TV show. "I'm afraid you've come just as we were about to leave for the evening. Is your business going to take long?" she asked, glancing at Sammy and finding his eyes locked on those of the beautiful young woman with Collins.

"I'm afraid it is, Ms. Whitmire," John said. "You see, we represent one of the largest law firms in Washington, and we're here to see about sending all of our people here on regular retreats. We feel that will keep them healthy and cut down on our insurance costs and even improve productivity in the long run."

Elizabeth smiled, seeing large dollar signs in front of her eyes. Suddenly, she was in no hurry at all to leave for the day. "Uh, just how large is your company, Mr. Collins?" she asked, her voice much warmer as she came out from behind her desk to stand close to Collins. Elizabeth was an attractive woman and she wasn't above using that attractiveness to further her business goals—within reason of course.

"Why, I believe we're currently over three hundred. Isn't that right, Marya?" he asked, turning toward the woman with him.

Elizabeth noticed the young lady never took her eyes off of Sammy when she answered, "Why, yes, Barney, that's correct."

Always one to exploit any advantage when it came to making money, Elizabeth quickly said, "Sammy, why don't you show Marya around the facilities while I have a chat with Mr. Collins about the details of our operation?"

Sammy's voice sounded almost drunk as he slowly nodded. "Okie dokie," he said, grinning as the beautiful woman took his arm and walked out of the office with him.

As soon as they were gone, Elizabeth put her hand on John's shoulder and led him over to a couch against the wall of her office. "Why don't you sit down there, Mr. Collins, and I'll fix us a little drink?"

"Call me Barney, Elizabeth," John said, his lips curled in a small grin. "Everybody does."

As Elizabeth turned to hand him his whiskey, she noticed

the bulge in the front of his pants. My God, she thought, her face blushing, he's huge . . . and he's obviously interested in me! This is one time I won't mind mixing a little pleasure with business, she reasoned, thinking him the most handsome man she'd seen in quite some time.

She sat very close to him and made sure her breast pressed up against his arm as she leaned into him. "A toast," she said, raising her glass, "to a very profitable friendship, for both of us."

"I'll drink to that," John said, draining his glass.

"Oh, not so fast, Barney," Elizabeth purred, sipping her drink. "There's no need to hurry. The rest of the staff have all gone home already, so we're all alone here."

John set his drink down and half-turned on the couch to face Elizabeth. "That's nice," he said, raising his hand and beginning to undo the buttons on her blouse.

Elizabeth blushed and tried to brush his hand away. "Uh, what are you doing, Barney?" she asked. She'd expected a pass, and in fact she welcomed it, but he was moving just a little too fast for her.

Quick as a flash, his hand was inside her blouse and slipping under the edges of her bra to hold her left breast. "Why, getting to know you, Elizabeth," he said, taking her hand and placing it on his lap.

Her fingers automatically curled around the hardness she felt there, causing her to gasp as his fingers pinched her nipple gently, making it as hard as a rock and starting a fire in the pit of her stomach that quickly spread downward to her groin.

"Oh, Barney," she whispered, pushing her breast against his hand as she began to unzip his trousers, all thoughts of caution thrown to the wind. When his erection sprang into view, she gasped again and licked her lips. "God, you're big!" she said.

"You haven't seen anything yet," John said, smiling and

continuing his massage of her breast. As he dipped his head down and covered her lips with his, a loud scream of terror came from the rear of the building.

Elizabeth jerked her head back, her eyes wide and frightened. "What was that?" she asked, letting go of his penis as she started to get up.

John's fingers tightened on her breast and he easily pulled her back down on the couch. "Oh, that was just your assistant getting a good look at Marya changing," John said.

Elizabeth's eyes were puzzled and a little scared as she asked, "Changing into what?"

With a quick jerk, John tore Elizabeth's blouse and skirt off. Pushing her back on the couch and climbing between her legs, he growled, "You'll see," as his own body began to melt and morph into his Vampyre form.

Elizabeth's mouth opened to scream, but John covered it with his own before she could make a sound, pushing his tongue deep between her lips.

Keeping her head down with his, he put his hands on her buttocks and jerked her hips up off the couch and onto his lap, impaling her in one brutal thrust.

She moaned deep in her throat and her eyes half closed in rapture as the hormones in his saliva began to work on her bloodstream. Her hands reached between them and cupped his balls as he pumped and thrust while his hands crushed her breasts and pulled at her nipples.

As she began to contract in a rapid, overwhelming orgasm and her eyes squeezed shut in rapture, he lowered his fangs to her neck and began to feed, making sure not to do too much damage.

After a few quick swallows, he reached up and made a slash in his neck with one of his claws. As his blood oozed out, he put his hand behind her head and pulled her lips to his neck. He felt her sucking his blood as he spasmed and exploded inside her, causing her to come once again.

She gasped in delight and put her hands around his neck and pulled him tighter against her lips—she couldn't get enough of him.

Marya was having a little more trouble with Sammy. Once they were alone, she'd let him know in several subtle ways that she was attracted to him and that an advance on his part wouldn't be amiss.

Used to having women clients come on to him, though none of them had been as pretty as this one, Sammy had immediately pushed Marya down onto one of the exercise pads in the gym and fastened his lips on hers.

Slipping his hand under her blouse, he was gratified to find she wasn't wearing a bra and that her breasts were every bit as magnificent as they'd appeared to be.

He smiled against her lips when her hand sought him out and slipped into his trousers without him even having to put it there. He was kissing her and fondling her breasts and pushing his erection against her hand when he suddenly felt a sharp sting on his tongue, which he had deep in her mouth at the time.

He jerked his head back, about to admonish her against biting, when he saw her face melt and change and huge fangs appear between her luscious lips.

He screamed and tried to get away, but she held him fast and pulled him back up against her. Unfortunately, the sight of her Vampyre body had driven all thoughts of sex from his mind and he was as limp as a strand of spaghetti.

"Oh, Sammy," she growled, her eyes on his wilted manhood. "I'm so disappointed."

She quickly pulled his face to hers and covered his lips with hers to stop his screaming. As her saliva mingled with his and her mind worked to get him back in the mood, he quit struggling and his eyes half closed and his expression became dreamy.

Suddenly, Marya noticed some wood in his member and she slowly stroked him back to full erection, still kissing and licking his lips.

His hands found their way back to her breasts and all was right with the world.

When she pricked her neck and put his lips to the wound, he whimpered like a baby suckling his mom and she smiled around her fangs as he drank her blood.

After a while, she gently pried his face away from her neck and climbed up on top of him, slowly easing herself down until he was in her to the hilt.

He smiled, his eyes still shut, and pushed back against her as she began to move up and down. His hands squeezed and pinched her breasts as she lowered her head and bit into his neck.

Just as she began to suck, he throbbed and exploded inside her. She growled and moved faster and faster until she was coming with him, making a major effort not to drain him dry in her excitement.

Her breasts swelled and her nipples pushed against his hands as she finally collapsed on top of him, satiated.

Chapter 16

Ed Slonaker glanced at his wife, Kim, as she tried to pack their suitcases for the trip to Maine to see Elijah. Her skin was as pale as the bedsheets and her hands were trembling as she tried to fold their clothes.

Coming off the vaccine was evidently hitting her much harder than it had him. He still felt the ever-present hunger, but to him it was still just a nagging emptiness in the pit of his stomach and an ill-defined ache for blood. He could tell for Kim it was much worse. Her eyes appeared sunken and vacant and she was constantly licking her lips as if she could almost taste the sweet saltiness of a blood meal.

He knew she must be feeling terrible because she was in a foul mood and tended to bite his head off every time he opened his mouth. Usually the sweetest tempered woman he'd ever met, one always with a joke or quip at hand, she was now shrewish and mean as a snake.

He'd tried giving her some of the test-tube blood that Elijah had provided, but though it did ease the symptoms for a short while, they were returning much faster than they had while they'd been on the vaccine.

They were due to fly out early the next morning, but Ed

knew he would have to do something before then. Kim was in no shape to fly on an airplane, or for much of anything else for that matter. It was time to take drastic measures.

He went to their closet and picked out a bright red dress, one from years ago when they'd both been much younger. The dress was cut low in the bosom and was so short Kim joked she didn't dare sit down in it.

He pitched it onto their bed. "Here, babe, put this on," he said.

Kim frowned and picked up the small scrap of cloth and looked at him, questions in her eyes.

"I think it's time we went out to a bar and find us something to eat."

"Are . . . are you sure, Ed?" she asked, her voice trembling in anticipation.

"Sure," he said, his heart breaking to see her in such pain. "We'll have to be very careful with this investigation going on at headquarters, but I think I can find a way around that," he added, grinning darkly.

Kim didn't even ask his how, she just stripped to her bare skin and pulled the dress on without bothering with underwear of any kind.

Ordinarily this would have excited Ed to no end, but he too was looking forward to later, when they could share a blood feast and engage in some quality lovemaking.

Ed parked the car in the far corner of the parking lot in front of a dive on the outskirts of Banff called Deuces Wild. It was the roughest bar in the county and the Mounties were called out there at least once or twice every weekend to mop up after bar fights or assaults.

He glanced at Kim and grinned. "Damn, you look good," he said. She'd put on extra makeup and was wearing a long, dark wig to cover up her short natural blond hair. A generous amount of cleavage was visible at the top of her dress and he could see the curve of her thigh leading to her groin just under the hem.

"I can't believe I ever let you out of the house wearing that dress," he said, shaking his head and smiling.

She reached over and touched his cheek. "Darling, back in our younger days you were so horny you didn't care much what I wore as long as I could get out of it fast."

She was obviously feeling better now that she knew a blood meal was at hand.

He leaned over and peeked down her dress, able to see clear down to her nipples. "Yeah, I remember, and that dress is bringing back the old feelings pretty good."

She leaned over, giving him an even better view and kissed him on the lips. "Now, you go on in there and find me a real bad apple. I wouldn't want some boy scout to come on to me and get eaten for his troubles."

Ed laughed. "Sorry, darling, there won't be any boy scouts in this place, but I'll go see if I can't find one who truly deserves to be our guest for dinner tonight."

Ed got out of the car and sauntered into the bar. He emerged less than ten minutes later and was smiling grimly as he got back in the front seat.

"Any luck?" Kim asked, the Hunger making her too anxious to wait much longer.

"Yeah. There's a real beaut of a guy in there sitting at the end of the bar. He's wearing a red-and-black cowboy shirt and a black Stetson hat." Ed hesitated and then he added, "His name's Ben Carter and he's been accused of rape at least five or six times, but every time we brought him in, the witnesses either showed up beat to hell and recanted their stories or just disappeared entirely."

Kim nodded, her eyes dark. "He'll do." She leaned over and kissed him lightly on the cheek. "You'll follow us when we leave?"

"I'll be right behind you," Ed promised.

"Good, 'cause if it's anything I hate, it's a rapist and abuser of women."

Kim walked slowly into the saloon and went right up to the bar, climbing up on a barstool one over from the man Ed had described. She crossed her legs slowly, giving him a good look at her upper thighs and dark patch of pubic hair and asked the bartender for a shot of whiskey and a beer chaser.

The barman got a worried look on his face, and as he put the drinks down in front of her, he whispered, "Listen, lady, I think you're in the wrong place. If I was you, I'd finish my drinks and get the hell out of here."

The man named Ben Carter snorted and moved over to take the stool next to Kim's. He leaned over and blatantly stared down her dress at her exposed breasts, smiling and licking his lips obscenely.

"Don't listen to old Wally," Ben said, his eyes never moving up to her face as he talked to her. "You're plenty welcome here, little lady, and I'll make sure nobody bothers you."

Kim turned on the stool to face Ben until her legs were between his, drained her whiskey, and followed it with half the glass of beer. She leaned over toward him, letting her dress fall open to give him an even better look at her breasts, and she said, "And what if I want someone to bother me, Mister Protector?"

She thought his eyes were going to bug out of his head as he slipped his hand up under her dress and began to move his fingers over her pubis region.

"Well, then, I'm your man for that too," he said, his voice becoming husky with desire.

Kim spread her legs a little and pushed her pelvis up against his fingers until they were on her lips and could feel her wetness.

She glanced down at the bulge in his pants and then over

at the glass of beer in front of him. "Why don't you finish your drink and we can get out of this place and go someplace more private?" she asked, licking her lips as she stared into his eyes.

His eyes were as dark and cold as a doll's eyes, with no soul in them. "The hell with my drink, little lady," he growled. "Let's get out of here right now!"

Ben took his hand out from under her dress, dropped a couple of crumpled bills on the bar, and followed Kim out of the door.

As soon as they were in the parking lot, he grabbed her upper arm and tried to pull her up against him, pushing his erection against her.

"Uh-uh, big boy," Kim said teasingly, pulling away. "I don't do it in parking lots. Find me a bed, quickly."

Ben's face turned mean but he pushed her roughly toward a big four-wheel drive pickup right in front of the door. "Get in," he ordered, opening the door, all traces of niceness gone now that he was sure of his conquest.

Kim climbed up into the seat and within seconds he was roaring out of the lot and down the highway back toward town.

Kim scooted over next to him and glanced out the rear window in time to see a pair of headlights follow them out of the bar's lot.

Ben grabbed her hand and shoved it down into his lap. Kim laughed and unzipped his zipper, bringing his penis out into view. It wasn't especially large, but it was hard and she could feel it throb under her fingers.

"Put it in your mouth," Ben ordered gruffly, hunching his pelvis forward.

"Uh-uh, darlin', not while you're driving," Kim said. "Wouldn't want you to have a wreck 'cause of me." She looked out the windshield and pointed at a turnoff just ahead. "Why don't you pull off onto that road and we'll see what I can do?"

Ben grinned and jerked the wheel, almost losing control in the small amount of snow and ice on the road as he turned down the dirt road.

He stopped about a hundred yards off the main road just around a bend in the dirt road and switched off the engine. Twisting on the seat, he looked at her expectantly.

Kim sat up and let the dress fall off her shoulders, exposing her breasts to his view, her nipples hardening in the chilly night air.

"Doesn't this seat recline?" she asked. "I don't want to get a crick in my neck."

"Sure baby, sure," Ben said. He reached down and flipped a lever and the back of the seat lowered until they had enough room to lie down on the seat.

Ben grabbed her breasts and pulled her down onto him. "Hey, just a minute," Kim said, letting her voice sound weak and frightened. "Not so rough, honey."

Ben made a fist and swung his hand at Kim, catching her in the jaw and snapping her head back. "Don't give me orders, bitch!" he yelled, backhanding her across the lips and making them bleed.

"Now," he said, grabbing her head and forcing it down toward his lap. "Suck my dick!"

Kim obligingly put her lips around his erection and began to move her head up and down, licking and sucking him until she knew he was about ready to climax.

She sat up, stripped out of her dress and straddled him, letting him glide into her wet groin.

He dug his hands into her breasts hard enough to bruise them, evidently unable to enjoy sex unless pain and subjugation of his partner was involved.

As he began to buck against her and his eyes closed with pleasure, Kim let herself begin to change, sending out a mental message to Ed whom she sensed waiting just outside the driver's door.

When the door opened and the cab light came on, Ben

opened his eyes and his heart almost stopped at what he saw. One monster straddling him, her fangs dripping red drool as she pumped against him, and another equally fearsome creature whose grinning lips exposed fangs almost four inches long beneath red-rimmed, glowing eyes from hell who was standing just outside the pickup door.

In spite of his terror, Ben felt himself begin to spurt just as both creatures lowered their heads to his neck and began to feed on him.

He got off one short scream before his throat was ripped open and his life's blood spurted into Ed's and Kim's waiting mouths.

A few minutes later, when Ben had been drained dry, Ed grabbed his lifeless body and jerked it out of the cab and threw it on the ground. He bounded into the cab and took Kim in his arms, pulling her against him.

She grinned around bloodstained fangs and put her hand on his chest pushing him down on the seat. "Here, darling, just let me get the taste of that bastard out of my mouth."

She lowered her head and encircled his penis with her lips and began to suck him into full erection.

After a moment, he could stand it no longer and he grabbed Kim and pulled her up alongside him on the seat. He kissed and caressed her breasts, told her how much he loved her, and then gently eased himself into her. She arched her back and dug into him with her claws. "Don't be gentle," she growled, "fuck me hard!"

And then they coupled in wild abandon on the pickup's seats, each howling in pleasure as they climaxed, their bloody lips locked together.

Exhausted and exhilarated at the same time, they lay back in each other's arms. "Now," Kim said, licking some blood splatters off his chest, "wasn't that better than using bottled blood?"

Ed glanced down at her and motioned toward his still-erect penis. "Do you have to ask?"

* * *

After a short rest period to calm their wildly beating hearts, Ed and Kim changed back to normal and got dressed. Ed put Ben's body in the passenger seat and turned the pickup around and drove back to the road with Kim following in their car.

He turned toward town and drove about four miles along the highway, searching for just the right spot. At a right angle curve on the edge of a high ledge, he stopped the car in the middle of the road, and pulled Ben's body over behind the steering wheel.

Kim appeared next to him holding a gallon can of gasoline, which he quickly poured over Ben's body. He shut the door, put the truck in gear, and as it moved off toward the curve, he flipped a match through the open window.

Flames engulfed the truck as it crashed through the barrier and became airborne, plummeting like a falling star toward the rocks a hundred and fifty feet below. Ed watched until the truck landed and exploded into a raging fireball, lighting up the night sky for miles.

He put his arm around Kim and walked with her back toward their car.

"You feel better now, sweetheart?" he asked kindly.

She reached around his waist and hugged him to her. "Oh yes, darling. Much better, but not nearly as good as I'm going to feel after we get back home and I get you in our bed for act two."

Ed grinned as his eyes flowed over her dress. "In that case, I'll make it home in record time."

Chapter 17

A long, sleek, black limousine eased into the parking lot of the Rejuvenatrix Spa and parked next to the walk leading up to the front doors.

Theo Thantos, Christina Alario, Brahma Parvsh, and Gabrielle de Lavnay exited the vehicle and stared up at the imposing edifice of the spa and hotel.

The building had been built to resemble a large Swiss chalet, with towers and spires and balconies with elaborately carved figures and designs on the railings. Tennis courts, an Olympic-size swimming pool, and even riding stables complete with dozens of horses could be seen dotting the property.

"Very nice," Gabrielle said, nodding her head as she surveyed the setup. "I've heard of this place from some of my friends, but I still don't know why you insisted we come all the way out here, Theo."

"Just be patient, my dear," Theo said, his mood expansive. "I told you I was going to explain how we could transform a lot of important people without anyone being the wiser, and this is part of my plan."

The large, double doors of the front entrance opened and John Ashby stepped out, followed by Marya and Elizabeth Whitmire and Sammy Akins.

Whitmire and Akins still looked a bit drawn and pale from the ordeal of their recent transformation, and the reason for their appearance wasn't lost on the visitors.

Brahma Parvsh sucked in his breath at the sight of Elizabeth, who was a striking looking woman. "I sense we have a couple of new recruits," he said, already planning on how he might persuade her to join him in his bed.

"They're the key to my plan," Theo said, ushering his visitors up the stairs toward the front entrance.

As they approached the front porch, Elizabeth smiled and spread her arms. "Welcome to my home, people. Come right in and we'll show you around."

Minutes later they'd all been introduced and Theo had assembled the group around one of the dining room tables. As Sammy poured coffee and tea for them, Theo elaborated on his plan.

"Elizabeth, this is not all of the group that is helping us. The others have jobs where they had to be and we didn't want to raise any suspicions this early in the game."

When she nodded, he continued. "Now, as you can see, Brahma and Gabrielle, we have control of a very tony establishment where our . . . um . . . prospective transformees can be kept for up to a week or two without anyone suspecting foul play."

Gabrielle nodded. "Yes, but what about the normal clients? Won't there be concern if their reservations are canceled?"

Elizabeth smiled. "There won't be any need for that, Gabrielle. In addition to the regular hotel style rooms you see at the inn, we also have a number of guest cottages scattered about the property. They are designed for complete isolation and are intended for the use of our many celebrity clients. I will simply make sure any of our new recruits get assigned to those areas."

"I didn't see any cottages," Brahma said as he sipped his tea.

"That's because they are located back in the woods that surround the spa," Elizabeth explained. "I think they will be perfect for what Theo has planned."

"Yes," Sammy Akins added, "And some of the cottages even come with adjoining facilities for servants and support personnel that some of our celebrities require, and they can be used to house the Secret Service agents that will accompany any governmental higher-ups we invite."

"Speaking of that, just how are we going to persuade our more important targets to come here?" Gabrielle asked. "Lord knows, even I have trouble getting them to attend one of my parties occasionally, and that's in town and not out here in the boondocks."

Elizabeth's eyes darkened momentarily at Gabrielle's description of her spa as being located in the boondocks, but Theo put a hand on her shoulder and spoke up. "That's already being taken care of," he said, smiling. "Some of the targets' family members are being told they've won a contest where the prize is a week or two at this spa, which should suffice for the media and judicial types. As far as the extremely high-up governmental targets, we're going to have to get them by first converting family members who have access to them and then let them do the transformations for us."

"Won't that be risky?" Brahma asked. "They're sure to call doctors at the first signs of illness in any of these people."

Theo nodded. "Good thought, Brahma. In fact, we've already decided some of our first guests will be the doctor for the Congress and we're even working on getting the president's own physician to attend."

"It certainly seems like you've thought of everything," Gabrielle said with admiration, her obvious flirtation with Thantos causing Christina to bristle. She opened her mouth to make a sarcastic comment, but closed it at a warning glance from Thantos and a mental command, "Not now!"

"I hope so," Theo said, trying to sound modest as he turned his attention back to Gabrielle. "However, one of the most important parts of my plan is you, Gabrielle."

"Oh?" she said, smiling and patting her hair, pleased both at his attention and at his compliment.

"Yes. One of the problems with targeting extremely important people in the government is getting access to them. They are, as you know, usually very insulated from the general public."

She nodded, starting to get his drift. What he was saying was true. It'd taken her the better part of ten years to become famous enough so that her calls to Washington royalty were always returned.

"So, we're going to need you to utilize your many Washington contacts to first spread the word about how great this spa is, and secondly to give out some guest passes as gifts to your political acquaintances," Thantos said.

"That should be no problem," she said. "Politicians simply love to be given expensive gifts, and they love even more attending beautiful places when someone else is picking up the tab."

"Good," Theo said. "Now," he added, glancing around the table, "I want all of us to make a list of fifty or so people that we think should be targeted. I'll call up the others in our group and have them do the same thing and then we'll get together and make our final list."

"Perhaps, before we do that," Brahma said, stroking his chin while his coal-black eyes bored into Elizabeth's, "Elizabeth might consent to give me a . . . um, personal tour of her beautiful facility?"

"Yes," Gabrielle said, smiling coyly as she glanced at Thantos, "and I would appreciate a more detailed view with you, Theo, if you have the time."

Thantos glanced quickly at Christina and saw her lips pressed into a hard, white line.

"Uh, I think it'd be much better, Gabrielle, if Sammy here showed you around. I've got some very important calls to make and I need to get right on them."

Theo watched as Gabrielle pushed her disappointment to the side and gave the muscular Sammy an appraising glance. Good, he thought when she smiled coyly at the young man. It wouldn't hurt to put a little icing on the cake with these two.

Elizabeth returned Brahma's look, letting her eyes roam over his hard body. "I wouldn't mind at all, Brahma."

Sammy glanced at Gabrielle's rather dumpy body and carefully shielded his thoughts as he said, "Me too, Gabrielle. It'll be a pleasure."

Chapter 18

Ed and Kim Slonaker exited their plane and walked through a large revolving door on the second floor of the Portland Jetport just before noon.

Elijah Pike held up his hand in greeting so they could see him over the heads of the other people waiting in a small crowd outside the door.

He gave Kim a hug and shook Ed's hand. "Everything go okay on your flight?" Elijah asked as they walked toward the baggage claim area.

Ed grinned, glancing at Kim, whose face wasn't nearly so happy. "Yeah, 'cept Kim got the full treatment by the security staff. Full search."

Elijah raised an eyebrow. "Oh?"

"I guess she just has a suspicious look about her," Ed teased, watching her out of the corner of his eye.

"Keep it up, big boy and I'll spread you all over this airport," she replied through gritted teeth, though Elijah could see a gleam of humor in her eyes.

As they walked down the corridor, she sighed and relaxed a little. "You know guys, when pale-skinned Canadian females start hijacking airlines or blowing themselves up with body bombs, then I will be able to understand why people like me are subjected to full searches, while at least three Middle Eastern types waltzed right through the check-in with a 'have a nice flight' from the guard and a big toothy smile."

"It's all in the name of political correctness," Elijah said. "The PC police won't let us check minority types because that might be racial profiling, even though it is precisely those minority races who pose the security check. Maddening isn't it?"

Kim glanced at him. "For a supposedly sophisticated country, you people down here in the lower forty-eight sure do manage to let a lot of idiots do your thinking for you."

Elijah chuckled along with Ed as they waited for the Slonakers' luggage to come up out of the conveyor. But, after a moment, he asked in a low voice, "Kim, I'm curious about something."

She cut her eyes at him. "You're wondering why I didn't just give the guard a little mental push to make them forget about me?"

"Exactly."

She shook her head. "I'm just not very good at that sort of thing," she said, a note of chagrin in her voice. "In terms of psychic ability, I come up way short in persuasion techniques."

"Don't let her kid you, Elijah," Ed said. "Kim may not be the best at controlling other people's behavior, but she rates second to none in other psychic abilities."

That peaked Elijah's interest. In his research over the years he'd found that members of his race varied widely in both the amount and type of psychic ability they had. In fact, this was one of the abilities he was hoping to influence with his new "share the blood" experiment back at his cabin.

"Tell me about it, Kim, if you don't mind," he requested. He also knew that some of his kind were very reticent to discuss that particular part of their makeup. He didn't know why, but for some reason, Vampyres who'd slaughtered thousands of innocent people to feed their hunger over the years would suddenly stammer and stutter and become totally tongue-tied when asked to discuss their particular psychic abilities.

She looked at Ed, who nodded. "Okay, I'm very strong on precognition, and I'm starting to develop some mild telekinesis ability."

Elijah's eyes widened. He'd heard of some Vampyres having precog abilities, but she was the first he'd come across to admit to telekinetic abilities.

"So, you can move things around?" he asked.

"It's more than that," Ed said. "Telekinesis involves mental power over all things physical."

"I don't understand," Elijah said. To him, telekinesis was about moving small objects like in the movie *Poltergeist*.

"Let me give you an example," Ed said, glancing at Kim, "If it's all right with you, sweetheart."

She shrugged and he continued, "A couple of months ago, Kim and I were out at dinner. When we finished and were walking back through the parking lot, a local thug I'd arrested a couple of weeks before stepped out of the shadows and pointed a .38 pistol at me at point blank range." He held out his hands, "I was so startled, I didn't have time to try and 'push' him mentally, so I was as surprised as he was when he pulled the trigger six times and nothing happened."

"What'd you do?" Elijah asked.

"I bitch slapped him unconscious and put the cuffs on him and we took him to the station on the way home."

When Elijah looked puzzled at the point of this story, Ed explained, "When we got to the station and I told the sergeant the story, he said, 'must've had bad ammo,' and he pointed the pistol out the window and pulled the trigger. The sergeant was as surprised as Kim and I were when all six bullets fired."

Elijah turned to look at Kim, who laughed. "I was as startled as Ed when that punk pointed his gun at us and I forgot for a moment that it couldn't hurt us, so I just kind'a pushed at the gun with my mind and made it not fire."

"Wow!" Elijah said under his breath. "That's amazing."

Kim shrugged again, a slight blush on her face. "I don't really have all that good a control over it, Elijah, but I do know that it seems to work best at times of high stress or fear."

"How about you, Ed?" Elijah asked as he and Ed bent to grab their luggage off the carrousel. "You have any strange talents?"

Ed pursed his lips as they walked toward the garage where Elijah had parked. "I guess about the only thing out of the ordinary is I'm pretty good at long-range telepathy."

Kim touched Elijah's arm, pride for Ed showing in her eyes. "And not just emotions, like most of us, Elijah. He can actually speak mentally over long distances."

"Show me," Elijah asked.

Ed squinted for a moment, and then Elijah's cell phone began to beep.

He glanced at Ed and answered it.

"Hey, Elijah," TJ said, "I just got the strangest thought in my head to call you. Is everything all right?"

Elijah laughed and told her he'd explain when they got back to the cabin. After he hung up, he helped Ed store their bags in the back of his Explorer and then they piled in and he took off.

He paid the guard and turned the car toward the Maine Turnpike. Once they'd gone through the toll, he asked Ed, "You obviously don't have to know the exact location of the party you're talking to, but are there any restrictions, like distance or personal knowledge of the person?"

Ed nodded. "Yeah, I have to have at least met the person before, and it helps if I've had some mental contact with them in the past as well. As far as distance, I really haven't spent any time testing it so I can't tell you for sure."

"Once, when he was in Toronto at a Mountie convention, he 'talked' to me and it was as clear as if he'd telephoned," Kim said, looking at Ed with admiration. "And that's over a thousand miles."

"My oh my," Elijah said. "I can't wait to tell the others about this."

"Elijah," Kim asked, "You told us when you called earlier that you had some ideas about passing abilities around among us. Is this the kind of thing you meant?"

He nodded. "This is exactly what I hope we can somehow learn to share with each other, Kim. I'm pretty sure it'll work with new transformees, since they'll be getting doses of all the different DNA samples at one time, but I'm less sure about whether old dogs like us can incorporate the new DNA into our systems without messing up our old DNA in some way."

"So," Ed said softly, "that means in addition to contributing some of our blood to the two young men, Matt and Shooter, we're also gonna be passing it around to you and the two girls?" Ed asked.

Elijah nodded. "As well as accepting some of our blood, Ed. This is hopefully going to make all of us stronger, faster, more intelligent, and better psychically."

"Sounds almost too good to be true," Kim said.

"Yes, it does, and I just hope it isn't," Elijah said, mentally crossing his fingers.

As they pulled up to Elijah's log cabin on the shore of a small lake, both Ed and Kim remarked how beautiful the spot was.

" 'Course, these little foothills you call mountains down here in Maine don't compare with the big boys we have up in Canada," Kim teased.

Elijah nodded and smiled. "You got that right, but when we got into the vaccine business and found out how much antipathy and resistance there was to the idea of helping Vampyres escape the curse of needing human blood to live, I decided to come up here and hole up due to the cabin's isolation." He looked around at the deep woods that surrounded the place.

"Not much chance of anyone finding us here unless we want them to."

As he reached into the back of the Explorer to get the Slonakers' luggage, the cabin door opened and Sam appeared.

As soon as Elijah saw the expression on her face, he knew something was wrong.

He forgot about the suitcases and straightened up. "Sam, what's wrong?"

She gave Ed and Kim a quick nod. "Hi, guys, good to see you again." Then she turned her attention to Elijah. "You'd better come in here. There's something you ought to see," she said, holding the door open wide.

The three of them followed her into the cabin and through the living room and into Matt's bedroom. Matt was covered with sweat, his face flushed with temperature, and he was literally writhing on the bed in pain, groaning even though he appeared to be unconscious.

"Jesus!" Elijah exclaimed, rushing to the bedside to feel of Matt's forehead. "He's burning up with fever. How long has he been like this?"

"It started this morning, right after you left for the airport." She shook her head, worry in her eyes. "His temp's been as high as a hundred and six."

Elijah's eyes narrowed. "And Shooter?"

She glanced at him. "The same. TJ and I have been continually bathing them in cool water to keep their temperatures down, but without much success."

Kim, who had been a Vampyre longer than Ed, and who had in fact transformed him to be her mate, stepped closer to the bed. She peered down at Matt and shook her head. "Elijah, I've seen a couple of transformations, and they didn't act at all like this. They got sick, but it was much milder, kind'a like the flu, eay?"

"You're exactly right, Kim. This is very unusual," Elijah replied, stroking his chin unconsciously as he thought.

"TJ and I think it's because of the . . . uh, rather special circumstances of their transformation," Sam said.

"Oh, you can speak freely around Ed and Kim," Elijah said, "I've told them about our experiment with multiple donors to the transformation process."

"How would that change things?" Ed asked.

Elijah motioned them to follow him out of the room. "Let's go out here to talk so we won't disturb Matt's sleep."

When they got to the kitchen, he took cups for everyone out of the cupboard and poured cups of coffee all around.

"In answer to your question, Ed, the sickness Kim mentioned that occurs to transformees is because of their bodies' reactions to the invading Vampyre bug, as we call it. Just like when you get the flu and your body causes fever to help fight it off, so does the body try to ward off the Vampyre bug."

"Uh huh," Ed said, as his nonmedical mind wrestled with the idea.

"However, in this case, instead of just one new bug to fight against, Matt and Shooter are fighting against three each."

Kim glanced at Sam. "You mean you and TJ and Elijah have all contributed blood to the boys?"

Sam nodded over the rim of her coffee cup.

Kim looked back at Elijah. "And what about the girls and you, Elijah? Haven't you all also shared blood?"

He nodded. "Yes, but we didn't get as sick as the boys probably because our Vampyre blood's resistance is very high to any kind of new infection."

"But even so, we did feel the effects, Kim," Sam said. "All of us ran a slight fever for a couple of days after sharing our blood, though not nearly so bad as Matt and Shooter's, and we had mild muscle aches and pains too, but again, not as bad as the pain Matt and Shooter are experiencing."

Kim looked at Elijah. "I know you asked Ed and I here to contribute to this experiment, but do you still think it's safe, considering how ill the boys are? Wouldn't more blood from two different donors make them even sicker, or possibly even kill them?"

"I don't know, Kim," Elijah said, a speculative glint in his eyes. "This is new territory for all of us, but perhaps you could be of help?"

Kim raised her eyebrows in question.

"Maybe if you used your precog talent, you could get some idea of how we should proceed."

"Precog, as is precognition?" Sam asked, her eyes moving to stare at Kim.

Kim nodded, shrugging. "Heck, it's worth a try, though like I said, it's not very predictable."

Sam moved to put a hand on her shoulder. "If it'll help Matt, please try."

Kim put her coffee cup down and walked back to Matt's room, with the others following close behind.

She sat on the edge of his bed and put her palms on his burning cheeks and closed her eyes.

"I'm imagining us all donating blood to Matt to try and see what will happen," she whispered.

After a moment, she gave a shiver and stood up, smiling. "I think it'll be okay," she said. "In my mind, after I pictured us all giving him blood, I saw him healthy and completely recovered."

Sam moved quickly to hug her. "Now, quickly, go and try it with Shooter. I know it'll be a great relief to TJ to find out he's going to be okay too."

Chapter 19

Secret Service agent Michelle Meyers slipped out of the door of the cottage and pulled a Marlboro out of her handbag. Strictly speaking, she wasn't supposed to smoke on duty, but what the hell, she figured. She was going to be stuck at this health spa eating tasteless food that was supposed to be good for her and watching rich brats lollygag around the swimming pool and ride horses while she stood around hoping someone would assassinate the little assholes for at least the next week, so she was going to treat herself to some nicotine every chance she got.

She put her lighter to the end of the butt and inhaled deeply. God that tasted good, she thought, glancing around at the heavily wooded area around the small group of cabins they'd been assigned to. It was beautiful here, and she supposed this duty did beat hanging around the vice president's mansion, ignoring the sexist comments of the other male agents assigned to the vice president while her charge, Allison Burton, spent the day on the phone or playing games on her computer.

She took a final drag, smashed the butt under her shoe, took a hit on some Binaca breath spray to cover her tobacco

156   *James M. Thompson*

breath, and reentered the cabin. If her highness was through with her morning shower, they could begin the day's activities, she thought.

Allison was sitting on the couch running a brush through her still-damp hair. She glanced up at Michelle and sniffed, her face screwing up into her habitual scowl. "You know I hate it when you smoke," she said tartly. "It makes you smell like an ashtray."

Michelle bit her lip to keep from replying in kind since it could cost her her job. "Yes, I know," she said, her voice tight as she glanced at her wristwatch. "We'd better go," she said evenly, trying to keep the disgust she felt for the young teenager from her tone. "It's time for your morning massage," she said, while thinking, *as if that's going to get rid of all that baby fat on your ass.*

Allison's face brightened and she jumped to her feet. "All right," she said, excitement in her voice.

Michelle grinned at the sudden transformation. "I see there's something here you like."

Allison smiled smugly. "Yeah. That Sammy Akins is a hottie, and I think he likes me."

Michelle's grin faded. "You mean the spa's assistant director has been giving you your massages?"

Allison shrugged. "Sure. Why not?"

"I thought only women were allowed to massage the female guests," Michelle said, moving toward the door and unconsciously checking her sidearm holster before opening it.

Allison smirked. "Well, you'd have known it if you didn't sneak out to suck on a butt every time I took my massages."

Michelle nodded. The kid was right. She *had* been shirking her duty, but no more. She intended to have a word about this with the head of the spa, Ms. Whitmire. She knew the vice president would shit a brick if he found out some man had his hands on his darling daughter!

* * *

Michelle accompanied Allison into the massage room and held up her hand when Sammy Akins moved to pick up the massage oil. "Hold on there, mister," Michelle said. "I need to have a word with Ms. Whitmire before you go any further."

Sammy shrugged and moved to lean back against the wall, his hands crossed over his chest. "Okay," he said. His words were addressed to Michelle, but his eyes were on Allison, and they were filled with hunger.

As soon as Michelle had left the room, Allison stepped behind the curtain in the corner of the room and began to undo her blouse. "You don't have to listen to that old biddy, Sammy," she purred, wrapping a large Turkish towel around her nakedness and moving toward the massage table. "She doesn't own me, she's just my bodyguard."

She hopped up on the table and lay on her stomach, letting the towel open to reveal her buttocks, as she always did.

Sammy grinned and moved to stand next to the table as he dribbled heated oil onto Allison's back. "Okay by me, kiddo," he said, placing his hands on her back and beginning to rub gently in small circles. "After all, you're the boss."

He felt himself getting hard and pressed his groin up against Allison's arm as he rubbed her. Elizabeth Whitmire had told him today was the day he got to begin the Rite of Transformation on Allison, and he could hardly wait. She was going to be his first and the thought excited him greatly— almost as much as the feel of Allison's tight young ass under his hands did.

Allison squeezed her eyes shut tight when she felt his erection against her arm. She was right: He did care for her.

Though she was still a virgin, she'd seen enough movies and talked to enough of her girlfriends to know what his hardness meant, and the very thought that she made him feel that way gave her a funny feeling in the pit of her stomach that shot right down to her groin.

She gasped and sucked in her breath as his hands moved

lower to knead and caress her buttocks. Wow! That felt good, she thought. She squeezed her hips together to make them feel firmer, concerned that he'd notice the dimples she'd gotten there when she gained her last few pounds. She vowed for the hundredth time to give up cheeseburgers and order salads instead.

After a few moments of this, his hand slipped between her cheeks and his oily fingers began to caress areas of her body that'd never been touched by anyone other than herself. At first, she felt a sudden fear that things were getting out of hand and would go too far, but after his fingers went a little deeper and slipped inside her, she began to worry that he would stop and things wouldn't go far enough!

Jesus, she thought, holding her breath when his finger began to draw little circles around her clitoris. That's unbelievably wonderful!

In spite of a nagging cautionary thought that she pushed far down in her mind, Allison's hips began to move with Sammy's hand, pushing back against him to make him go deeper inside her. Faster, harder, she called out to him in her mind, and it was as if he could hear her thoughts for he did indeed begin to move his hand faster and harder, pressing down in exactly the right spots to make her quiver and shake under his touch.

When his hands moved to slide around her and lift her up so he could cup her breasts, she wondered why she wasn't fighting him off, but the thought soon evaporated under his skilful caresses and she moaned and groaned with the pleasure his hands were bringing.

When he finally turned her over onto her back, she didn't resist letting the towel slide to the floor, and she arched her back when he bent his head to take her right nipple between his lips.

Moments later, she opened her eyes to find a naked Sammy easing up on the table next to her. She opened her mouth to protest, but he filled it with his tongue before she could make a sound.

She felt woozy, as if she'd had too much to drink, and her arms went around him and pulled him down as he moved on top of her and nestled down between her legs. When he entered her and moved his mouth to kiss her neck, she whispered his name over and over.

She didn't mind either the pain between her legs or the sharp stinging in her neck—they both felt wonderful, and when he pressed the bleeding hole in his own neck against her lips, she sucked the sweet, coppery blood down hungrily.

Michelle was in no mood for an argument when she burst into Katherine Whitmire's office. "Ms. Whitmire," she began in a stern voice, "I've got a complaint!"

Katherine Whitmire smiled graciously and got to her feet, indicating with a sweep of her arm that Michelle should take a seat in front of her desk. "Of course, Michelle, but you must call me Kathy," Whitmire said, her voice as smooth as silk and seeming to be slightly more husky than Michelle remembered.

Suddenly, Michelle was having trouble remembering just what it was she was so angry about. She shook her head, trying to clear it of the clouds that swam before her eyes. The last time she'd felt this befuddled had been in her college days when she'd shared a joint with her roommate. She wondered briefly if she could somehow have been drugged, and had a fleeting glimmer of panic that perhaps it was a plot against her charge, Allison, but the thought disappeared into more clouds before she could act on it.

She barely noticed Whitmire moving around behind her to lock and bolt the door, and she somehow wasn't surprised when the lady stepped up close behind her and began to rub her shoulders.

"Uh . . . Ms. Whitmire . . . uh . . . Kathy," Michelle struggled to remember why she was here. Her face felt numb, her lips didn't seem to work right, and her tongue felt as if it was covered with fur or something else that was keeping it from obeying her mind's commands to protest this treatment.

"That's all right, dear," Katherine crooned behind her ear, "You just relax for a moment and all will become clear to you."

Michelle leaned her head back against the chair. Damn, that did feel good. Maybe it wouldn't hurt to just relax for a change and let someone else take care of her for a while.

For some reason, when Katherine's hands moved off her shoulders and began to knead and caress her breasts, Michelle said nothing, even though she was strictly heterosexual and had never in her life been with another woman. She was just so damned relaxed she couldn't seem to muster the energy to protest.

Michelle closed her eyes and gave herself in to the feeling, opening them moments later to find her blouse undone and her bra open at the front. Katherine was kneeling in front of her, her lips on one of Michelle's nipples while her hand was moving under Michelle's dress.

This wasn't right. This wasn't supposed to be happening to her. She was an agent in the Secret Service, and there were rules against this sort of thing. She had to do something, anything to make this woman stop what she was doing.

To her utter surprise, Michelle felt herself lift her buttocks and spread her legs so Katherine would have easier access to her groin, which seemed suddenly to be very hot and very wet. Michelle felt as if there were a thousand tiny needles prickling her vagina, which throbbed and pulsed under their attack.

As Katherine's fingers pushed her panties aside and entered her wetness, Michelle laid her head back against the chair and groaned, thus missing the change in Katherine's face when her fangs grew and her features melted and coalesced into something horrible.

Michelle started when the fangs entered her carotid artery, but she could hear Katherine in her mind telling her to relax and enjoy it . . . and so she did.

Bitsy McCormack, Allison Burton's best friend and her invited guest at the Rejuvenatrix Spa, looked at her watch and frowned. Allison was supposed to have joined her for lunch and she was already twenty minutes late. She shook her head. Her father, Black Jack McCormack, chairman of the Joint Chiefs of Staff, would never tolerate such laxness of discipline. He'd have somebody's head on a platter if they ever dared to keep him waiting like this.

Bitsy blushed and laughed at the thought. Dear God, she thought, please don't tell me I'm turning into my father.

The phone rang, interrupting her thoughts. She grabbed the receiver. "Allison, is that you?" she blurted, intending to give her friend a piece of her mind for being so selfish and rude.

"Hello, Bitsy," a male voice said.

"Uh, yes?" she answered.

"This is Sammy Akins, and Allison asked me to tell you to meet her at the pool. She has something she wants to show you."

"Okay," Bitsy said, her voice a bit arch at the way Allison was ordering her around. She fully intended to tell her about it too, as soon as she got to the pool.

Bitsy put on her bikini and threw a robe on over it and walked as fast as she could to the pool house.

She entered the cavernous space and noticed there was no one else around. The large building was completely empty.

Suddenly, the door opened behind her and a tall, thin man with dark hair drawn back into a ponytail walked through the doors. He was wearing only a tiny Speedo bathing suit and Bitsy couldn't help but notice that he had a full erection and was making no effort to hide it.

She blushed and tried to brush past him to get to the door, knowing she was in some sort of danger.

"Not so fast, little one," Theo Thantos said, reaching out to grab her arm. He pulled her to him, using his mind to calm her fears enough so that she wouldn't resist, but not so much that the fear entirely left her. The taste of fear added a certain spiciness to the taste of blood that Theo quite liked—he said it was the perfect aphrodisiac.

He pressed his groin against her as he reached around her and unfastened her bathing suit top. When it fell to the ground, revealing small, perfectly formed teenaged breasts, Theo felt his penis throb and pulsate against the girl's groin.

Her eyes opened wide and she tried feebly to pull away from him. "Stop . . . stop . . ." she croaked through a mouth gone suddenly dry. "Don't hurt me, please mister," she pleaded, pulling away from him and starting to cry—something she hadn't done since she was six years old and fell off her bicycle onto a sharp rock.

"Don't be afraid, child," Theo purred, taking her hand and slipping it inside his suit. When her fingers tightened on his erection, he bent to kiss her lips, saying, "This won't hurt a bit . . . I promise!"

Chapter 20

John Ashby and Marya Zaleska drove out to Gabrielle de Lavnay's house on the shores of the Delaware River to attend the latest meeting of Theo Thantos's conspirators.

Just before they got out of the car, Marya turned to John and put her hand on his arm. "Johnny, what are we doing here?" she asked, a puzzled frown on her face. "Why are you so determined to help this madman in his insane quest for power over the Normals?"

John sat back against the seat and sighed. It was a question he'd been wrestling with himself for weeks now, and he wasn't sure he knew the complete answer.

"It's hard to put into words, baby," he said, his voice low and somber as he stared out of the windshield at the roiling current of the river across the wide expanse of de Lavnay's yard. "Ever since I can remember, I've been a sort of outcast, never really fitting in, not even in my own family." He turned to look into her eyes. "As a kid, I had eight brothers and sisters, and all of us were physically abused by my dad, who when he wasn't drunk, was pretty much crazy angry. Later, after I was transformed, I went back home and he was the first one I killed. He was down on his knees, crying and pleading for mercy, just like us kids had done all those years ago when he stood over us with his four-inch-wide belt and beat the shit out of us."

He chuckled to himself, though there was no humor in the sound. "I gave him the same mercy he gave us—I ripped his head off, though I couldn't force myself to drink the bastard's blood."

Marya moved over on the seat and put her head on his shoulder. "Poor baby," she murmured, stroking his arm with her hand.

"And later," he continued, his eyes focused on something only he could see, "after I was changed, things were pretty much the same—I was still different, still outside the window looking in on everyone else's life." His eyes dropped to hers, "That's why I still feel such a kinship and love for Ed and Kim Slonaker even after all that's happened lately—they took me in and treated me like family when I came to work for Ed, more like family than my own relatives did."

He shrugged and gave a self-deprecating chuckle. "Hell, maybe this way if Theo Thantos does manage to take over the world, I'll be one of the ones on the inside looking out instead of the other way 'round."

She tilted her head up and kissed him lightly on the lips. "Well, if it's good enough for you, then it's good enough for me, lover."

"So you don't mind hanging with the crazies for a while?" he asked, stroking her face.

"Not if it makes you happy, but one thing I won't do is ever turn my back on either Thantos or Christina. Neither one of them are worth our trust."

He kissed her again on the lips and then they got out of the car and went into the house, arms locked together.

Theo, as was his habit, paced back and forth in front of the group gathered at de Lavnay's house as he talked. "I've asked you all to join us here for a progress report on our endeavors so far," he said in his rather pedantic and pompous tone of voice.

Marya glanced at John and rolled her eyes, but was careful not to let anyone else see her do it. The son of a bitch was so full of himself he looked about to burst with self-importance.

"So far, Elizabeth and Sammy have done an admirable job with the prospects we've sent them," he said in his condescending tone of voice. "Each and every one has been transformed without any suspicions of foul play."

"Uh, Theo," Augustine Calmet called, raising his hand like a schoolboy trying to get the teacher's attention.

Theo frowned, hating to be interrupted in mid-speech. "Yes, Augustine?"

"Just whom are we talking about here?" he asked, his cultured tones almost dripping with both condescension and sarcasm. "Mid-level flunkies or people high up on the Washington food chain?"

Theo sneered back at the man, thinking just because he's on the staff of the *Washington Post* he believes he's big shit. Well, just wait until he hears whom we've managed to snare in our net. "Well, Augustine, how does the daughter of the vice president of the United States, the daughter of the chairman of the Joint Chiefs of Staff, and the daughter of one of the Secret Service agents who guards the president himself sound to you? Is that high enough up on the food chain?" he ended, trying a little sarcasm of his own.

Augustine's eyebrows raised and he gave a low whistle. "Wow," he said, his self-important manner suddenly gone. "That is impressive, Theo. I had no idea you'd reached so high into Washington society."

Theo accepted the compliment with grace, and with a smug smile continued, "And that's not all. Currently we're working on even more members of the elite of Washington, targeting influential members of the media, both print and televised, as well as some foreign diplomatic types who will be sent back to their native countries to continue our work there."

Augustine glanced at the front of the room where Elizabeth Whitmire and Sammy Akins sat. "Bravo, people, bravo," he said, clapping his hands softly together until he was joined by everyone in the room.

Theo beamed, holding up his hands as he smiled. "Now, for the most important part of the meeting. I want all of you to take the time to write down the names of people in your fields or who you know should be targeted—people who either can do us good on their own or who have access to people higher up in society than they are."

He turned and pointed at Brahma Parvsh and Christabel Chordewa. "Brahma, you and Christabel drive everyone who is anyone to every important party and function in the city. Pick out some that we may be able to get to."

He looked over at Johannes Cuntius. "Johannes, you can tell us who we should target in the TV industry. Remember, we want the men and women who make the final decisions on network news policy: not just the Indians, we want the chiefs."

Ronnie Ranger raised his hand. "I can do the same thing as far as radio, Theo," he said, beaming when Theo nodded and gave him a thumbs up.

"Now, once we have your lists"—he glanced at Gabrielle de Lavnay—"we'll have Gabrielle schedule a huge party on some pretext or another and we'll make sure everyone on the list is invited. Then, we'll make sure we know all their weaknesses or predilections and we'll see how many we can get started transforming that night."

"What do you mean about their weaknesses and predilections?" Augustine asked.

Theo sighed. The man might be high up in the newspaper business, but he was still an idiot. He wondered how the man had gotten as high up as he had since he obviously had no nose for conspiracy or subterfuge. "Well, Augustine, suppose one of our guests has a thing for young boys. We'll simply make sure an attractive young man invites him up to one of Gabrielle's more isolated bedrooms for an assignation. Once there"—Theo shrugged and grinned—"we can go to work on him without fear of being interrupted."

"That brings up another question, Theo," Christabel said. "The Rite of Transformation takes several days, at least. How are we going to accomplish it in one night?"

Theo smiled again. "I'm glad you asked that. One of the first things we did was to target several doctors around town who handle the carriage trade. Once we start the rite, the person will wake up the next day with symptoms of fever and muscle aches. We'll make sure by mental commands that he or she calls the correct doctor to make a house call, and the doctors will continue the rites on their patients until they are far enough along so they will seek out their transformers themselves for their blood meals."

Augustine nodded, his eyes shining. "It seems you've thought of everything, Theo."

Theo gave a depreciating wave of his hand. "Probably not, Augustine, but with all of us here working on the plan, hopefully it will go off as expected."

That night, the vice president of the United States knocked softly on the door to his daughter's bedroom.

"Allison, honey, it's Daddy," Jonathon Burton called softly.

"Come in, Daddy," Allison answered.

Jonathon opened the door and stepped a little way into the room. He squinted his eyes, trying to see in the gloomy darkness. "I just wanted to make sure you were okay and that you've gotten over that nasty flu you had last week," he said, wondering why she had the lights out at such an early time of night. She usually stayed up until well past midnight chatting to her friends on the phone. Maybe she hadn't fully recovered from her illness yet.

"I'm feeling much better, Daddy," Allison said in her little-girl voice. "But I'd feel even better if you'd come over here and tuck me in like you used to when I was little."

Jonathon grinned in the darkness, shaking his head as he moved toward the bed. She must still be delirious from the fever, he thought. The last time he'd tried to give her a kiss good night on the cheek she'd had a hissy fit and told him she was too old for that foolishness.

As he got closer he could make out her form sitting up in bed, her back propped up against the wall with pillows behind her. His eyes flicked once across her breasts, outlined and plainly visible beneath her sheer nightgown. Jesus, he thought, averting his gaze and flushing in embarrassment. Where in hell did she get that nightgown? She's a full-grown woman and I haven't even noticed.

He reached down and pulled the blanket up as she scooted down in the bed, her arms outstretched toward him. "Give me a hug and a kiss good night, Daddy," she said, smiling up at him with a strange glint in her eyes.

He put his hands on her shoulders and leaned down to kiss her cheek, when she suddenly turned her head toward him and placed her open mouth on his, sticking her tongue almost down his throat.

He recoiled and tried to pull back, but she grabbed him with surprisingly strong arms and pulled him down on top of her in the bed.

"Come on, Daddy dear," she said, her voice growing suddenly low and harsh. "You can do better than that."

As he struggled to get up off of her, she shifted in the bed until she was lying next to him and grabbed his hand with hers and placed it on her breast, which had somehow come out of her nightgown.

She leaned over him and with her index finger she made a small slit in her neck over her jugular vein. When he opened his mouth to ask her what in the hell had gotten into her, the blood from her neck dribbled into his mouth, making him sputter and spit and shake his head.

As he swallowed the coppery, salty liquid, he felt it spread out and travel through his body like a wildfire out of control. All of a sudden he could hear her voice in his mind, telling him to relax and enjoy it.

The fire caused by her hormones raging throughout his bloodstream seemed to go straight to his loins and he realized with a start he had a sudden, massive erection and his hand began to fondle his daughter's breast of its own accord, pinching the nipple and squeezing the firm young flesh over and over again. He was horrified at his actions.

Though he tried to fight it, telling himself this was craziness, he reached up and put his hand on the back of her neck and pulled her down to his waiting lips and sucked her blood as fast as he could swallow.

Allison moaned and pressed her neck against his lips while her hand was busy unfastening his trousers and pulling his erection out into view.

"Oh, Daddy," she moaned as she stroked him and turned her head to the side to sink her teeth into his neck while he groaned and pushed himself against her hand as hard and as fast as he could, his mind completely under her control.

At almost that exact same moment, Bitsy McCormack was opening the door to her father's bedroom. Black Jack McCormack and his wife had slept in separate bedrooms ever since he'd come back from the Gulf War. His nose had been broken in an automobile accident there and he now snored so loudly she refused to sleep in the same room with him.

Bitsy stood just inside the door and watched her father as he sat propped up in the bed, reading intelligence reports from the morning's briefing at the White House.

After a moment, he jumped when he caught sight of her

out of the corner of his eye. "Oh, hi darlin'," he said, putting the stack of papers down on his lap and smiling at her over the pair of half-glasses perched on his nose. "I didn't see you come in."

Bitsy reached over and flipped the light switch off, plunging the room into almost total darkness.

"What . . . ?" McCormack began, until Bitsy cut him off.

"I've got something to show you, father," she said, her voice deepening as she began to change as she moved toward him through the darkness.

"But how . . . ?" he asked, his voice choking off as she leapt onto him and fastened her lips to his neck and began to feed.

Chapter 21

Matt opened his eyes, smacked his lips, and stretched. For the first time in as long as he could remember, he felt great! No aches, no fever, and no pain of any kind afflicted him on this fine winter morning.

He bounded out of bed and moved to the window, flinging it open and taking a deep breath of the frigid Maine air, which for some reason didn't seem to cause him any discomfort whatsoever. Jesus, what a beautiful day!

As he lowered the window, he thought he could hear faint voices behind him and he turned, surprised to find the room empty. "Huh," he mumbled, "that's strange." He was about to conclude he was hallucinating when he heard the voices again, but this time he could tell the sounds were in his mind, not his ears. Whoa, this mind reading shit is neat, he thought, grinning as he focused a little to listen in on the thoughts coming from the other room. He soon realized the entire group was already awake and discussing his and Shooter's transformation. He also found each voice in his mind was distinct, just like their real voices were, and that he could identify who was thinking what just as if they'd been talking directly to him. Better get out there with them before they think he's a lazy bones.

He started to go through the door when he realized he was naked. That won't do, he thought. He turned around and went to the closet. He grabbed some jeans and a pullover sweater and put them on before leaving the room. Since the cold didn't seem to bother him, he didn't wait to put on shoes but proceeded out the door and into the living room in his bare feet.

"Well, lo and behold, the wonder boy awakens," Shooter said when Matt appeared. Matt stared at his best friend for a moment, realizing Shooter looked somehow younger than he used to, with all the stress lines around his eyes and mouth completely gone.

Matt looked around the room, surprised to see in addition to Elijah, TJ, Sam, and Shooter, both Ed and Kim Slonaker sitting in the room. He hadn't noticed their thoughts in the mélange of voices in his head before. One drawback of telepathy, he realized, is when you're in a group, everyone is thinking at the same time and it's hard to pick out individual thoughts. It isn't like a group conversation where only one person speaks at a time. Oh well, he'd probably get used to it sooner or later.

Sam jumped to her feet and rushed over to throw her arms around his neck and give him a resounding kiss on the lips. "Darling, I'm so glad you're finally awake," she said, rubbing her cheek against his and then pulling back and frowning at the beard stubble there. He picked up the thought "porcupine" from her before he was interrupted by Elijah Pike.

"Good morning, Matt," Elijah said, smiling and nodding his head in greeting. "You look like you've survived the Rite of Transformation with no ill effects."

Kim Slonaker laughed from across the room and smoothed her hair back. "Well, he wasn't feeling any pain last night when I gave him my donation of blood, I can tell you that," she said, thinking of how sore her breasts still were after their session in his bedroom the night before.

Matt, who could read her thoughts as easily as if she'd spoken out loud blushed and glanced at Sam, worried that she might be jealous.

Sam laughed and ruffled his hair. "Oh look, Kim," she said lightly, "You've made the poor man blush."

Kim laughed too. "Serves him right for what he put me through last night—the man was an animal!"

"Hey," Shooter said indignantly, "what about me? I seem to remember you coming to visit me too last night."

"Yes, dear," Kim said indulgently, "but you were a pussy-cat."

Everyone laughed as Shooter looked around with an embarrassed expression on his face.

"That's okay, baby," TJ said, rubbing his thigh. "I still think you're an animal even if no one else does."

"Oh, thanks a lot!" Shooter said, grinning himself now. He muttered "pussycat" and shook his head ruefully. No female he'd ever been with had called him that before.

"I'll get you some coffee, sweetheart," Sam said, "while you tell everyone how you're feeling."

Matt smiled and looked around the room. "I feel great," he said and took a seat on the couch where Sam had been sitting.

"That's not what she meant, chum," Shooter said, shaking his head. "They want to know what effects the transformation has had on us, what we can do now that we couldn't before."

"What did you tell them?" Matt asked, arching one eyebrow and tuning into Shooter's thoughts.

Shooter smiled and shrugged, thinking back at Matt, let's do this out loud so the others can hear. "Mainly that it seems I can now read thoughts pretty much at will," he said. "I really haven't tried anything else yet."

"Same for me," Matt said. "I can hear the sound of everyone's thoughts in the back of my mind, kind'a like background music that I can ignore or listen to whenever I want to."

Elijah looked skeptical. "You mean you boys can both hear our thoughts even when we're not trying to contact you?"

Sam reappeared with a steaming cup of coffee and handed it to Matt as she took a seat next to him.

Both Matt and Shooter nodded, glancing at each other as if to say it was no big deal.

"I want you to try something," Elijah said, leaning back in the chair he was sitting in and pursing his lips in thought. "I am going to think of something and try to block it from anyone reading it. I want everyone in the room to try and read me and we'll see what happens."

He shut his eyes and his brow furrowed with the strength of his concentration.

After a moment, Matt and Shooter looked at each other and smiled, sharing the thought between them that this was too easy. The man was an open book, as was everyone else in the room.

Minutes later, Elijah opened his eyes and looked around the room. TJ, Sam, Kim, and Ed all shook their heads, indicating they couldn't get any hint of his thoughts.

Both Matt and Shooter said almost in unison, "You were thinking that this is shaping up to be a much colder winter than last year."

When Elijah's face showed his astonishment, Shooter stared at him and sent the thought, "At least that was what you were thinking on the surface. Underneath you were worried that if we could read your mind we'd find out about how strong your feelings for TJ still are."

Elijah's face paled and he murmured, "Jesus!"

"Don't worry, pal," Shooter continued, still thinking thoughts that only Matt and Elijah could 'hear,' "your secret's safe with me . . . and Matt."

"This is amazing," Elijah said, shaking his head. "I've never seen anyone who could break through a mind block before."

"I wonder if they have any other powers that are as strong," Ed Slonaker asked, regarding the boys with speculative eyes. "Like telekinesis or long-distance telepathy or precog abilities, things like that."

Matt glanced at Ed and his eyes narrowed as he stared at the coffee cup on the table next to Ed's chair. The cup slowly rotated on the table and then moved up to hang suspended several inches in the air.

After a moment, the cup returned to its place and Matt took a deep breath. "There's your answer, Ed. I can do it, but it takes full concentration and is very tiring."

Shooter turned his head to look at TJ and suddenly the buttons on her blouse popped open and her blouse opened slightly to reveal the cleavage of her bare breasts. She gasped and grabbed the edges of her blouse and gave him a stern look.

He laughed. "Don't worry, babe," he said, "I didn't open it too far."

Sam and the others all laughed, and even TJ gave a half-smile, but it was clear from the glint in her eyes that she intended to have a serious talk with Shooter later.

"I think this psychic stuff is gonna be fun," Shooter said, smiling lasciviously at TJ, "except what you're thinking about me right now does not bode well for an enjoyable evening."

"Yes, and it will be quite useful to our work too," Elijah said, glancing around at the group. "Of course there is a down side to this."

"What's that, Elijah?" Sam asked.

"It means that the rest of us are going to have to double up on our sharing of each other's blood, and that in turn means we're going to have to remain off the vaccine for a few more days at least."

Kim and Ed glanced at each other, and then Ed spoke.

"That might be a problem, Elijah. Both Kim and I are having a rather tough time controlling our hunger. Remember, we hadn't been on the vaccine nearly as long as you and Sam and TJ before we had to stop it to donate blood to the boys." He took a deep breath. "I'm afraid we might do something rash if something isn't done to relieve the hunger."

Before Elijah could answer, Matt looked at Shooter and they mind-spoke at each other. After a second, Matt said, "Elijah, I think you should know that just about everyone here is feeling the same way, except for Shooter and me. We haven't been Vampyres long enough for the hunger to build yet, but you are all struggling with it."

Elijah sighed. "I know. I was hoping it was just me, but now I can see the signs on all of us—the irritability, the nervousness, and the general air of waiting for something to happen."

"Elijah," Sam said, "If we're going to try and share out blood among ourselves to attempt to gain some added powers, then we've got to stay off the vaccine. What are we to do? This area is too small and lightly populated for any killings or missing persons to go unnoticed."

"You're right, Sam, so I think the only solution is for us to leave here for a short while. Maybe a trip to Portland would give us the chance to assuage our hunger and to still keep our existence a secret."

TJ cocked an eyebrow at Elijah. "What have you got on your mind, Elijah? I know you detest the idea of killing innocent people to satisfy our hunger—in fact, that is the entire reason you invented the vaccine in the first place."

Elijah grinned and for a moment all two hundred years of his cunning and his experience hunting humans for food could be seen in his eyes. "Who said anything about killing innocents?" he asked. He inclined his head toward the morning's newspaper lying on a nearby table. "There was an interesting article in the Portland paper this morning," he said. "It concerned a vicious gang of thugs who've been shanghaiing innocent townsmen and putting them to work on oceangoing freighters."

"You think that's enough to justify killing them?" Shooter asked with some ambivalence evident in his voice.

"Not that alone," Elijah answered, "but the paper went on to say that just before reaching port, the poor suckers who were shanghaied are thrown overboard and left to either drown or be eaten by sharks."

When everyone frowned at the barbarity of these acts, Elijah smiled again and there was no mirth at all in his expression. "What say we give them a taste of their own medicine?"

"Do you think there's enough of them in this gang to satisfy all of us?" Kim asked.

Elijah shrugged, the evil glint in his eye sparkling. "If not, there are plenty of other lowlifes in Portland that can easily be found."

Kim's face lit up and she took Ed's hand in hers and squeezed it. "Oh, a road trip," she said gaily. "That sounds like fun!"

Chapter 22

At five o'clock the next morning, Elijah tapped on the door to Matt and Sam's room.

Matt, unlike his previous disposition to have to be driven out of bed and plied with coffee before waking up, came immediately awake and felt refreshed and more alive than he ever had before.

He cast his mind out and found that it was Elijah at the door and called, "Come in, Elijah."

Elijah stuck his head in the door and had a rueful smile on his face. "I can see there's going to be no keeping secrets from you from now on."

Matt grinned back. "Nor from the rest of you guys once we all share our blood."

Elijah entered the room and tried to keep his eyes, and his mind, off the sight of Sam's body as she sat up in the bed and stretched with the sheet down around her waist revealing her bare breasts. "Hey, what's up, Elijah?" she asked.

"I'm waking everyone up early today. After you all went to bed last night, I got to thinking that in addition to needing to feed, we have some vaccines ready to send out. So, I figured this would be a perfect opportunity to kill two birds with one stone, so to speak. I spent the night preparing dozens of batches of serum and I have the boxes all addressed and loaded in the back of the Explorer. I thought we'd all drive into Portland and you and Matt and TJ and Shooter could fly off to different cities and mail the boxes from there so there wouldn't be any trace of our location."

Matt pursed his lips as he looked into Elijah's mind. With his new powers, Elijah wasn't even aware he was being read. "There is a secondary benefit to your plan," Matt said.

Elijah just nodded and Sam looked at Matt. "What?" she asked.

"It spreads us all out in different areas of the country so we can all feed to satisfy the hunger without the authorities in any one place seeing a rash of missing or dead people."

"I'm afraid it's necessary, Sam, at least until we finish our sharing of blood among ourselves and get back on our vaccines," Elijah said, his tone apologetic.

Sam jumped out of bed, completely unconcerned about the fact that she was naked, and walked toward the bathroom. "No problem," she said, glancing back over her shoulder. "We'll look on it as a vacation. I just love staying in motels—it makes Matt even more horny than usual."

Elijah grinned. "Don't use up all the hot water," he warned. "Everyone else is going to be showering too."

Matt threw the covers back and followed Sam toward the bathroom. "In that case, we'll conserve by sharing the shower and using only half as much water."

Elijah knew what that meant. "Fine," he said, "just don't take too long. We've got to be at the airport by eight o'clock and it's an hour's drive."

Sam stuck her head back out of the door and grinned at Elijah. "Don't worry, dear," she said, "Matt never takes too long in the shower when I'm in there. As a matter of fact, he's quick like a bunny rabbit."

Elijah could see Matt's hand reach around the door and yank her out of sight. "We'll see about that," he heard Matt say.

Matt and Sam, their faces still flushed from their exertions in the shower, piled into the car along with Shooter and TJ and Elijah.

"We'll swing by the Bear Mountain Inn and pick up Ed and Kim on the way," he said. Ed and Kim were staying at the nearby bed and breakfast as Elijah's cabin only had two bedrooms.

"You think they're awake yet?" Shooter asked. "After all, they didn't get to bed until really late."

He was referring to the fact that the previous night had been spent with the group playing musical beds as they all went from person to person to take small drinks of each other's blood. Some of the visits had lasted longer than others when hormones began to rage and playful sex was engaged in. Just as Elijah had foretold, even Shooter had lost his monumental jealousy under the influence of the Vampyre Bug. Of course, having the beautiful Kim to keep his mind off what Ed was doing with TJ helped quite a bit.

"I'll bet they're already up and at 'em," Sam said. "Kim is really anxious for this trip. It seems the hunger is especially strong in her."

Sure enough, both Ed and Kim were waiting in the inn's driveway when Elijah pulled up. Shooter and TJ got in the rearmost seat, leaving Kim room to squeeze in beside Matt and Sam while Ed got in the front seat with Elijah.

"How are you guys feeling?" Elijah asked.

Ed replied, "Not too bad, all things considered. We're both running a slight fever and have some muscle aches, but not nearly as bad as the first time we went through the Rite of Transformation."

"Speak for yourself, my cuddly little bear," Kim said from

the backseat. "It's been so long since I had any kind of sickness, I'd almost forgotten how rotten a fever makes you feel."

"Have either of you noticed any changes in your abilities yet?" Matt asked.

Ed looked over his shoulder. "Yeah, we both think so. At least, we feel like our psychic abilities are getting stronger."

"Last night, after Elijah let us off at the inn, we could both sense almost every other guest's thoughts and dreams. It was really weird."

Matt smiled. "It is at first, but you'll soon find you can shut them out entirely, or let them kind'a run at the back of your mind like when you're talking to someone and there's a TV playing in the background. You hear it but you don't really listen to what's being said."

"I hope so," Kim said with feeling, "otherwise, I'm going to go crazy."

Ed winked at Matt. "What she means to say is she'll go crazier!"

"Cuddly bear," Kim said, her voice low and dangerous but her eyes still holding a glint of humor. "You know how cranky I get when I don't get my sleep and those damned psychic thoughts kept me awake all night. You're already living on borrowed time, so watch it!"

Rapidly changing the subject, Ed turned to Elijah. "By the way, I was wondering how you got all those names on the boxes of vaccines we're going to be sending out."

"Through my e-mail," Elijah said. "I opened an account on AOL with one of my old names and addresses on it so it couldn't be traced. A friend, Ramson Holroyd, has spread the word about the vaccine and asked everyone he told to tell all of their friends and to give them my e-mail address. Those that are interested have e-mailed me they'd like to try it. So far I've gotten several hundred inquiries." He laughed, "And not a few threats and diatribes about how what we're doing is going to ruin the race, etcetera."

Ed whistled low in his throat. "Wow, that's gonna cost a

bundle to provide that many of our kind with the vaccine, since I know it can't be cheap."

Elijah grinned. "You're right, Ed, and even though I'm not exactly hurting when it comes to money, most of the people wanting the vaccine have agreed to donate what they could to a Swiss bank account number I provided when I e-mailed them their instructions on how to take the vaccine and what it could and couldn't do for them."

"You mean they're really sending donations when you told them they could get it for free?"

Elijah nodded. "That's right. Last time I checked, my account had grown by over a million dollars in the past two weeks."

"Jesus!" Ed whispered. "Now I feel really bad about not paying you anything for Kim and my vaccines."

"Don't worry about it, Ed. I realize you and Kim are living on a policeman's salary and don't have a lot to spare. Remember, most of my . . . uh, clients or patients, are still actively hunting and killing Normals. That usually means they have a steady supply of shall we say ill-gotten gains. They can certainly afford it."

"Still," Ed said, unconvinced, "We're gonna find some way to help you pay for all this."

Elijah pulled into the Portland Jetport driveway and eased the big SUV up to the passenger unloading area. Everyone got out of the car and he opened the rear hatch door. There were two large trunks lying there. He bent in and easily lifted both out and put them down on the sidewalk.

"Okay, you guys. Each couple take one trunk and head out to some airport somewhere and when you get there use a FedEx service to send out the packages inside. The addresses are marked on each box of vaccine and be sure and pay cash."

He reached into his pocket and brought out a large wad of

cash, handing each couple several thousand dollars in hundred dollar bills.

"Elijah, you haven't told us where to go," Matt said, putting the cash in his billfold.

Elijah shrugged. "It doesn't matter, as long as it's at least two connecting flights from here. That'll make it much tougher for anyone to trace, just in case Morpheus's old gang is still looking to prevent the disbursal of the vaccine."

Sam and TJ stepped forward and gave Elijah a kiss on the cheek. "See ya soon, Elijah," TJ said.

"Hey, boys," Kim said, winking at them, "Don't stay away too long—we still have some unfinished business to complete."

Matt and Shooter gave her a wave, inclined their heads at Ed, and led the girls through the big revolving door into the terminal.

Sam took Matt's arm in hers and leaned against him, her face filled with excitement. "Where shall we go, darling?"

He pursed his lips for a moment, looking at the big bank of computer screens that held departure information. "Hey, how about Houston?" He pointed at the screens. "See, we can leave here in an hour, connect through Newark, and from there head straight to Bush International." He turned to her. "We can be there in time to have supper with Shelly and Barbara and catch up on old times."

"Wonderful," she said.

Shooter said, "I think we'll head for New Orleans. I miss that good ol' Cajun cookin' we had while we were there last year."

"Yeah, and we can stop by and say hi to that nice policeman—what was his name?"

"Boudreaux," Shooter said, "Bill Boudreaux." He narrowed his eyes at her. "I remember the way you looked at him when we were there before. You had a crush on him, didn't you?" he asked sternly, though there was a hint of teasing in his voice.

TJ nodded. "Yes, dear. I'm afraid it was the uniform. I'm a sucker for a man in uniform."

He shook his head. "And to think I was a detective in plain clothes—just my luck."

She squeezed his arm. "Yeah, but remember I came after you in spite of the fact that you didn't wear a uniform. What do you think that means?"

He gave a grin and a shrug. "That I'm so handsome I don't need a uniform to make you hot?"

She leaned back and punched his arm. "Sexist pig!"

"That means I'm right . . . right?" he asked.

"Yeah, darn it, you're right," she admitted.

At that moment, Jonathon Burton was stepping out of the limousine driven by the Secret Service agents assigned to him. He made his way up the walkway to the White House and entered by the private door on the side.

When he got to his office, his secretary glanced up and raised her eyebrows. "Good morning, sir," she said.

"Hello, Mary Ann," he replied.

She got to her feet and gave him a close look, frowning at his bloodshot eyes and pale, waxen complexion. "Goodness, sir," she said, "you don't look like you're quite over the flu just yet."

He glanced at her, his eyes narrowing a bit. "Yes, Mary Ann, it was a rather nasty case." He paused, thinking for a moment, and then he added, "I hope you don't get it."

She smiled. "Oh, I doubt I will, sir. I took my flu shot already this year."

He wlked toward his office. "Put on the 'do not disturb' light over my door, Mary Ann, and come into my office. I want you to go over the mail with me."

When he got to his desk, he turned and began taking his coat off as she entered the room and shut the door behind her. Her eyes widened a bit when he loosened his tie and began to unbutton his shirt as well.

"Sir," she asked, "what are you doing?"

He smiled as he began to give her mental commands to relax and be quiet. "Well, I wouldn't want to get blood on my clothes, now would I, Mary Ann?"

"Blood?" she asked, suddenly feeling as if she'd had a couple of drinks too many. Her mind was fuzzy and she felt very relaxed, almost sleepy. She reached her hand out and put it on the back of a nearby chair to steady herself. She felt as if she was going to faint.

When Burton's face began to change and melt, she felt a slight anxiety, but for some reason she didn't call out or turn to run, but simply stood there, her notebook in her hands as he moved across the room toward her, scarlet drool dripping from his smiling lips.

As he bent down and sunk his fangs in her neck, she moaned and felt her sex become wet. With trembling hands and a wildly beating heart, she began to undo the buttons on her blouse. She didn't have a spare in the office and she too didn't want to get blood on it.

When the vice president reached down and made a tiny slit in his left wrist, she knew instinctively what he wanted her to do. She took his hand in hers, kissed the palm once, and then fastened her lips on the wound and began to suck.

She'd never tasted anything as good as the salty sweetness she swallowed greedily.

Chapter 23

Matt and Sam rented a car at Bush International airport and drove toward downtown Houston. While Matt fought the freeway traffic, Sam took out her cell phone and dialed a number by memory.

A female voice answered, "Hello?"

"Barbara," Sam said excitedly, "This is Sam."

"Why, Sam, how nice to hear from you," Barbara Silver said. Her happiness at hearing from her husband's old protégé was evident. "How are you doing, dear?"

"Fine, Barbara. Matt and I are in town for a short while and if you and Shelly are going to be home and don't have other plans, we'd like to see you, maybe take you out to dinner."

"Oh, good, we'd love to see you. Shelly should be home in a little while. But forget going out to dinner. I can cook for us here. Did you two have a big lunch?"

Sam laughed. "Only some peanuts on the airplane."

"Then I'll whip something up . . ." Barbara began.

"No, Barb, how about we stop by a deli and pick up some food for us to eat? That way we won't have to worry about dishes and we can spend the whole time talking."

"What a delightful idea."

"As I recall," Sam said, "both you and Shelly prefer Reubens, with plenty of hot mustard and sauerkraut and potato salad."

Now Barbara laughed. "You know Shelly, dear, the hotter the better, and I'll make sure we have some bicarb for later tonight."

Both Sheldon Silver, professor of pathology at Baylor College of Medicine and Sam's old boss, and Barbara were delighted to see Sam and Matt. Hugs were exchanged all around, and Sam even lied a tiny bit and told Shelly it looked like he'd lost weight since they left Houston.

"Bless you my child," he said, beaming and patting her cheek, "but the truth, as I'm sure you can tell, is that my lovely Barbara keeps fixing such wonderful meals that I've actually managed to gain a few ounces."

"Oy," Barbara said, placing her hands on her cheeks and looking heavenward. "Ounces the man says. God forgive him for such a falsehood."

Matt and Sam both laughed and Shelly led them all into the living room, where Barbara already had a light white wine chilling in an ice bucket.

The dinner was spent catching up on gossip around the medical center and talking about the good old days when Sam was studying under Shelly and Matt was head of the Emergency Medicine Department.

Shelly and Barbara, who'd been deeply involved with Matt and Sam in discovering that it was Elijah who was killing people in Houston some years back, knew about TJ's conversion to a Vampyre and Shelly had helped the young doctors to try and figure out a way to cure her.

Finally, after they'd polished off their deli dinner and two bottles of wine, Barbara left them at the table while she went into the kitchen to prepare coffee all around.

Shelly, though he was a professor of pathology, was an astute diagnostician. He'd noted the telltale signs of Vampyrism on both Sam and Matt—the bloodshot eyes, the slightly phosphorescent teeth, the pale skin, and the piercing gazes. After he looked over his shoulder to make sure Barbara couldn't hear, he leaned across the table and whispered, "I see there have been some changes since you two left here with TJ and Shooter."

Matt, who knew from his thoughts that Shelly suspected they'd been transformed, nodded. "Yes, Shelly, there have. If you'd like, we'll tell you and Barbara about the adventures that led up to them."

Shelly leaned back in his chair and pursed his lips as he thought over Matt's offer. Finally, he reluctantly nodded. "I must admit, dear friends, that you have indeed piqued my curiosity. If this was a voluntary transformation on your parts, then I am left wondering what could possible induce two such level-headed people to do such a damn fool thing, and if it was involuntary, then I am also left wondering why you haven't approached your old friend Shelly to help you reverse this process."

Both Matt and Sam laughed at Shelly's convoluted though sensible verbalization of the situation. Barbara appeared just then and looked at Shelly with upraised eyebrows. "Have I missed something?" she asked as she put her tray down and poured everyone coffee into heavy mugs.

"Let's go sit in front of the fireplace, dear," Shelly said, picking up his mug. "Our friends have a tale to tell us that I'm sure will be most interesting."

Once they were all settled in front of the fire Shelly had going in the fireplace, even though the temperature in Houston was in the low sixties, Matt gestured for Sam to begin.

She started with the last time they'd seen the Silvers, when they told them the year before that they wouldn't be coming back to their practices in Houston. They hadn't gone into detail then, merely told the Silvers that they were no longer in danger from Michael Morpheus.

"Remember how we said we were going to work with Elijah Pike, whom you knew as Roger Niemann, to perfect the Vampyre vaccine?"

Shelly and Barbara nodded.

"Well, we got it down pretty good, so that a Vampyre can take it and it stops the hunger, the Vampyre's insatiable desire for fresh blood. While on the vaccine, the Vampyres are able to live an almost normal life, taking only small amounts of test tube blood occasionally."

"The problem, as we found out," Matt continued, "is that not all Vampyres want to be changed, or cured as we call it."

Shelly glanced at Barbara with sad eyes. "That shouldn't have been such a surprise, Matthew. Ever since man left the Garden of Eden, there have been souls who are evil, and who do evil, vile things for evil's sake alone."

"You're right, Shelly, it shouldn't have surprised us, but it did," Matt agreed.

"At any rate," Sam continued, "we found ourselves in a war with a group of Vampyres on the other side who wanted to stop the vaccine production and its distribution to members of their race who want to change, to become normal once again."

She then told them in some detail of the apocalyptic fight in the snow of Canada with Michael Morpheus and his minions and how some of his followers were still on their trail, vowing to stop the virus production.

"Is this war the reason that Matt has decided to become one of you?" Shelly asked, drawing a grunt of surprise from Barbara, who hadn't noticed. "Because you need more 'soldiers'?"

"Only partially," Matt answered. He reached over and took Sam's hand in his. "Actually, it was more because of Sam. The Vampyre virus was keeping us apart, keeping us from ever being fully together. I changed so we could be as one for the rest of our lives with nothing to keep us apart."

"And Shooter?" Shelly asked. "I assume he has done the same thing for TJ's sake."

Matt and Sam nodded, still holding hands. "Both Shooter and Matt are involved in some research to see if the abilities of the Vampyres can be improved by"—she hesitated, not wanting to get too graphic—"by technical means."

Shelly looked at Barbara, who smiled back at him with tears in her eyes. "Well," he said, also smiling, "you have our blessings, not that you need them."

They spent another hour or so letting Shelly fill them in on the various promotions, divorces, transfers, and other personal goings on at the medical center and then they took their leave with tears in all of their eyes, promising once again to keep in touch.

After another hour or two spent visiting with Matt's parents, who, much to Matt's embarrassment, chided him for not "making an honest woman" out of Sam and marrying her, they pled extreme fatigue and told his parents they were going back to their hotel room to get some much needed sleep.

Once they were in their rental car, Matt turned to Sam. "How about it, darling, are you hungry?"

She gave him a slow smile, knowing that he wasn't referring to hunger for normal food. "Why, as a matter of fact, I'm famished."

"Do you want to go shopping down at the warehouse area at the docks or take in one of the rougher clubs downtown?"

She grinned and fluffed her hair. "How about a club? We haven't gone dancing in a while."

Matt put the car in gear and headed for a section of town the emergency docs had named Knife Alley for its propensity to provide the local emergency rooms with stabbing victims, and worse, over the years.

As he pulled up in a parking lot lit only by the glare of a nearby club's sign, Sam put her hand on his arm. "Darling, since this is your first hunt since your transformation, I want you to pick out our guest for dinner."

He grinned. "Oh, I plan to let our guest pick us out," he said, getting out of the car and opening the door for her.

They entered the door to a place named The Jive Joint and walked through a crowded hallway until they came to a table that was empty. Except for a few white women who were obviously prostitutes that were dancing with black men, they were the only nonblacks in the place.

After a few moments, a young black woman wearing only pasties and panties approached their table. She was carrying a tray in one hand and was obviously a waitress. She leaned over and whispered loud enough to be heard over the roar of the speakers, "If I was you two, I'd leave this place as fast as yore little white feetsies can carry you!" She glanced around at the angry eyes staring at them from every corner of the room. "You in real danger here, whitey," she said to Matt, "or don't you care nothin' 'bout your girlfriend what may happen to her if'n you don't get your butts outta here?"

Matt grinned back at her. "Two Tanquerays and seven, please, with wedges of lime."

The waitress shrugged. "Well, it's your funeral," she said as she moved off toward the bar area.

Matt took Sam's hand and led her out onto the dance floor, where they began to dance. As people moved away from them, giving them plenty of room, Matt frowned and leaned his head down close to Sam's face. "We're being watched," he said.

"No shit, Sherlock," she replied gaily, not getting his meaning. "I think every eye in here is on us."

"No," he hissed, taking her hand and leading her off the floor. "I mean there's one of us here, and I think I know who it is."

They took their seats, finding their drinks already on the

table. Before he could explain further, two large black men stepped in front of them and leaned down, putting their fists on the table. "Can we dance with your date, whitey?" one of them asked in a sarcastic, hostile tone.

"Both of you at once?" Matt asked, his voice full of good humor, with not a smidgeon of fear in it.

An even larger black hand appeared on the man's shoulder before he could answer, and his eyes opened wide and his face screwed up in pain as he was whirled around. "Go and mind your own business, Dawg, these folks are friends of mine," Ramson Holroyd said in a low, menacing tone of voice.

The other black man at the table made the mistake of challenging Ramson, pulling his fist back like he was going to swing, when Ramson grabbed him by the neck and squeezed until the man dropped to his knees. "You got anything else to say, nigger?" Ramson asked, his voice now even and almost friendly.

"No . . . no . . ." the man croaked as his friend helped him to his feet and led him off.

"Mind if I have a seat?" Ramson asked, smiling.

"Not at all," Matt answered. "Can we buy you a drink?"

"No, I won't be here that long," Ramson replied. He stared at Matt for a moment and Matt felt him try to probe his mind. Matt shut him down and pried Ramson's mind open even though he was trying to block it. Matt immediately saw why Ramson had joined them.

"I see you're now one of us, Doctor Carter," Ramson said, still unaware his mind had been breached. He glanced around. "Are you two here for the music, or are you shopping for your next meal?"

Matt nodded. "Yes, I am one of you, Ramson, and as for our purpose here, that is none of your business. Now, why don't you tell us about this group of renegades that's on your mind?"

Ramson's face showed his surprise that Matt could so

easily read his thoughts through his mind-block. "How did you . . . ?"

"You're as easy for me to read as a newspaper, Ramson," Matt said, "and I already know what you're gonna say, but why don't you spell it out for my lady friend here?"

Droplets of scarlet sweat began to appear on Ramson's forehead. He glanced at Sam, who smiled innocently back at him.

He pulled a wadded-up kerchief out of his jacket pocket and mopped his brow, leaving the linen cloth stained red. "I assume you are still in contact with our mutual friend, Elijah Pike, or know how to get a message to him?"

Both Sam and Matt nodded. Sam felt Ramson trying to get into her mind, but it was already strong enough after just a few sharing of blood episodes that she easily repelled him, causing him even further consternation.

"That will do you no good, Ramson, so please just get on with your story," Sam said, still in a friendly, conversational voice.

"Maybe . . . maybe I will have that drink you mentioned," he stuttered, confused about the strength of the minds of these two relative newcomers to the Vampyre race. "A scotch and soda if you don't mind."

Matt used his mind to signal the waitress to bring another drink for their guest, causing her to think he'd somehow shouted the instructions to her.

"It's on the way," Matt said, indicating Ramson should continue his story.

"Well, it's like you said. There's this group of renegade Vampyres," Ramson began, "that want to fundamentally change the dynamic between us and the Normals that has existed for hundreds of years." He went on to outline Theo Thantos's plan to take over the Normal word by changing important persons into Vampyres in this and other nations.

"That's crazy," Sam said. "Such a plan would never work."

Ramson shrugged. "I agree, but the problem is if the delicate balance between our two races is upset, there is no telling how much damage this zealot and his friends might cause. It could eventually mean the beginning of another pogrom against us like there was in the Middle Ages which might even lead to the extinction of one or the other of the races."

"Why didn't you send this message to Elijah over his e-mail network?" Matt asked. "He told us you had his e-mail address and were helping him get the word out about the vaccine."

"This is too damned important to be broadcast over the Internet," Ramson said. He glanced around, as if someone might be watching or listening to them. "Beside, Thantos has some very influential and important friends on his side already. There is no telling how much they know, or what they can find out."

"So," Matt said, already knowing the answer, "why aren't you organizing some opposition to this takeover?"

The droplets of sweat on Ramson's head reappeared and began to run down his face now. He wagged his head, slinging sweat to and fro. "I . . . I can't. In the first place, he has spies everywhere. If I approach the wrong person, I wouldn't last the night. Hell, a couple of people who made the mistake of criticizing his plan publicly have disappeared completely and others have been warned they're next if they don't keep their mouths shut."

"So, you're leaving it up to Elijah and us to stop this madness?" Matt sneered.

"If you can, and if it's not already too late," Ramson said, downing the drink the waitress placed before him in one long swallow. "Now, you've been warned. What you do with the information is up to you. I wash my hands of the entire matter."

"So said Pontius Pilate," Matt said, causing Ramson to frown and look back over his shoulder as he walked rapidly away to disappear in the crowd around the dance floor, wondering how the waitress knew to bring him a drink, and even more, how she knew what drink mix to bring.

"So much for a fun evening out," Sam said, getting to her feet. "Let's go give Elijah a call on his cell phone and then we can go hunting someplace else."

Matt threw two twenty-dollar bills down on the table and took her arm and they walked out to the parking lot.

After he put her in the passenger side, he walked around and was about to open the driver's side door when the two men who'd been at their table moved up to flank him.

"First, we're gonna take your money, honky, then we's gonna take your woman," one of the men said as he pulled a .38 caliber pistol from his pocket.

Matt smiled and leaned down to look in his window. "Should we take both of them, or will one do?"

Sam yawned. "Oh, I've kind'a lost my appetite, dear. I think one will be more than sufficient."

The two men looked at each other, frowns on their face. The white man was supposed to be frightened to death, and that snooty white bitch with him should have been shitting her panties. Instead, he was acting like it was him in control and not them, and she didn't look the least bit concerned.

The man who'd made the threat backed up a step, thinking something was seriously wrong with this situation.

Matt straightened up and stared at the man with the gun, focusing his mind on him. The man frowned, then looked terrified as his gun hand slowly moved to point the gun it was holding at his friend.

He winced and tears formed in his eyes when he squeezed the trigger and put a slug in his best friend's chest. Before the man's dead body hit the ground, Matt had opened the back door to the rental car, made the man drop the gun next to the corpse, and then ordered him to climb in the backseat.

As the man meekly moved into the backseat, his eyes half-closed as if he were sleepwalking or stoned on some particularly potent drug, Matt got into the front seat and smiled at Sam.

"Let's go someplace a little more private for our meal. I don't feel like dealing with any more interruptions tonight."

"Sure thing, sweetheart," Sam said, smiling at the man in the backseat. "Whatever you want."

As they drove off, an astonished Ramson Holroyd watched from the shadows of the building, his mind racing. Something seriously strange was happening here. He'd never seen anyone as powerful as these two, and yet they acted like their extraordinary powers were no big deal—they hadn't even tried to impress him by demonstrating their powers.

He stared at the dead man in the parking lot and stroked his jaw, trying to determine where his interests lay. Should he try and curry favor with Thantos by calling him up and telling him about this new development among Pike's friends, or should he keep his mouth shut and wait and see who came out on top in the upcoming war.

This decision was easy. He knew if he betrayed Pike and ever got within a hundred feet of those two he'd met tonight, they would know instantly of his betrayal and would kill him without the slightest hesitation.

No, better to sit back and wait and see what happened. He'd managed to keep his head for a long, long time now. No need to risk it with nothing to gain for it.

Chapter 24

Special Agent Michelle Meyers of the Secret Service knocked on the door to Russell Cain's office at precisely five-thirty in the afternoon. The appointment she'd made was for five-thirty and Cain was a stickler for punctuality. *When he sees what I've got to show him, he's going to wish I were late,* she thought, grinning at the door.

Michelle had told Cain, who was the special agent in charge of all of the Washington, D.C., agents, that she needed to see him on a matter of national security and that the meeting had to be kept just between the two of them. Cain had reluctantly arranged to meet her in his office after everyone else had gone for the day.

"Come," he said at her knock.

She walked in and smiled, reaching behind her to lock the door to his office. "Thank you for agreeing to meet with me, Sir."

He frowned when he heard the metallic snick of the door lock being set. "I don't like this, Agent Meyers. It goes against protocol for us to be meeting alone like this." He opened his middle desk drawer and pulled out a small tape recorder. He pushed the record button and sat it in the middle of his desk. "So, to protect both of us, I'm going to record this meeting."

Michelle's smile never wavered as she continued across the office until she was standing right against the front of his desk. "Are you afraid I might sexually harass you, Sir?" she asked, a mocking tone in her voice.

"No," Cain snapped, "but in this day and age, I don't want any questions of propriety raised."

She inclined her head at the recorder, already spinning on his desk. "I don't think you want to do that, Sir," she said, her lips still curled in a smile.

"Oh," he asked irritably, "why not?"

Without another word, Michelle leapt across the desk, her hands already turning into claws as they wrapped around Cain's neck. The impact of her body against his drove his chair back until it hit the windowsill and flipped over backward, sending them tumbling.

"Goddamn!" he had time to utter as his right hand went for the 9 mm Glock semiautomatic he had in his shoulder holster and his back thudded against the back of his chair as it slammed down on the floor.

Michelle's teeth fastened on his neck just as he managed to free the pistol and stick it against her stomach. The sound of the shots was muffled against her clothes as he fired twice.

Her body bucked and jumped under the impact, but her grip never wavered, nor did she stop drinking until his eyes glazed over and rolled back in his head and he fainted.

Once he was unconscious, she rolled off him and cursed as she ripped her clothes off and examined the damage to her abdomen. "Shit!" she said, groaning and doubling over into a fetal position with the fiery pain of the bullet wounds. Though she knew they wouldn't kill her, it was going to take some time for her to recover, possibly as much as twenty-four to thirty-six hours.

Not wanting to waste the blood flowing from her wounds, she stuck her fingers in it and then pried Cain's mouth open and rubbed them against his lips. After a moment, with her mind telling him what he had to do, he began to suckle her bloody fingers like a newborn baby, whimpering in his sleep.

Minutes later, with the hormones in her blood racing through his bloodstream, he awoke. After a moment regaining full consciousness, he blinked several times, a wild, hungry look in his eyes. He let his gaze roam over her naked, wounded body lying on his carpet, and she could see the effect she was having on him.

His mouth dropped open and his eyes became hooded while they glittered with lust.

She held out her arms to him and his eyes glazed over and his expression softened, as if he didn't quite know where he was or what was happening to him. After a moment, he gave a slight quiver and moved into her arms. She moaned with satisfaction and pulled his head down onto her abdomen and let him suck the blood from the bullet wounds he'd caused.

As her body began to heal and knit the wounds and the bleeding slowed, Cain sat up and stripped his clothes off until he too was naked. Still with a somewhat befuddled expression, like a sleepwalker in the middle of a dream, he climbed between Michelle's legs and entered her with a quick thrust as her fangs fastened on his neck once again and she began to suckle.

Later, as he lay curled up with his hands between his knees like a little boy sleeping, sweating with the fever that was already coursing through his body, Michelle sat at his desk and made a phone call. She had her discarded blouse wadded up and pressed against the almost healed bullet wounds to ease the pain her every movement caused.

When Christina answered, Michelle explained that she needed a cleanup crew at Cain's office as well as some clothes for both of them since theirs were soaked with blood.

Christina asked if there were any other problems the crew would have to deal with, any collateral damage that would have to be covered up.

Michelle felt of her abdomen, which was still tender and sore and throbbing, though the bullet holes had completely knit together and there were only two slightly pink, puckered scars remaining.

"No," she said tiredly. "Not really."

Elijah Pike walked down the dark street toward the Portland harbor, stumbling a bit as he whistled off-tune, appearing to be very drunk indeed.

Ed and Kim were just behind him, arm in arm with Ed singing something about putting the lime in the coconut and drinking it all up while Kim giggled like an idiot. She had her blouse half-unbuttoned and her breasts were hanging half out of her bra in plain sight.

Suddenly four men stepped out of an alleyway just ahead of them. Their leader, a man with a full beard, grinned, revealing a mouth that was missing several teeth. "Well, boys, lookit what we got here," he said in a voice roughened by too many whiskeys and too many cheap cigarettes over the years.

Elijah stumbled into the man and reared his head back, gasping at the rancid smell that wafted off the man. "Oh, I beg your pardon," Elijah mumbled as he stepped out into the street to go around the man.

Ed stopped his singing and just stood there, wobbling a bit as he put his arm protectively around Kim's shoulders. "What . . . what do you want?" he asked, slurring his words and trying to appear frightened.

The apparent leader of the group laughed harshly and moved over to stand directly in front of Kim, his hungry eyes moving up and down her body.

"Hey, Bobby," one of the men in the rear called, laughing, "He wants to know what we want."

Bobby laughed again, his horrible breath making Kim's eyes water. He reached over and shoved Ed to the side and grabbed Kim by the shoulder with one hand while he tried to stick his other hand down the front of her dress. "I'm going to fuck your woman, mister," he said, glancing at Ed as he squeezed Kim's breast roughly, "and then we're going to put your asses on a ship that's sailing for Indochina at midnight."

The man who'd called out took a length of pipe from under his coat and raised his hand to smash Elijah in the head.

As he brought his hand down, Elijah straightened up and grabbed the man's wrist. He grinned as he squeezed until the sound of bones breaking echoed down the deserted street.

The other two men pulled out long-bladed knives as their companion screamed in pain and dropped to his knees, tears of pain coursing down his cheeks.

Elijah let himself begin to change as he backhanded the first one hard enough to send him flying backward against the wall of the warehouse they were standing in front of.

The second man, upon seeing the monster emerging before him, screamed like a girl as a urine stain blossomed on the front of his trousers. He dropped his knife and turned to run, only to find Ed, grinning around large, scarlet-tinged fangs, standing in front of him.

"Now, what was it you were going to do to us?" Ed growled, reaching out and grabbing the man by his neck and lifting him up until his feet dangled in midair. The strong smell of ammonia coming from the man made Ed wrinkle his nose in disgust.

Bobby glanced back over his shoulder at the sound of his friend screaming and tried to pull his hand out of Kim's dress. She clamped her claw on his wrist and growled through lengthening fangs, "Oh, my. Is the foreplay over so soon?"

He looked back at her changing face and his bowels let loose in terror; he moaned as he shit himself.

Kim wrinkled her nose and twisted his wrist until it snapped like a twig. "Damn," she said, turning to drag him into the alley. "I wish you hadn't done that."

Ed, who was right behind her and still holding his man in the air, chuckled, "Maybe we should dunk 'em in the harbor before we eat them. Might make them smell better at least."

"I don't intend to linger over this meal, darling," she replied. "This is just a quick snack to take the edge off until we can find someone more suitable to spend some quality time with."

Elijah entered the alley behind Ed and Kim, dragging his two men by the scruff of their necks. "I asked this one where they lived and he said they were bunking in this warehouse. Why don't we take them inside so we won't be disturbed?"

Ed nodded and moved up the alley until he came to a door with a single dim lightbulb over the entrance. He tried the door, found it locked, and stepped back and kicked the door open.

"Maybe there'll be a shower in there and we can rinse 'em off first."

Inside, they found several cots lined up against the wall, a small bathroom that smelled almost as bad as the man Kim was dragging, and a couple of seaman's trunks next to the cots.

Kim eyed one of the cots and arched an eyebrow. "I don't think I want to lay on that. I'd probably get cooties."

"Then I guess we'll just have to eat standing up," Ed said, "kind'a like at a buffet." He bent his man's head back and lowered his face to his neck. The man's scream of terror ended in a gurgle as Ed ripped his throat open and began to drink his blood.

Bobby, when he saw this, moaned and would have fallen to the ground if Kim hadn't been holding him. "Oh, no you don't," she said, licking crimson drool off her lips. "I want you to be fully awake to enjoy this." She smiled around her fangs at the look of terror on his face. "After all, you had such a fun night planned for me."

She reached down and buried her claw in his genitals, and when he threw his head back to scream, she opened her mouth wide and sliced open his carotid artery, letting the spurting blood run down her throat until he died.

Ed was just finishing his man off when a sudden thought interrupted his meal. These guys must get paid pretty well for shanghaiing sailors, he mused. He quickly finished drinking and dropped the man's lifeless body onto the floor. He glanced in the corner and saw that the only remaining ambusher was still unconscious and so he moved over to the row of seaman's trunks next to the cots.

Their locks were no impediment to his strength and he quickly hooked a claw under the edges of the locks and snapped them open. When he looked in the trunks, he found all of them filled to the brim with grimy, crumpled hundred dollar bills.

Grinning he tipped one of the trunks over so Kim and Elijah could see what was inside. "Look guys," he said, "more capital for our vaccine business."

Elijah dropped his man and walked over to Ed. "Damn," he said, eyeing the loot, "these assholes must do a thriving business."

Kim cocked her head to the side and scrunched her eyes, as if listening to a far-off sound. "Hey, I think there's someone in the warehouse."

Elijah and Ed both concentrated and then nodded. "You're right, Kim," Elijah said, moving to a door in the wall that was hidden behind some boxes.

They followed him through the door, crouching with claws extended in case of trouble.

Their eyes widened at the sight before them. In the middle of the warehouse was a cage made up of iron bars. It was over twenty feet wide and twenty feet long. It was filled to the brim with men dressed in ragged clothes; most showed evidence of bruising and rough treatment in the recent past.

Though Elijah and Ed and Kim could see clearly in the near darkness of the warehouse, the men couldn't see them.

"We'd better change back to our normal forms before we free them," Elijah said. "No need to frighten them any more than necessary."

"Hold on a minute," Ed said, taking hold of Elijah's arm. "Shouldn't we do something about those guys in the next room before we set these men free?"

"You're right," Elijah said. "We don't want them found like that or it'll raise too many questions in the authorities' minds."

"I saw a couple of bottles of whiskey on their dresser," Kim said. "How about I start a little fire while you two open that cage?"

"Perfect," Elijah agreed, looking around the warehouse to see what else it contained besides the captive men. "This warehouse is isolated enough that the blaze won't spread and the fire will obliterate any evidence of how they died."

By the time Kim was pouring two bottles of whiskey over three dead bodies and one live but unconscious one in the next room, Elijah and Ed had changed into normal forms and were busting the lock on the makeshift jail in the warehouse.

Only a few of the men in the compound were fully conscious, the others having been beaten so badly they were still out cold.

"What's goin' on?" one of the men asked wearily. "You takin' us to the ship now?"

"No," Elijah replied. "We're setting you free. The men who captured you are in the next room, dead. Now, pick up the men who are unable to walk and get out of here. This whole place is going to go up like a bonfire in about five minutes."

Kim and Ed and Elijah watched the show from the shadows of a nearby alleyway as fire and police vehicles arrived on the scene scant minutes later. As far as they could tell, all of the men who'd been shanghaied had made it out of the warehouse before it turned into a blazing inferno.

"Well, that was a good night's work," Elijah said as he bent to pick up the seaman's trunk lying next to him on the ground.

"Yeah," Kim said, also lifting a trunk to her shoulder. "Now, let's get these back to the car so we can maybe find someone less distasteful to spend some quality time with before we go back to the cabin."

Elijah grinned. "My but you're hungry tonight, Kim."

"Hey," she said, her eyes flashing at him in the semi-darkness. "Ed and I've been on the wagon for some months now. Surely you're not begrudging us one night out to have some fun before we settle back down."

Elijah laughed and held up his hands palms out. "Not me, Kim," he replied. "As a matter of fact, I've been on the straight and narrow myself for quite a while and I find my appetite is like yours, unsatisfied by our recent experience with the sailors. You mind if I join you two or would you rather hunt alone?"

Kim looked at Ed and shrugged, a suggestive smile curling the corners of her lips. "Fine with me, big guy, but you'd better ask Ed."

Ed shrugged. "Hey, far as I'm concerned, the more the merrier."

Kim handed Ed her trunk and hooked her arms in his and Elijah's as they walked up the street. "A hunting we will go, a hunting we will go," she sang gaily as they walked, mimicking the song the dwarfs sang in the *Sleeping Beauty* film.

Chapter 25

Elijah awoke from a sound sleep and looked around the room. He could have sworn he heard Matt's voice calling to him.

Inside his mind, a thought appeared, "Elijah, get your lazy butt out of bed and get everyone together. Sam and I are on our way to the cabin and we need to have a meeting."

Elijah thought back, "Are you communicating with me all the way from Portland?"

"Yes," Matt replied, the words sounding as real as if they'd been spoken from a few feet away instead of dozens of miles. "Our plane has just landed from Houston and we have some important news. Have TJ and Shooter gotten back yet?"

Elijah climbed out of bed and moved toward the bathroom, covering his mouth as he yawned. He'd only been in bed a little over three hours. "Yes, they got in last night."

"Good. Wake them up and see if you can get Ed and Kim to the cabin by the time we get there."

"Is it that urgent?" Elijah thought as he bent over the sink and began to wash his face.

"We'll let you guys decide, but I think it's something you'll all want to hear."

* * *

As usual, even though it was only a little over thirty-five miles from Portland to the cabin in North Waterford, the drive took Matt and Sam slightly more than an hour because of the small, twisting roads they had to take.

When they arrived, TJ came running out of the front door and threw her arms around both of them. "Welcome back you two," she said. "I missed you."

"We missed you, too, TJ," Sam replied, hugging her friend back.

TJ released Sam and grabbed Matt, kissing him full on the lips. Matt rolled his eyes to look over TJ's head to see if Shooter, who was watching from the porch minded her sudden friendliness.

"Not at all, pal," came the words in Matt's mind, showing Shooter was as adept at reading thoughts as he was.

"Good," Matt thought back, " 'Cause your woman's giving me a woody."

Shooter burst out laughing on the porch, making Elijah and Ed and Kim look at him strangely, none of them being privy to this exchange of thoughts.

"She is very good at that, buddy," Shooter thought back when he'd gotten his laughing under control.

They gathered in the living room of the cabin and everyone stared at Matt expectantly, waiting to hear why he'd made such a fuss about all of them coming together.

"While we were in Houston," he began, standing in front of the chair Sam was sitting in, his hand on her shoulder. "We ran into an old friend of Elijah's."

He glanced at Elijah who narrowed his eyes with effort but still couldn't manage to penetrate Matt's thoughts, even though his own psychic abilities were growing stronger day by day with fresh infusions of blood from the group. Matt smiled back at him and sent him a quick thought, "Be patient, Elijah."

To the rest, he spoke out loud, "Ramson Holroyd approached Sam and me and gave us a message to bring back here."

"Jesus old son," Shooter interrupted irritably, "get to the meat and quit fooling around."

"Okay. The good news is that our old enemy Theo Thantos and his cohorts have apparently given up trying to kill us to prevent our distribution of Elijah's vaccine."

Elijah's forehead wrinkled in puzzlement. "You wouldn't have made such a fuss about getting us all together just for that, so I'm assuming you must have some bad news to add to this rather good news."

Matt nodded solemnly. "Yeah, it seems that instead of coming after us, they've gone completely crazy and have hatched some scheme to have Vampyres take over the world."

Everyone laughed except Elijah, who sat back in his chair with a worried, thoughtful look on his face.

"You can't be serious," Shooter said, a wide grin on his face. "What does he plan to do, have all the Vampyres in the world take up arms and march on their countries' capitals?"

"He must be mad," Kim added, echoing Shooter's sentiments. "From what I have gathered over my years of being a member of the race of Vampyres, there can't be over a couple of hundred thousand of us at the most—and that number is scattered among hundreds of countries around the world."

As everyone nodded, Elijah sighed loudly. "I'm afraid you are all wrong," he said, his lips tight and white.

"What do you mean?" Matt asked. "You think Thantos's plan actually has a chance of working?"

Elijah shrugged, but his eyes remained worried. "It all depends on just how smart he is," he answered. "I know I could devise a plan that would do just that—put Vampyres in charge of every country on earth."

Sam glanced at Matt, and then she turned her eyes to Elijah. "How, Elijah?"

He stood up and began to pace back and forth as he often did when addressing the group. Sam had asked him about it once and he said simply that he thought better on his feet.

"First of all, you've got to remember that we Vampyres operate on a different time schedule than Normals. After all, we live several hundred years at least so there is no need to hurry any plan we might devise."

"But still," Matt began to argue until Elijah cut him off with a wave of his hand.

"Let me finish, Matt, then you can make your arguments." He paused to gather his thoughts and then he continued. "Now, our second big advantage is that we can increase our numbers in a matter of weeks instead of years like it takes Normals, and furthermore we can do it selectively so that anyone we choose to have join our ranks can already be in a position of authority."

He glanced around at the group. "Do you understand what that means, dear friends? I would say that within a matter of a few years at most, Thantos could have the leadership of every major country in the world in his camp."

As the group members thought about what he was saying, their expressions slowly became, like his, worried.

"But, if that is true, how can Thantos and his minions be stopped?" TJ asked. "He already has a couple of months' head start on us and there's no telling how many people he's transformed to help him, or even who they are."

Here, Elijah smiled for the first time since he'd heard of Thantos's plan. "So far, I've only given you Thantos's advantages," he said. "He also has some serious disadvantages."

Matt shook his head. "After what you've said, I can't think of any."

"First and foremost"—Elijah said, leaning back against the front windowsill and crossing his legs at the ankles—"is that just because he transforms someone into one of us does not mean that the person will agree with Thantos's plans or will be able to be controlled by him. Remember, he is going to be transforming some of the most powerful and egotistical people in the world. They are not necessarily going to suddenly become docile followers of Thantos, or to blindly accept that Vampyres should be the rightful leaders of the world."

Ed nodded his agreement. "That's right. I remember when I was transformed," he said, glancing at Kim and smiling. "It took me a long time before I truly felt like I was a member of the community of Vampyres, before I could accept that I was going to be one for as long as I lived."

Kim chuckled. "And even then, neither one of us really joined the community of our new race. We hunted because we had to, but we certainly didn't seek out other members of our new race."

Elijah inclined his head. "And that's just what Thantos is going to be facing. Vampyres tend by nature to be loners, fiercely independent, and they rarely become good followers unless it is to their advantage. It is going to take him a while to gain control over his new converts, and he is bound to fail with at least some of them."

"What else does he have against him?" Matt asked, " 'Cause I think it is just like you said. He is going to be transforming men and women who are already in power, and most of them are going to want to remain in power, or even increase their power if possible." He gave a sour smile. "If there's one thing that is almost universally true, it's that politicians and leaders rarely voluntarily give up their positions of power."

Now Elijah grinned, and there was more than just a touch of evil in his smile. "The most important thing that is going to prevent Thantos from succeeding in his plan to take over the world is . . ." He paused for a moment and stared into everyone's eyes before he finished, *"Us."*

Shooter nodded and let his lips curl in a cruel smile also. "Good. So we're going to go up against this bastard and make sure his evil plan doesn't succeed?"

"Exactly," Elijah said with more certainty than he felt.

"But, what about the vaccine program?" Sam asked. "We aren't going to give that up, are we?"

"Hell no," Elijah said. "But we've got another couple of months' supply already made up. There's nothing to say we can't do what we've been doing from Washington, D.C."

"How do you know Thantos is in Washington?" Ed asked.

Elijah shrugged and spread his arms out. "Where else, if he's seeking the most powerful people in the country, would he be?"

Shooter looked around and grimaced. "And I suppose the seven of us are going to just waltz into Washington and defeat Thantos and his perhaps hundreds of followers?"

Elijah nodded. "Uh-huh."

"And just how are we going to manage that without getting our heads lifted first?" Shooter asked.

"I also neglected to mention our other great advantage," Elijah said, smiling at each of them in turn.

"And that is?" TJ asked, her hand on Shooter's shoulder as she stared back at Elijah.

"Why, our newfound powers," Elijah explained. "We're going to keep sharing blood until every one of us is as powerful as ten other Vampyres. Hell, boys and girls, when we finally are ready to attack, they won't know what hit them!"

Chapter 26

"Good evening, ladies and gentlemen," Theo Thantos said, speaking into a hand microphone as he paced across a small stage set up in the Rejuvenatrix Spa main building. There was a group of more than thirty people scattered around the room, and they were all either the original conspirators in Thantos's scheme to take over the government of the United States or they were new converts that had been transformed to help him carry out his plan.

"This is the first and it will be the last time that we all convene together in one location," he continued, still pacing as he spoke. "It is far too dangerous for us all to ever again gather at the same time and place, and in this city of conspiracy theories, if anyone noticed our congregation, it would raise far too many questions.

"I plan to organize us along the lines of any good terrorist or guerrilla organization, into cells that are small in number and anonymous to the other members, so that in the event one of us is compromised, he or she can't name more than a few others in our group."

He paused to take a sip from a glass of water that was on a stool on the stage. "In a few moments, our cell leaders will be circulating among you to take you to a group of rooms or cottages where they will give you your assignments and fill you in on what you need to know about where we are in our plan to take control of the country." He looked around at the faces looking at him and let his face grow stern. "But first, I have something to say about our feeding. The hunger is new to most of you, so you'll have to learn how to handle it fairly rapidly since we don't have time for an extended training period. Usually the one who does the transformation teaches the new recruit how to feed and what precautions to use to avoid getting caught or to give away the existence of our race, but that's not going to happen now. It will be up to you to ask questions about this sort of thing of your cell leader, who will be more than happy to share his or her knowledge with you. Suffice it to say that with the large number of new recruits we are expecting over the next few weeks in this town, I am making an executive order that no one feeds within fifty miles of Washington, D.C."

He smiled evilly at the crowd. "Disobeying this order is grounds for immediate termination, and I promise you it will be done in such a manner as to cause you more pain than you can possible imagine!"

When the crowd stirred and began to murmur among themselves, Thantos held up his hands. "The order is not open to discussion, but you should know that as long as you feed every couple of weeks, the hunger will remain manageable and you will have plenty of time to select your victims with care, and to dispose of them in such a way that our feeding habits do not become obvious."

He turned his head to the side of the stage where the original conspirators were sitting in a group waiting for his signal.

When he nodded, they consulted papers in their hands and began to move among the crowd, picking out members of their cells to take to private rooms and begin their training.

Christina bounded up on the stage and put her arms around

his neck, her eyes excited and glittering with respect for his new position as leader. "Oh, Theo," she gushed, squeezing him tight. "You were wonderful."

He grinned back at her, thinking she was right: he *was* wonderful. "So you think the talk went well?" he asked, fishing for more compliments.

"Absolutely!"

"Good. Now, I've got to go and meet with Augustine Calmet's cell. I have some things to clear up with them that can't wait."

Augustine Calmet's cell consisted of Russell Cain, Michelle Meyers, Allison Burton, and Bitsy McCormack. The two girls' fathers, who were much too famous and too well watched to attend this meeting, would be filled in by their daughters later about what was expected of them.

Calmet's group was meeting in a cottage on the edge of the property, and Thantos entered without knocking, just in time to hear Cain grumbling about being kept in the dark and having to take orders from a nonprofessional concerning security.

Thantos entered the room and moved just inside the door, leaning back against the wall and crossing his arms in front of him. "You were saying, Russell?" he asked, his voice hard and his face expressionless.

Russell didn't drop his eyes and his voice was confrontational as he replied, "It's no secret how I feel, Thantos. You're walking around up there like you're some big expert on everything, but as far as I can tell, you've never been in the military or any sort of law enforcement organization. So, I was just wondering what makes you think you know enough about security and planning to be in charge of this group?"

Thantos was furious at his ability being questioned, but he kept his voice level and calm as he replied, "In the first place, Russell, it's been a hundred and eighty some odd years since I was transformed, and in all that time I've killed and eaten well over a thousand people." He narrowed his eyes. "And I've done it without once even coming close to getting caught or leaving any clues that would point to the existence of our race."

Cain sneered, "So what? Any fairly competent criminal could do the same thing, and it's easy not to leave clues when no one in the world even suspects that our race exists. But this is bigger, much bigger than just killing a few innocent bystanders. This is planning the overthrow of a government, and I have a feeling that you have no idea how it functions on a day-to-day basis."

"You're right about that, Russell," Thantos said, letting a little scorn creep into his tone. "I am not an expert on government bureaucracy, and that's exactly why I ordered Michele to convert you to our cause. But don't confuse being a long-time bureaucrat with being able to plan and carry out a guerrilla war because the two are vastly different."

"How so?" Cain asked, grinning insolently.

"In the first place, bureaucrats push papers and plan meetings, leaders implement plans, plans that often mean someone has to die." As he finished speaking, Thantos changed quickly into his Vampyre form, catching everyone in the room by surprise. He launched himself across the room at Cain, grabbing him by the throat and sinking his claws in deep, behind his esophagus and trachea, squeezing so the man could hardly breathe.

"Have I got your full attention now, Russell?" he growled in a deep, gravelly voice.

Cain couldn't speak, but he nodded quickly, his eyes wide with terror.

"With one flick of my wrist I could tear out your throat and then rip your head from your shoulders and your miserable life would be over. Do you want me to do that?" Thantos asked again, his red-rimmed eyes glowing fiercely and his fangs inches from Cain's face.

He relaxed his grip enough so that Cain could croak, "No."

"No what, Cain?" Thantos taunted.

"Uh, no Sir!" Cain answered.

With a contemptuous shrug, Thantos picked Cain up by this throat and flung him across the room to smash up against the far wall and then sink to the floor.

"Now that we've established who the alpha male is, are there any other questions?" he asked the rest of the group.

All quickly shook their heads negatively.

He slowly changed back to his human form and straightened his clothes. "Good. Now the reason I've come here, girls," he said to Michelle and Bitsy and Allison, "is to discuss the rather ticklish matter of how your fathers are going to feed."

The two girls looked at each other, surprise on their faces. It was clear that they hadn't considered the difficulty of the vice president or the chairman of the Joint Chiefs of Staff getting off alone so they could kill and eat someone.

Thantos smiled. "I can see that you haven't given this much thought." He turned his gaze to Michelle. "Since it's obvious these two men can't go running off to nearby towns to feed every time they get hungry, it's going to be up to you and Mr. Cain over there to see that suitable food is brought in for them on a regular basis. I assume there are ways to get people into the vice president's mansion and into General McCormack's home without being observed?"

Before Michelle could answer, Bitsy and Allison glanced at each other and giggled.

Thantos turned his attention to them and raised his eyebrows.

Allison sobered enough to speak. "Sure, Mr. Thantos, that won't be any problem at all. Bitsy and I've been sneaking in and out of those old houses for years. We've found ways to get in and out right under the noses of the Secret Service agents assigned to guard us."

When Michelle blushed and gave Allison a stare, the girl

shrugged. "We had to, or we'd never have gotten to do anything fun."

Thantos laughed. "Good for you, Allison. Now I want you and Bitsy to coordinate with Michelle and Mr. Cain so that they can bring . . . uh, food in for you and your parents. It will also be up to them to make sure that any Secret Service Agents assigned to either of your residences are among our converts."

"That won't be a problem, Sir," Michelle said, showing some deference after seeing what Thantos had done to Cain, one of the toughest men she knew.

"And you, Russell," Thantos asked the man who had just managed to scramble around and sit with his back against the wall, "do you think you can handle that?"

Cain nodded, his hand massaging his throat. "Yes . . . uh, yes Sir," he answered.

"Good," Thantos said simply. And then he turned his attention to Augustine Calmet.

"Augustine, I put you in charge of the cell with Allison and Bitsy because with your long association with the *Washington Post,* I know you're friends with both the vice president and the chairman."

"Yes, Sir," Augustine said, being sure to show Thantos the proper respect. He didn't want to end up with his throat ripped out.

"For that reason, it will be perfectly natural for you to visit both of them occasionally, ostensibly to do interviews for your paper, but in reality to pass messages back and forth that are too sensitive to be done on the phone or in an e-mail."

Calmet nodded. "It won't be a problem. Both men are used to being interviewed by various members of the press so it won't cause any suspicion for me to visit them."

Thantos nodded. "Good, now go on with your presentation to the newcomers about feeding and such matters."

Chapter 27

When Sam woke up the next morning, it seemed as if every muscle in her body ached. She rolled on her side and threw her arm around Matt, who was still sleeping soundly.

"Matt, darling," she murmured against his neck. "Did you beat on me with sticks last night?"

He snorted and smacked his lips and came immediately awake. Turning to her and kissing her lightly on the lips, he grinned, which irritated her to no end. She was still not a morning person, and Matt had since his conversion been unbearably cheerful in the early morning hours—something Sam felt was vaguely immoral. He didn't even need to have his coffee to get him going when he got up, and Sam thought anyone who didn't need caffeine to get their motor started was abnormal.

"Just what are you grinning at, you heathen?" she asked, moaning with both pain and desire when his right hand reached over and began to massage her breast. It felt bruised, and her nipple was raw and still swollen from the night before when it had received rather more attention than was good for it.

"Sore, are you?" he asked, with no trace of sympathy in his voice.

"Yes, I am. Aren't you?" she asked, letting her hand move under the covers to caress him. She found him already hard and ready for her.

"Only certain parts of my anatomy," he answered with an even wider grin.

She sniffed and squeezed his penis maliciously, causing him to moan softly in pain. She'd teach him to be so cheerful in the morning. "Well, I can see why, after the way you went after TJ and Kim last night," she said, referring to their ritual sharing of blood the night before. In order to augment their abilities to the max, Elijah had them all sharing blood with one another on a nightly basis, which usually resulted in what in any other situation would be called a mass orgy.

He laughed, "Yeah, that's true. But I don't really recall you fighting Elijah and Shooter and Ed off during your little trading blood episodes either." In spite of his soreness, he pressed himself against her hand and began to slowly move his hips in and out.

She blushed slightly, remembering why her breasts were so sore this morning. It seems they'd been quite popular with the other men in the group, all of whom had done some serious massaging and sucking on them for an extended period of time while they shared their blood.

Matt, who could read her mind like an open book, felt himself getting even more aroused again by her memories. "So it was that good, huh?" he asked, moving closer to her in the bed and easing his hand down between her legs, which spread and accepted him eagerly.

"You know you're not supposed to get in my mind like that without asking," she murmured as he put his lips on hers, causing her to immediately become wet and aroused. She moved her hand faster and pushed her groin against his hand, willing his fingers to enter her.

"How about my getting in other parts of your body this morning?" he asked with a husky voice.

"Ummm, that sounds good, as long as you promise to be

gentle, since the other parts of my body are just as sore as my breasts."

"I think the exercise will be good for both of us," he said, moving on top of her and positioning himself between her legs.

"Nothing like a little EMI to get the blood flowing and the heart pumping," he said, his lips against hers.

"EMI?" she asked, flicking her tongue against his and lifting her hips off the mattress to push him further inside her.

"Yeah," he answered, pushing back and driving her hips back down with the force of his pumping. "Early Morning Intercourse."

Later, they walked hand in hand out to the kitchen to see if they were too late for breakfast. Just as Sam was pouring them both mugs of steaming coffee, Ed and Kim knocked briefly at the front door and entered without waiting for an answer.

"Hey, Ed, Kim," Sam called, holding up the coffeepot, "You want some caffeine?"

Kim nodded vigorously. "Please, dear," she said. "Ed rushed me out of the Bear Mountain Inn so fast I didn't have time to grab any there."

Ed smiled. "Yeah, Sam, give her a double dose. She's been as cranky as a bear the last few days."

Kim gave him a flat look as she accepted the cup from Sam. "It's these damned muscle aches and this blasted fever I'm running," she said, adding after a moment, "not to mention the soreness of certain rather sensitive areas of my body."

"Me, too," Sam said, nodding her head sympathetically. "And when your mate," she added, glaring over her shoulder at Matt, "insists on sex every hour on the hour, it just makes it worse."

Matt called, "Hey, I resemble that remark, sweetheart. You weren't complaining an hour ago when I was . . ."

Sam grinned and held up her hand. "That's enough, dear," she said, "I'm sure our guests don't need a blow by blow description of our activities."

"Blow by blow, that's quite a pun, Sam sweetie," Shooter said, shuffling into the kitchen, his hair mussed and a blue shadow on his cheeks showing he hadn't shaved yet this morning. "Remember dear, now that all of our psychic abilities are geared up from sharing blood, we're all acutely aware of what the others are thinking . . . and doing," he added, taking the cup our of Sam's hands and upending it over his mouth.

"Yes, Sam," TJ said, coming into the room behind Shooter, her eyes dancing and her hair equally tangled. She was wearing only a T-shirt that barely covered her hips, and it was obvious there was nothing on underneath it.

"I want to thank you and Matt," she teased. "When you two got amorous this morning, it gave Shooter over there some ideas of his own and I barely got my eyes open before he was on me like a duck on a June bug."

Kim looked over at Ed, who was blushing. "So, my big, cuddly bear, that's what got into you this morning?"

He shrugged. "Can I help it if Matt and Sam were transmitting on all frequencies? What's a man to do?" he asked, holding out his hands.

Kim smiled and reached up to pat his cheek. "You did plenty, big guy, and don't think I don't appreciate it—just next time wake me up first!"

Everyone laughed and sat at the kitchen table to a pile of donuts and pastries piled high on a plate in the center of the table.

Elijah walked in, joining in the laughter. "I hope all of you had fun this morning, 'cause I was also receiving Matt and Sam's transmissions, only my bed was empty of a partner. So I had to get up and head down to Tut's to get our breakfast to keep my mind off all the nefarious goings-on here at Casa Pike."

"And don't think we don't appreciate it, pal," Shooter said around a mouthful of donuts, holding up his coffee cup in a toast to Elijah.

"Here, here," everyone said, also holding up their cups and laughing heartily. Each of them had never felt better or more alive in their entire lives, notwithstanding the soreness and slight fevers the blood sharing was causing. It seemed to each of them as if they were twenty years younger.

"Speaking of work," Elijah said, moving over to the counter to pour himself a cup of coffee. "How is everyone feeling this morning? Lots of aches and pains and fever?"

Kim nodded, "And by the way, Elijah, your theory must be correct about how much our abilities are going to improve since the bear over there picked up Matt and Sam's mental transmissions all the way over at our inn, and the fact that they weren't even trying to contact us makes it even more amazing."

Elijah smiled, "And Kim, remember it's not only our psychic abilities that I think will improve, but all of our Vampyre characteristics: immunity from disease, recovery from injury, strength, intelligence—in short, just about every trait that can be transmitted by DNA should do better."

Shooter swallowed his donut and drained his coffee, a puzzled expression on his face. "Say, Elijah, I've been thinking about your theory . . ." he began.

"Uh-oh," TJ said smiling tolerantly at Shooter.

He stopped in midsentence and glanced at her. "What's uh-oh supposed to mean, dear?" he asked, sarcasm evident in his tone.

She looked back at him salaciously, waggling her eyebrows up and down in a caricature of Groucho Marks, "Well, sweetheart," she drawled, accentuating her southern accent, "of all your traits that endear you to me and make me love you so much, thinking isn't one of them."

"Ouch," Matt said, chuckling.

Shooter looked over at him and smiled. "That just means

my *other* traits are so much stronger that they overshadow everything else, Matt my boy."

"Uh, you were saying, Shooter, about my theory?" Elijah interrupted.

"Oh, yeah. I was just wondering about this transferring DNA stuff back and forth between us when we share blood . . ."

"Yes?"

"What happens if we share blood with someone dumber, or weaker, or less psychically gifted than we are? Why doesn't that diminish our abilities like sharing with someone stronger or better increases them?"

"That's an excellent question, Shooter," Elijah said, "and I'm wondering why our medical experts present didn't come up with the same idea?"

"Uh, just never thought about it," Matt said lamely, while Shooter beamed with pride and looked at TJ, licking his index finger and making a move in the air like he was chalking one up for him.

Sam's eyebrows knit together and she said, "I think the answer would be that if you already have an ability, like strength or quick recovery from injuries or intelligence, getting a transfusion of DNA which is less good in that area doesn't take your better DNA away, it just doesn't do anything one way or the other."

"Bravo, Sam," Elijah said, clapping his hands. "At least, that's the way I figure it also. Remember guys," he added, "transfused DNA doesn't *replace* our own natural DNA, and so whatever we have to begin with when we share blood, we'll always have. However, if the new DNA has something we're missing or that we have less of, it will *augment* our own DNA to make us better." He spread his hands, "So, you see, Shooter, sharing blood can never make us less than we already are, it can only make us better if we're deficient in some areas to the DNA we receive."

"Whew," Shooter said, wiping his forehead as if to remove sweat. "I was afraid taking my blood was gonna dumb you guys down to my level."

TJ sighed and put her arm around Shooter's shoulders. "Shooter, you're not dumber than us by any means. You're just smart in areas different from medicine and science."

"Yeah," Sam said, leaning over to kiss him on the cheek. "I'd like to see any of us fix up our security like you have, or track down a killer, or interrogate witnesses like you can," she said.

Shooter held up his hands, "Okay, okay," he said, laughing. "It's nice to know I'm appreciated, but let's not go overboard, all right?"

TJ grinned and glanced at Sam as she spoke to Shooter, "Sam's not being entirely truthful, dear. It's not just your excellent security abilities that make her quiver with delight when you two share blood . . ."

Just then, a bell went off and a red light began flashing from a small control box on a nearby table.

"Speaking of security," Shooter said, happy to change the subject as he jumped to his feet, his hand immediately going to his shoulder holster. He jogged over to the box and flipped on a small monitor screen next to the flashing red light.

A UPS truck could be seen coming down the quarter mile long driveway toward the cabin.

Shooter glanced over his shoulder at Elijah. "You expecting a UPS delivery?"

Elijah nodded. "Yes. I called a friend of mine in San Francisco when we heard about Theo Thantos's plot and had him send me some supplies I think we're going to need. The truck was scheduled to arrive this morning."

Shooter drew his 9 mm pistol and picked up a shotgun from the corner and flipped it to Matt, who'd jumped up at the same time he did.

"Matt and I'll take up stations just outside in the bushes next to the driveway, just in case," Shooter said. "We wouldn't want any surprises so early in the morning."

They bounded out the door and got hidden just before the large, brown truck pulled to a stop in front of the cabin.

Elijah opened the door and moved out onto the deck, his coffee cup in his hand and a welcoming smile on his face as he approached the truck.

The driver stepped out and consulted his clipboard as he came around the front of the truck. "Jesse Brown?" he asked, referring to one of the aliases Elijah used while in San Francisco.

"Yeah," Elijah said, taking the clipboard and scrawling his signature at the bottom.

As the young man unloaded several large cardboard boxes from the back of the truck, he said, "Had a helluva time finding this place. It ain't on no maps."

Elijah smiled as he mentally counted the boxes. "That's the idea," he said simply.

"Huh?" the driver asked over his shoulder as he pulled the last box off the truck.

"Never mind, just glad you could follow the directions I left with the shipper."

"Oh," the driver said, dusting his hands off and reaching for the clipboard. "You have a nice day."

"You too," Elijah said, waving as the driver climbed back in his truck and drove back down the driveway.

Once the truck was out of sight of the house and the sound of his engine had faded away, Matt and Shooter stepped from the bushes nearby.

"That's a lot of boxes," Shooter said, sticking his 9 mm back in its holster.

Elijah picked one up and threw it over his shoulder. "Wait until you see what's in them," he said, enigmatically.

Chapter 28

The vice president of the United States, Jonathon Burton, was sitting at the dining room table with his head in his hands when his daughter, Allison, entered.

"Hey, Dad," she called, stopping in midsentence when she saw the troubled look on his face.

Burton's wife and Allison's mother had died two years before without ever getting to see him elected to the second highest elected office in the United States. Since that time, Allison and he had been rocks for each other, developing a much closer relationship than most fathers had with their teenaged children.

Allison stood in the doorway and cast out with her mind to try and use her new psychic powers to see what was troubling her dad. Even though she could usually read him like a book, this time all she could get was his emotional state of mind, and she was unable to "hear" any specific thoughts. She could tell, however, that he was severely depressed and worried, but just what he was so worried about eluded her.

Finally, she went to the refrigerator and took out a carton of orange juice and poured herself a glassful. She took it and sat at the breakfast table across from him, drumming her fingers on the wood and staring at his red-rimmed, bloodshot eyes and pale, pasty skin. If he goes to the office looking like this, she thought, they'll call in a doctor for sure.

Even though the family dining area was off-limits to the Secret Service agents who guarded them, she glanced around to make sure no one was within earshot before she asked, "Hey, Daddy, what's the problem? Why are you so glummy-jaws this morning?" she asked, deliberately using the term he always used with her when she was down in the mouth.

He sighed heavily and raised his head, smiling sadly at her as he took a drink of his coffee. He made a face, saying, "It's cold." He got up to refill his cup with fresh coffee, walking with the slow, shuffling gait of a much older man, or one with the weight of the world on his shoulders.

"Well?" she demanded, not willing to let him put her off this morning. She fully intended to give him no rest until he came clean with whatever was bothering him. After all, since Mom died, they'd always looked out for each other, and she wasn't about to let that change now just because of a little thing like being changed into Vampyres.

Instead of sitting back down at the table, he leaned back against the kitchen island and crossed his legs at the ankles as he sipped his morning brew, watching her over the rim of the cup as he drank. She could tell nothing from his expression, which remained blank, giving her no clue as to his thoughts.

"Will you open your mind to me before I answer?" he asked, raising his eyebrows.

Allison shrugged. "Sure," she answered. She didn't mind because since she'd transformed her father into a Vampyre like her, she had no real secrets from him. And even though they'd had a brief sexual episode during the transformation when both were under the irresistible influence of the raging hormones the act stirred up, it had been the last one between them. And so it was that they couldn't read each other's mind like true mates can often do. In fact, they'd reverted back to the same kind of father-daughter relationship they had before the transformation, only even closer now.

She hoped when she opened her mind to him, he would return the favor and reciprocate by letting her fully into his thoughts and fears. Maybe then she'd be able to help him with whatever was bothering him.

She leaned her head back and closed her eyes, granting him full access to her thoughts and feelings. It was a measure of the trust between them that she held nothing back, not even her innermost thoughts, as embarrassing as those sometimes were.

When he entered her mind, she giggled. It felt like someone was tickling her brain with a feather—not an unpleasant feeling, merely strange. In fact, the warmth she felt with him in her mind reminded her of the times when she was a small girl and she would climb up into his lap and he'd put his arms around her, hugging her close—making her feel protected from all the bad things in the world.

After a few moments, he grinned and moved to sit next to her at the table. "I'm glad to find out that you're not really tied to this Theo Thantos's scheme for Vampyres to take over the world," he said, lowering his voice so it wouldn't carry more than a few yards.

She laughed. "Dad, as if someone my age could get all caught up in that . . ." she hesitated and then said with some distaste, *"political* shit."

He almost automatically told her to watch her language until he caught himself with a smile. After all she'd been through recently, he guessed she had a right to curse occasionally. "Well, I'm relieved to find it out anyway," he said. "It makes me feel a lot better about some things I've been thinking about."

She narrowed her eyes and looked into his. "Why, Pops? I thought you'd be all gung ho for this kind'a stuff. Isn't running the world what you've worked your entire life to achieve?"

He sighed again and leaned back in his chair, surprised

that she didn't know him better than that. "No, dear, not this way. Not by subterfuge and stealing the government from the people without their knowledge and approval. In fact," he added somewhat stiffly, "it's just that sort of thing that prompted me to go into politics in the first place—I wanted to give the people more of a say in their government."

She nodded and gave him a half smile. "You really are, down deep under all that political bullshit, you really are a true patriot, aren't you, Dad?"

He blushed and returned her smile self-consciously. "I guess I am after all, even though when you say it out loud like that it sounds kind'a schmaltzy." He shook his head. "Boy, would your mother be surprised to find me turning down the job of being the next president."

Allison reached across the table and put her hand on his arm. "No, she wouldn't, Dad. Mom always knew you were a boy scout at heart. She told me more than once that she didn't know if you were cut out to be in politics—you were just too decent a guy for that kind of career."

He threw back his head and laughed, tears forming in his eyes. "Your mother knew me too well, baby, and about the only thing that kept me going when she died was the fact that you remind me so much of her."

"Now," Allison said, again looking over his shoulder to make sure no one was around, "what are we gonna do about this Thantos and his plans? Can you go public to someone in the government who can stop him?"

He shook his head. "No, not without exposing the entire Vampyre race to public scrutiny."

She shrugged. "So what?"

"No, Allison, that wouldn't be right. I'm sure that ninety percent of the people in the world who've been transformed as we were, against our will, are decent souls who don't deserve to be hunted down and killed like animals."

"Even though they, and we for that matter, will have to kill others to get the blood we need to survive?"

"Somehow, as horrible as it sounds, I just can't see killing to stay alive as morally wrong," he said. "It may not be fair to those who are killed and used as food, but then the cows probably wish we didn't like hamburger so much either."

She nodded, seeing his point. "Well," she said, squeezing her hand in his, "you've always taught me that there are two sides to every argument, especially in politics."

"Yes, so?"

"Then if that's true, there must be a group of Vampyres who are against this Thantos and what he's trying to do. All we have to do is contact them and get them to work with us to defeat the son of a bitch."

Burton nodded slowly. She was right. The answer had been right under his nose the whole time. His face got serious. "You're right, baby, but we've got to be very careful. Remember, these people we're dealing with can read minds, or at least emotions. We're going to have to lock our thoughts and feelings down very tightly whenever we're around any of them until we can find someone to help us."

"How are we going to do that, Dad? Find someone who's on our side, I mean."

He wagged his head, his lips tight and white. "I don't know, sweetheart. I just don't know right now."

"Maybe I could kind'a feel out some of my new Vampyre friends and see if they've run across anyone who's opposed to Thantos."

His eyes grew worried and she felt his hand under hers become damp with fear-sweat. "No, that's much too dangerous, Allison. They'd see right through you and our lives wouldn't be worth spit."

She grinned conspiratorially, "Now Daddy, you're forgetting who I'm related to—one of the master politicians of our time. If I can't pull the wool over some Vampyre from the sticks, then I don't deserve to be your daughter."

He smiled back hesitantly. "Do you really think you can do it?"

"No *problemo*," she answered, quoting one of her favorite old movie stars.

He sighed and leaned back, looking at her with affection. "By the way," he said, hesitantly, "speaking of needing blood to survive, have you felt what Thantos calls the hunger yet?"

She shrugged. "A little, I guess, but so far it's not overpowering or anything. I figure I've got another week or so before I need to do something about it."

"Me, too," he said. "Though sometimes I feel like a man who's trying to quit smoking—I think about drinking blood several times a day and I can feel myself getting . . . uh . . . excited," he finished, blushing slightly at the admission.

"Don't worry, Dad," she said, putting her hand on his, "we'll think of something before it comes to that."

Chapter 29

Elijah had the boxes spread out in the middle of the main room's floor in his cabin. One by one, with the others watching intently, he went from box to box and opened them. As he spread the contents out on the floor, stacking the contents neatly into separate piles, Shooter gave a low whistle.

"Man, that is some *serious* firepower you got there, Elijah."

"Yeah," Ed echoed, fingering one of the instruments curiously. "If I ever want to start a war, I'll know who to call to get my weapons."

Elijah's face was serious and he didn't join in the banter as he usually did. It was a good indication of just how worried he was about their upcoming course of action. "What we all need to understand is that this action we're about to take *is* a war, and it's a war to the death—either theirs or ours."

He looked from one to the other of his friends, each in turn. Even though with their new powers, the group was able to communicate solely by telepathic means, it was much simpler and more convenient to continue in the way they always had before, by talking things out.

"Make no mistake about it, my friends," he continued, "Thantos and his cronies will give no quarter, and neither will we." He sighed, staring into their eyes so they'd know the seriousness of his words. "Once we go after Thantos and his minions, it won't be too long before all-out war is declared on us. We all know and remember from our previous encounter with he and Michael Morpheus that Thantos and those like him are the worst kind of megalomaniacs, and anyone who has the temerity to disagree with their beliefs is a dreaded enemy, to be defeated or killed. Everyone in his group will be charged with the task of trying to find us and eliminate us and the risk we represent to their ambitions of global conquest."

"And you're sure that there's no other way?" Kim asked, shaking her head slowly. " 'Cause to tell you the truth, Ed and I have never been exactly what you'd call revolutionaries. Even after we became transformed, we never really immersed ourselves in the so-called Vampyre culture or community."

Ed smiled at her and took her hand, waiting for Elijah's answer.

"No, I'm afraid there is no other way that I can think of, other than to go after them with everything we've got," Elijah said. "We can't expose them publicly without also exposing thousands of innocent members of our race at the same time, which would lead to yet another kind of war—one with the Normals that we would stand no chance at all of winning."

He turned back to his weapons and emptied the last of the boxes out onto the floor.

"Why don't you take us through all of this stuff and explain how some of it operates," Sam said, eager to get off the subject of war, even if it meant discussing the very weapons they'd be using in that war.

Elijah looked at her and nodded as he squatted down next to a row of seven long swords and scabbards, each of which had a shorter version next to it. "These, as most of you know, are Japanese *katanas*. The typical long swords favored by the Samurai warriors in the old days. They're razor sharp and will cut through stainless steel if you swing hard enough."

He took one in his hand and whipped it back and forth, almost twirling it in his dexterity. The group could hear a faint whistling as the wicked blade swished back and forth through the air. "These are handmade by a friend of mine and are exquisitely balanced and, despite their strength, light as a feather."

"Why do you have the long ones *and* the other short ones over there?" Shooter asked, pointing to the other pile of shorter bladed swords lying nearby. "You don't expect us novices to use one in each hand like they do in the martial arts movies, do you?"

"No," Elijah answered, lightening up and laughing for the first time since he'd opened the boxes. "The longer *katana* are easier to use and can be used from a distance, but they're much harder to conceal. You have to be wearing an overcoat or long coat to keep them from view."

"Yeah," Matt said, grinning and joining in the lighter mood, "who'd want to walk around Washington carrying a big honker sword in their hands?" He glanced at the others, "Hell, you'd have women and children running screaming in the streets and every cop within two miles calling for the SWAT teams."

Elijah chuckled. "Exactly. So the shorter versions are for use when it'd be impossible to carry the longer ones. They're just as sharp and just as effective, but you've got to get up close and personal to use these—at least within a foot or two." He hesitated, "And believe me, at that distance, when you cut someone's head off, you're sure to be showered with blood, so we'll probably only use these in isolated areas where we'll be able to clean up before going out in public again."

"I understand the swords," Ed said, "since you have to be-head a Vampyre to kill him. But what about the other things?" he asked, pointing to some handguns with long, pointed snouts on them. "I know those are pistols, but I don't recognize the make."

"Those are Desert Eagle 50 caliber automatic pistols, each fitted with what looks like a Ryerson Silencer," Shooter broke in. "They're the most powerful handguns in the world, as Clint Eastwood once said, though he was talking about a forty-four magnum—a much less powerful weapon." Shooter raised his eyebrows at Elijah to see if he was right.

Elijah smiled and nodded. "That's correct, Shooter, and I've got a case of Glaser Safety Slugs for the pistols, enough for each of us to have plenty of bullets."

Shooter gave a low whistle.

"Huh?" TJ said. "What the heck are Safety Slugs?"

"They're hollow brass cartridges filled with tiny BBs immersed in silicone liquid," Shooter answered. "Nasty little fuckers act like shotgun shells, exploding on impact and tearing a hole as big as a basketball in whomever they hit." He glanced at Elijah, a slight frown on his face. "They've also been outlawed for the past few years, ever since they earned the reputation as cop-killer bullets. I didn't even know they were still making them."

Elijah gave a deprecating wave of his hand. "They're not, but you can still find them on the black market—if you know the right people, that is."

"If they're so big and bad, why are they called Safety Slugs?" Matt asked.

"I think it's because they won't penetrate Kevlar bulletproof vests," Shooter said. "The cops' initial thought was for only cops to have them and if they used them they wouldn't be liable to kill one of their comrades, all of whom would be wearing vests." He shrugged. "Trouble was, they somehow got out on the black market like Elijah said and every mother's son who wanted deadly bullets started using them. That's when they were outlawed."

"But Elijah," TJ protested, "Bullets can't kill us, so what good will these things do?"

"While it is true that bullets can't ordinarily kill one of us, TJ, these weapons are special. In the first case, a hit to the chest will make a hole you can stick your fist through. Not fatal to one of us, but it will certainly put the target down for an extended period of time, long enough hopefully to do something of a more permanent nature while he's down and out and helpless to defend himself."

He paused and grinned. "On the other hand, if you manage a dead center hit to just about any part of the head with one of these Safety Slugs, it will take the head clean off, which should do the trick, even for one of our kind."

Matt reached down and picked up one of the pistols, bouncing it in his hand as he examined it. "Jesus, Elijah, these things must weigh over two pounds. How do you expect the women to use them?"

Elijah laughed. "Matt, obviously you have not been paying attention to the women lately."

As Matt turned and looked at Sam, she smiled and flexed her arm, showing him a sizable muscle.

"He's right, Matt," she said. "Since we've been sharing our blood, TJ and Kim and I have all gotten quite a bit stronger." She waggled her eyebrows lasciviously. "In fact, if you want to try me out in a little wrestling match . . . ?"

He laughed and held up his hands. "Maybe later, darling, but your point is taken, my dear."

"She was kidding, but she was also correct, Matt," Elijah said, turning serious once again. "By my estimation, the women are just as strong physically as we are at this point, and probably much stronger than any 'normal' male Vampyre who hasn't been sharing blood as we have."

TJ gave Sam a high five and grinned maliciously, "It won't even be close; the bastards won't know what hit them!"

Shooter wagged his head, muttering "Women," and moved over to the stacks of equipment. "I know about the swords and the pistols, and even the sawed-off shotguns, Elijah," he said, nodding at a pile of short-barreled twelve-gauge gauge Beretta pump shotguns at the end of the pile of weaponry, "but what in the heck are those canisters there? They look like cans of hairspray."

Elijah smiled. "You're right, Shooter, and I even have the

name of a popular hairspray on the label, but they're nothing so innocuous. In fact, they're designs of my own that I have made up for me in San Francisco."

"But what exactly are they?" Ed asked.

"Actually, they're miniature flamethrowers," Elijah answered proudly. "The cans are filled with a sort of napalm mixture, kind of like jellied gasoline, that I devised a while back, and I've had it mixed with some Freon gas as a propellant. All you have to do is push the button on top of the can and a little diode there makes a spark and you've got a flamethrower effective up to about eight feet."

"Are they dangerous to the user?" TJ asked, a doubtful expression on her face.

Elijah shrugged and gave her a lopsided grin. "Well, if you're carrying one and it's hit by a bullet, you can probably expect a pretty severe hotfoot, but other than that they're as easy to use as a can of hairspray."

"But, if we cut their heads off, do we still need to burn them?" TJ asked. "I don't remember us having to do that up in Canada during our last confrontation."

"No, not if the head is completely severed," Elijah answered, "But if even a sliver of tissue remains connecting the head to the body, the enemy will be able to regenerate—eventually."

"So, to get this straight, the only two ways to kill the bastards we're going after is to behead them or to burn them to crispy critters?" Matt asked.

Elijah shrugged. "That's the only two ways that are practical. Practically anything that totally destroys the body will work—immersion in acid or lye or other caustic chemicals—but decapitation and fire are the easiest to use in the field."

"Are you sure killing them is the only way, Elijah?" TJ asked, and Sam nodded her head. Neither of the women were particularly violence prone and both hoped there was some other way to deal with the threat posed by Thantos and his minions.

Elijah looked into their eyes. "Well, girls," he said, calling the women girls as he always did though his voice was not condescending at all. "What we're dealing with here is a group of fanatics who want to take over the country, if not the world, in order to make it safe for them to totally subjugate Normals and use them as a food source. Do you seriously think they'll be open to a reasoned discussion with us about the error of their ways?"

Matt looked around at the array of equipment on the floor. "So, let's see now," he said, stroking his chin with his lips pursed. "We're supposed to trek all the way down to Washington, D.C., looking for Vampyres with absolutely no idea where they might be or even who they are, and all the while we'll be carrying what looks like about twenty pounds of illegal firearms and flamethrowers." He glanced around at his friends. "Is that it?" he asked.

Elijah's grin faded and his voice sounded a bit testy when he replied. "No, that's not it, Matt. In the first place, we'll only have to carry the equipment when we go out hunting for a particular Vampyre, not while we're walking around on the street; and in the second place, while it is true that we don't know where our targets are hiding out, we do know that they must have converted some high-ranking administration officials and possibly some Congress persons. So, with our newfound ability to use our psychic powers at fairly good distances, we should be able to ferret some of them out without too much difficulty and hopefully then find out from them the identities of the other members of their group."

"Plus our new strength will be an added asset when we find and confront them," Sam said, glancing from Matt to Elijah. "Those fuckers won't be expecting us women Vampyres to be stronger than they are."

Matt blushed at the rebukes by Elijah and Sam. "I'm sorry, Elijah. I don't mean to be a naysayer. It's just that I'm afraid we might be taking on more than we can handle." He paused before adding with a sour look on his face, "And it sounds to me like we're gonna need every little advantage we can get."

"You got that right, podnah," Shooter added. "Us seven are going up against no telling how many unknown opponents, and, if that's not enough of a challenge, there's something else you haven't thought about."

"What's that, sugar?" TJ asked.

"We're gonna be going to war in the middle of Washington, D.C. What do you think the authorities are gonna do when they're suddenly confronted with scores of headless dead bodies, especially when the medical examiner finds out that some of them are hundreds of years old?"

"Well, what about burning the bodies with Elijah's napalm?" Kim asked.

"Same problem, darling," Ed answered. "There isn't enough napalm in those cans to burn the bodies to ash, so the authorities are still going to be left with a lot of dead people to investigate."

"No," Shooter interrupted, "not dead *people,* Ed, dead Vampyres, and that's a whole other ball game."

Sam and Matt both nodded their agreement. "Yeah," Matt said, "that was one of the things that put us onto Elijah in Houston back when we first met. He'd killed a couple of Vampyres and burned their bodies, but the autopsy showed their flesh was over two hundred years old."

"It does present some rather unique problems," Sam said, her brows knitted in thought.

"Of course, a lot of the ones we end up killing will be new converts, so the age of their tissue won't be too much of a problem," Ed added, "but the pattern of decapitation is sure to raise some eyebrows down at police headquarters."

"No, you guys are all right," Elijah said, standing up and stretching his cramped muscles, a concerned expression on his face. "We should try and figure out some way to keep from inundating the Washington police with bodies, either of the headless type or the crispy critter type."

He glanced from one to the other. "Any ideas, teammates?" he asked.

Ed's eyes narrowed and he assumed a thoughtful expression "I've got an idea, Elijah. Let me work on it and I'll let you know how it pans out."

Immediately all of the other members of the group focused their minds on his, attempting to use their new, stronger mind-reading powers to get some inclination of just what his idea consisted of. They were met with a stone wall.

He grinned and shook his head when he felt their probes, shutting them out completely. "Uh-uh, boys and girls," Ed said with a grin. "No fair peeking."

With an enigmatic expression on his face, Ed got up and walked off toward the deck of the cabin, humming softly to himself.

The group followed him with their eyes, looking at each other and shrugging when they saw him pull out his cell phone and lean against the banister of the deck as he dialed.

"Well, since it looks like we'll just have to wait until Ed is ready to tell us his plan, why don't we spend our time getting as much of the vaccine ready to ship as we can and getting all of this equipment packed and ready to head to Washington?" Elijah suggested.

"How about I get on the phone and see about finding us someplace to stay?" Sam suggested.

"Good idea," Elijah said. "Pick a large chain hotel like Howard Johnson's or Marriott on one of the freeway loops around the outskirts of town," he advised. "That way, the hotel personnel won't notice our comings and goings if it's late at night and we'll be far enough out of the inner city traffic that if we have to leave town in a hurry we can go in any direction and get away fast."

Shooter's eyes narrowed. "You think we might have to cut and run?" he asked.

Elijah's grin was grim. "I told you all this is going to be a war, and we're going up against some of the richest and most powerful people in the free world, so anything's possible.'

He hesitated, and then he added cryptically, "If there's one thing I've learned by being on the outskirts of society for a couple of hundred years, it is to prepare for the absolute worst-case scenario and you'll never be surprised when it comes to pass."

Chapter 30

Allison Burton called her good friend, Bitsy McCormack. When she answered the phone, Allison said, "Hey, girlfriend, what's up?"

Bitsy, who was the quintessential spoiled Washington brat, immediately began to complain.

"Oh, hi Allison. I'm just sitting here twirling my thumbs and looking at the mess in my room. The old man has said I'm grounded until I clean it up."

Allison shuddered. She remembered the last time she spent the night at Bitsy's she found some month-old pizza under the bed. "Yeah, well, get your ass in gear, girl," Allison said, laughing. "Today's Saturday and the mall is gonna be full of mall rats. I thought we could meet and have some lunch and scope out the better looking ones."

Bitsy seemed to perk up at this. "Oh, great! The old man has always had a thing for you, Ally, so I'll tell him you're gonna come by and pick me up and I'll bet he'll let me go."

"Sure thing, I'll have my Secret Service agent drive us. So, I'll be by in about an hour, okay?"

"Yeah, and Allison," Bitsy said, her voice dropping to almost a whisper, "wear something low cut. You know how the old man likes to get an eyeful every time you come over."

Allison grunted noncommittally and was about to hang up when Bitsy suddenly said, "Oh, wow, I almost forgot! Did you hear about Jamie and Connie after the school dance last week?"

Allison made a questioning noise and settled in to listen to Bitsy go over the latest gossip, something she loved almost more than fast food. Allison was in no hurry to get off the phone, for she fully intended during their outing to explore Bitsy's mind to see if she was as fully committed to this Thantos guy's scheme to take over the world.

She was pretty sure Bitsy's dad, General Black Jack Mc-Cormack was fully supporting the plan, since Allison knew from previous conversations with her dad that McCormack was a full-on hawk and had some pretty severe political aspirations of his own.

Of course, she told herself, Bitsy *wasn't* her dad, not by a long shot, and she knew they didn't get along very well. Bitsy had once confided to her that he beat her mother, which Bitsy thought was gross and terrible. As far as Allison could tell, the two barely spoke to one another.

However, she warned herself, that could all be different now that Bitsy and her dad were both Vampyres. In fact, the last couple of times she'd seen them together, she got intense sexual vibes from both of them and she wondered if the old man was hitting on his daughter now that she'd transformed him.

Allison glanced over her shoulder, watching Michelle Meyer, the Secret Service agent assigned to protect her, sitting by the door reading a magazine.

Michelle must've sensed her scrutiny with her mind-reading abilities, for she turned and stared back at Allison, making no attempt to hide the probing as she tried to get inside Allison's mind to see what she was up to.

Allison clamped her thoughts down tight, thinking, Snooty Bitch! She'd never liked Michelle, and since her transformation, her attitude hadn't changed a bit. The broad was just a little too right wing for Allison, kind'a like Bitsy's father.

She was going to have to be very careful in her meeting with Bitsy today. She hadn't dared to try and *read* Michelle's thoughts. The bitch was just too powerful and Allison was afraid that if she got in the agent's mind, she'd catch on that Allison and her dad were attempting to find other Vampyres who weren't in favor of Thantos's scheme to rule the world.

She watched Michelle frown when she was unable to read Allison's mind, and she gave her an innocent grin and went back to her telephone conversation with Bitsy, only half listening as her friend told her all about Jamie and Connie's big fight after the dance.

As Bitsy talked on and on, Allison wondered briefly about how easy it was for her to shut out other Vampyre's psychic attempts to read her mind. Allison had as long as she could remember had what she called "hunches" such as knowing the phone was going to ring seconds before it did, and even usually knowing who was calling. Perhaps, she thought to herself, she'd had some latent psychic abilities prior to her conversion to being a Vampyre. If so, then she ought to be able to safely look into Michelle's mind without any danger.

She absentmindedly chewed on her thumbnail as she weighed the risks against the possible benefits from this attempt. She realized it would be best if she put all thoughts out of her mind about her and her dad's attempts to contact others who felt as they did. She'd just think about something else when she tried to probe Michelle's mind.

She fixed a firm picture of Joey Grayson in her mind. He was a boy at school that she thought was cute as a button, and he'd even flirted with her a time or two. All that had changed the moment she'd been transformed; she was afraid if she went out on a date with him she might have him for dinner instead of just going to dinner with him. She thought about how good his smile was as she ignored Bitsy's voice on the phone and cast her mind out at Michelle, trying her best to "tiptoe" through it instead of stomping around willy-nilly.

At first all she got was Michelle's emotional state, mainly boredom and frustration that she wasn't being promoted to a higher pay grade even though she'd been the one to transform her boss, Russell Cain, into the Vampyre race.

Suddenly her thoughts came through to Allison as clear as if she'd been speaking directly to her: "That misogynist son of a bitch," Michelle thought bitterly. "He'd rather cut off his right hand than give a woman a break."

As Michelle's thoughts continued in this vein, without any apparent knowledge that Allison was invading her privacy, Allison decided to dig a little deeper. She imagined she was a cat moving silently through the dark, her feet not making a sound on the grass.

This was a little tricky, as she'd never attempted to do this without the subject's consent before. She and her dad did it all the time, but they always asked first and got each other's permission to go after the deep thoughts that lay far beneath the surface of the mind.

Allison smiled as she moved through Michelle's mind, being as gentle as she could. It was almost like her favorite video game—Dungeons and Dragons—that she played for hours each day. In the game, she had to navigate through miles and miles of tunnels and caves, searching for the treasure without being found out by the dragons that guarded the underground maze.

Only, she was amazed to discover, this was easier. It was as if she were invisible to Michelle and could move anywhere in the woman's thoughts that she wanted.

She was startled to discover how bitter Michelle was, not only against her boss but also against the entire Vampyre movement. She found the agent hated Thantos with a vengeance, and that she was terrified that her thoughts would give her away to the "madman" as Michelle thought of him. She even found some fantasy thoughts of Michelle's where the agent imagined herself tearing Thantos's throat out and drinking his blood until it ceased to flow.

Digging further, Allison found that Michelle really respected and admired her dad, but she thought Allison was a spoiled little bitch who didn't deserve a father like him.

Allison grinned. Well, Michelle was right about that—she had given the agent hell on many occasions, and before her transformation, she *had* been a bit of a bitch. Well, in fact she'd been a lot of bitch, not a little she admitted to herself.

Allison was even more surprised to discover, after probing a little deeper, that in spite of Michelle's opinion that she was a bitch, there was also an undercover smidgeon of respect and admiration for Allison about how well she'd coped with her mother's death and her father's busy work schedule. Hell, Allison realized, Michelle even sees a little of herself as a young woman in me!

She was also amazed to learn that Michelle, like her dad, was an avowed patriot, and that she was furious at the way Thantos and his cronies were leading America's elected officials around by their noses. She got the feeling the agent would love to scuttle Thantos's plan, if only she could think of a way to do it without getting herself killed.

After only a moment's hesitation, Allison decided to make a move she would never have contemplated only a little while before. She was going to confront Michelle with her feelings against Thantos, though just to be on the safe side, Allison decided not to mention that her dad felt the same way.

She broke in on Bitsy's soliloquy about her miserable dating life and told her she'd see her at lunch. After she hung up, she took a deep breath and swiveled around in her chair.

"Hey, Michelle," she called, her voice trembling a little at the chance she was about to take. "Can we talk for a minute?"

Michelle's eyebrows went up in surprise. Allison had never once spoken to her as one woman to another, or practically even as one human being to another. In fact, usually the little worm treated her like she was a servant, put on earth to do her bidding. Wondering just what was going on, Michelle nodded and got up from her chair near the door and walked over to sit on the edge of Allison's bed, regarding her quizzically. "Sure, Allison. What is it you want to talk about?"

"Well," Allison began nervously, "I need to know what you think about this Thantos guy and his plan to take over the United States."

Michelle unconsciously glanced at the door, making sure no one was around to hear this heresy spoken by her young charge. "Uh . . . ummm, why exactly do you want to know this, Allison?" Michelle asked, her voice full of suspicion. "Did Theo ask you to see if I was loyal, or what?"

Allison leaned forward in her chair, "No, Michelle, I promise it's nothing like that. I need to know, because . . . because I think you hate him and what he has planned as much as I do!" she blurted out.

Michelle leaned back, more in surprise than to distance herself from what Allison was saying. Allison could hear Michelle's mind turning her words over and over, trying to determine if this was some sort of elaborate trap, if Allison was trying to make her admit her feelings against Thantos.

"What makes you think that?" Michelle started to ask, and then she nodded to herself. "Of course, you've been reading my thoughts."

Allison blushed and nodded. "Yeah, but just a little, Michelle, and just this once," she said.

Michelle's face flushed with anger. "And just what do you think gives you the right . . ."

"I'll tell you what gives me the right," Allison almost yelled back, her face red and burning. "Not too long ago I was raped and transformed into some hairy beast because of that son of a bitch Thantos, and then I find out he's trying to take over a country I happen to love! I think that gives me the right to do just about anything I can to stop the bastard!" she finished, her voice croaking with emotion and anger. "And if that's not good enough for you, then go fuck yourself!"

Michelle opened her mouth to voice a retort, hesitated, and then she did the thing Allison least expected: she smiled.

Shaking her head, Michelle stuck out her hand. "Shake, partner," she said, still grinning.

"You mean you *do* feel the same way?" Allison asked, happy that she'd been correct in her reading of Michelle's thoughts and emotions.

Michelle nodded. "Yep, right down to the son of a bitch part you called Thantos."

Allison reached out and took Michelle's hand. "Good, 'cause now I'm going to do something very dangerous," she said. "I'm going to open my mind and let you read everything in it, so long as you promise you won't do anything until you've read every part."

"Okay," Michelle said, her voice serious as she took both of Allison's hands in hers. She knew what an effort it took for Vampyres to voluntarily open their minds to another, especially one not their mate.

Fifteen minutes later, Michelle released Allison's hands and leaned back against the headboard. "Whew, and I thought you were just a spoiled little rich shit who only thought about herself and her shitty little rich friends."

Allison blushed as she said, "Well, I was wrong about you too, Michelle. I thought you were a power-hungry bitch who lived and breathed only work."

Michelle shrugged. "That's okay, kid. You weren't far wrong, at least until this Vampyre thing happened to us."

"Now," Allison asked, "What are we going to do about this now that you and dad and I all want to stop that bastard Thantos?"

Michelle's expression became thoughtful. "First of all, we've all got to be very, very careful. Thantos and his followers wouldn't hesitate to kill us all to keep their plans secret, so we've got to go around with our minds locked down tight at all times so he doesn't discover us."

"I've already been doing that," Allison answered. "In fact, I even try to avoid the son of a bitch whenever I can, just to make sure and stay out of range of his psychic abilities."

Michelle's eyebrows went up. "And just how do you know what his range is?"

Allison waved a dismissive hand. "Oh, he's not so good at the psychic stuff, Michelle. Heck, I'm a lot stronger at it than he is."

Michelle slowly nodded. "I wondered how you've been able to shut me out so easily." She smiled. "At first, I thought it was just 'cause you didn't have a thought in your empty little head."

When Allison smiled back, Michelle continued, "But then I came to realize it wasn't that, it was just that you were much better at this psychic thing than I was." She tilted her head to the side, "But I didn't realize you were stronger than some of the Vampyres who've been at it a lot longer than we have."

Allison wagged her head. "Oh, that has nothing to do with it, Michelle. It's not how long you've been psychic, it's how psychic you were before you were transformed and . . ." she paused, thinking for a second, "and probably how strong the Vampyre is who transformed you."

"If that's true, you're going to have to watch out for Sammy Akins, since he was the one who initiated you into this mess."

Allison laughed. "Don't worry about Sammy. He's cute but he has a brain the size of a peanut. No, I think I got my psychic powers more from my mother. She was always seeing and knowing things before she should've been able to."

"Good," Michelle said, "then since you're psychically much stronger than either your dad or I, you're going to have to be our 'point-man' in our search for allies."

Allison smiled and spread her arms out wide. "As I told my dad earlier, *no problemo!*"

Chapter 31

Allison and Michelle made careful plans for her luncheon date with Bitsy McCormack. They needed to find out if Bitsy was truly committed to Thantos's scheme or if she was just going along to keep peace with her dad. They decided Allison was to distract Bitsy with lively gossip and girl-talk while Michelle surreptitiously tried to read Bitsy's thoughts.

They planned it this way for even though Allison's psychic ability was far superior to Michelle's, there was no way Michelle could distract Bitsy as well as Allison could.

Michelle drove the car assigned to the agent to use while transporting her charge and stopped by Bitsy McCormack's house so that Allison could go in and get her.

As she climbed out of the car, Allison began to have doubts about their elaborate plans. She just knew they weren't going to work and that Bitsy's father, General Black Jack Mc-Cormack, would see right through her deception. The man had always been friendly to Allison before this and had never threatened her, but nevertheless his aloof nature and stern manner had always frightened her whenever she'd come to visit Bitsy.

Now she could feel her heart pounding and fear-sweat

forming under her arms at the thought of having to try and deceive him in his own house.

She walked up the sidewalk and looked back over her shoulder, just about to run back to Michelle and cancel the entire plan when the door opened before Allison had a chance to even ring the bell, and there stood Black Jack McCormack in the flesh. He stepped back from the door and motioned Allison in, a wide grin on his face.

Allison had followed Bitsy's instructions and worn one of her peasant top blouses and a push-up bra that showed her small breasts off to their best advantage. Maybe Bitsy was right; maybe it would distract McCormack and keep his mind off of hers.

McCormack's eyes moved down to her chest and he grinned even wider, holding his hands out wide. "Come on, Ally, and give your uncle Black Jack a big hug," he said, his eyes remaining fixed on her breasts.

It was the first time he'd ever called her Ally in all of the times she'd been over to visit Bitsy. Allison clamped down hard on her thoughts so he wouldn't pick up on the revulsion she felt at his lecherous staring, and she moved into his arms.

He wrapped his arms around her and pulled her tight against him, and she could feel his erection even through her jeans as he ground his groin against hers. Jesus, she thought, what a scuzzball.

"Nice to see you again, Mr. McCormack," she said, quickly moving back out of his grasp, but with a supreme effort, she kept her false smile glued on her face.

He immediately put his arm around her shoulders, letting his hand fall as if by accident to rest against the side of her right breast, which he slowly massaged with his thumb.

"Oh, call me Black Jack, dear," he said in his oily voice as he led her into the house.

Allison was saved from further conversation by the appearance of Bitsy bounding down the stairs two at a time. "Hey, Ally," she called, frowning a bit when she saw how her father was trying to feel her best friend up right in front of her.

"Hey, Bitsy," Allison responded, shrugging out of McCormack's grasp and running to hug her friend.

"Ready to go?" she asked.

"I'll say," Bitsy said, glaring at her father over Allison's shoulder. "Bye, Dad," Bitsy said, hurriedly moving Allison toward the door.

"Aren't you girls going to give old Black Jack a kiss good-bye?" he asked, holding out his arms again.

"No time, Dad," Bitsy said, shoving Allison ahead of her out the door. "We're late meeting some friends at the mall."

"Well, don't be gone too long," McCormack said, disappointed. He watched them run down the sidewalk for a moment, his dark eyes narrow, and then he turned and headed toward his study.

"Jesus, girlfriend," Bitsy gushed as soon as they'd both flopped into the back seat of the car. "I feel like I've escaped from prison every time I get a chance to get away from the old man for a while." As soon as she saw the front door close and McCormack could no longer see them, she began to take the barrettes out of her hair so it could fall down around her shoulders.

Allison nodded sympathetically. She too thought Bitsy's father was a bit of a jerk. Imagine, getting a hard on from a glimpse of one of your daughter's friend's boobs—what an asshole!

When they got to the mall, they walked around for a while, Michelle staying discretely in the background, and flirted with various boys they knew from school. By the time they adjourned to the food court, all three of the women had healthy appetites.

Bitsy handed Michelle the sacks of clothes she'd bought, treating her like a servant. Michelle's eyes flashed but she said nothing as she took the bags and put them next to her chair. She was sitting at a table next to Bitsy and Allison's, in order to give the girls a little privacy.

While Allison and Bitsy scarfed down burgers and fries and joked and talked about the boys they'd seen, Michelle sipped a cup of hot tea and played with a chicken salad sandwich as she focused all of her energies on getting into and out of Bitsy's mind without making her presence known.

It only took her a few minutes to find out what she needed to know since Bitsy wasn't at all complicated—what you saw was pretty much what you got: Bitsy hated her father, both for the way he'd treated her mother and for the continued sexual abuse she was still enduring ever since she'd transformed him into a Vampyre. Evidently, the brief sexual episode during the transformation had whetted his appetite for even more of the same, and it was now almost a nightly ritual, more importantly, one that Bitsy detested.

Michelle also discovered that Bitsy wasn't a bit political and that she had no strong feelings one way or the other about Theo Thantos's plans of world domination. But, Michelle did think the girl would do just about anything to hurt or destroy her father, *if* she thought she could do it without getting caught—she was still deathly afraid of him.

When Michelle was sure of what she'd learned, she waited until the food court was almost deserted except for them and then she took her tea and joined the girls at their table.

"Hey, how about a little privacy?" Bitsy complained grumpily at Michelle's arrival.

Allison just looked at her with upraised eyebrows.

Michelle nodded. "She's okay. I think she'll want to join us."

Bitsy looked from one to the other, her eyes wide. "What's she talking about, Ally? Join you in what?"

"Let's get us another Coke and I'll tell you, Bitsy," Allison replied. "It's a helluva plan."

"Does this plan of yours have anything to do with my

dad?" Bitsy asked, her eyes narrow and suspicious as they flicked from Michelle to Allison. Evidently she wasn't quite as dumb and simple as Michelle had thought.

"Yeah," Michelle answered.

"Will it piss him off?"

"Oh, yeah," Allison answered.

Bitsy grinned. "Then I'm in, no matter what it is! The son of a bitch has whatever you've got planned coming to him, and I won't mind a bit seeing that he gets it."

Michelle got to her feet. "You fill her in, Allison. I'll go get the Cokes."

Gen. Blackmon Taylor, head of USAMRIID (U.S. Army Medical Research Institute of Infectious Disease) at Fort Detrick, Maryland, where all of the U.S. germ warfare agents are stored and studied, was just sitting down to lunch at his home on the outskirts of Washington, D.C., when the phone rang.

"Damn," he said irritably to his wife who was sitting across the table from him. He glanced at the calendar on the wall, even though he knew full well what day it was. "It's Saturday, for Christ's sake! Why the hell are they calling me instead of the Officer of the Day."

"Maybe it's not work related, dear," his wife said amiably as she put a forkful of salad into her mouth.

"It's always fucking work related," Taylor said, getting to his feet and throwing his napkin down on the table. "Who else would be calling us? The fucking kids certainly never call anymore."

"Mind your language, dear," his wife admonished as she chewed her salad, her eyes as blank as a cow's.

Taylor went into his study and snatched the phone off the hook. "This better be pretty goddamned important!" he growled into the receiver.

"Hey, Blacky," Black Jack McCormack said evenly.

"Oh, sorry, Black Jack," Taylor said, calming down a little bit. He and McCormack were old friends from their army days and often played golf together on weekends when the weather was good. "I thought it was those assholes from the fort calling to fuck up my day. It seems the only time they ever have emergencies is at night or on the weekends."

McCormack chuckled. "Well, you're safe this time, Blackmon; it's just your old friend calling to see if you had anything on for today."

Taylor glanced at his watch. "No, nothing, but it's a little late for golf, Black Jack. We'll never get a tee time this late in the day."

"Uh, it's not about golf, Blacky," McCormack said. "If you and your wife are not too busy, I'd like to come by for a little chat."

Taylor shrugged, wondering just what McCormack was up to. He wasn't the sort of man to just drop by unless he had a damned good reason. "You know you're always welcome here, Black Jack," he answered, feeling a little uneasy. "Mind telling me what it's about?"

McCormack chuckled again, low in his throat. "No, I'd rather it be a surprise."

"Is it a good surprise or a bad surprise?" Taylor asked suspiciously, not able to think of a single thing the chairman of the Joint Chiefs of Staff could want with him.

"Oh, I think you'll really like what I have to show you, pal. It's gonna change your whole life around."

Brendan Fraser was sitting in a beach chair on famous Seven-mile Beach on Grand Cayman Island, working on his tan and sipping a tall fruity drink of some kind while he watched seminaked women half his age cavorting in the surf. As head of the National Security Council and chief advisor and best friend of the president of the United States, he'd managed to come to the island without having to drag his wife along by telling her he was meeting with various heads of state of some unnamed Caribbean countries as a favor to the president.

Actually, the only person he was meeting was a nineteen-year-old intern from his Washington office who'd promised him if he paid her way here she'd make it well worth his while.

So far, she hadn't disappointed him at all. In fact, he was still a bit sore from their frolicking the night before. When he thought of her, he unconsciously tugged at the front of his bathing suit, hoping the bruises she put on him down there wouldn't be noticed by his wife when he got home.

The intern was still asleep in their hotel room, so he thought he'd use this time to scope out the other action on the beach, just in case he tired of the teenager and decided to send her home early.

"Jesus," he muttered to himself, sitting up and pulling his sunglasses down a bit on his nose so he could get a better look at the dazzling beauty that was walking up the beach toward him.

She was tall and lanky, with dark, coal black hair hanging down almost to her hips, and she had a figure that was about a twelve on a scale of one to ten. He could tell her figure was good because she wasn't hiding much of it—her bathing suit consisted of three Band-Aid size patches of white cloth.

She must have an allergy to the sun, he mused, noticing her skin was still very pale in spite of the clear sky and bright sun over the island. As she got closer to him, he saw that she was coated with a thick layer of sunscreen covering every inch of exposed skin, and there were a lot of inches to cover.

Just as she came abreast of his chair, she stumbled in the sand and spilled her drink. As she bent to pick it up, he was rewarded with a view of her magnificent dark nipples when her bathing suit top pulled away from her chest.

He immediately jumped to his feet and rushed to her side. "All you all right?" he asked, kneeling in the sand to pick up her empty plastic glass.

She gave him a smile that made his heart almost stop and sent shock waves all the way down to his wounded crotch. "I'm fine, but I'm afraid I've lost my drink."

"No problem," Fraser said quickly. "Let me buy you another one."

"Why, how gallant of you, kind sir," she said, sticking out her hand. "My name is Christina Alario."

"Hi, Christina, I'm Brendan Fraser," he said, taking her hand and shaking it.

Christina glanced up at the clear sky and the sun shining overhead. "I'd love to take you up on the drink, but I'm afraid I need to get inside. My skin never seems to tan, and I've had a bit more sun already today than is good for me."

Fraser licked his lips. He just couldn't let this one get away. She was by far the best-looking woman on the entire island and he had the feeling that if she left he'd never see her again. "Well," he said hoarsely, "how about the hotel bar?"

She smiled and glanced down at her skimpy bikini. "You think they'd let me in like this?" she asked.

He pursed his lips. She was right. The bar had a strict dress code—no bathing suits were allowed.

When he hesitated, she moved closer to him and he could smell the heat coming off her skin—it smelled like the musk of some exotic wild animal and made his groin grow heavy.

"I know," she said, her eyes lighting up as if she'd just had an idea. "Why don't you come up to my room and I'll change into something . . . more suitable." When he hesitated, thinking of the intern in his room, she added in a sultry voice, "We can have room service bring us a drink while I change."

"Okay," he croaked through a suddenly dry throat, thinking he was the luckiest son of a bitch on the island.

Once in her room, Christina moved toward her bedroom while Fraser went to the phone to order them both drinks.

Christina undid the tiny straps to her bathing suit top as

she walked, calling back over her shoulder, "I'm going to take a quick bath to get this sunscreen off, if you don't mind waiting."

He shook his head when he caught a glimpse of very full breasts as she turned to enter her bathroom, thinking he'd wait all day if necessary.

After the bellman dropped off their drinks, Fraser carried them into the living room of the hotel suite, calling, "Drinks are here," toward the half-open bathroom door.

Her voice came floating out of the door along with waves of billowing steam, "Why don't you bring them in here, Brendan? The water is just too delicious to leave."

Fraser picked up the drinks and walked into the bathroom, weaving his way through the clouds of fragrant steam that smelled like vanilla until he saw Christina leaning back in a large Jacuzzi tub, the jets blowing soft bubbles around her floating breasts.

She smiled seductively. "Care to join me?"

He almost choked at the sight of her breasts bobbing on the bubbles, waiting for him in the steaming water.

He sat the drinks down on the cabinet and stripped out of his bathing suit, ignoring the aches and pains in his penis as it grew heavy and stiff, and seconds later he was next to her in the tub, clinking glasses and offering a toast to new friends.

She emptied her drink and sat the glass down on the edge of the bathtub before leaning forward and covering his lips with hers.

When he felt her hand on his penis, he grabbed her breast and closed his eyes, reveling in the moment and moaning from both pain and lust.

He opened his eyes and screamed against her mouth when he saw what she was becoming, but it was too late . . . much too late!

Chapter 32

John Ashby poured two cups of coffee and took them to the table where Marya Zaleska was sitting across from Theo Thantos and Christina Alario. John had requested a meeting with Thantos prior to his scheduled meeting with the cell leaders of his followers. He'd told him that he and Marya were tired of being kept in the dark and treated like they weren't important enough to know what his plans were.

"So," John said after he'd handed Marya her cup, "what's going on, Theo? Where exactly are we in your plan to take over the country?"

Thantos puffed up like a toad with self-importance and put his hand on Christina's shoulder. "We're almost there, Johnny. Now that Christina has converted Brendan Fraser we have an ally sitting on the president's right hand with complete and total access to the number one man in the country. In addition, General Black Jack McCormack has managed to convert General Blackmon Taylor and his wife, and they are soon to start working their way through the higher echelon of officers and their wives at Fort Detrick."

"Fort Detrick?" Marya asked, completely ignoring Christina and focusing all of her attention on Thantos.

Thantos nodded eagerly. "Yes, it's the country's main storehouse for both chemical and biological weapons. Once we have it completely under our control, the government and the people of the United States will have to do whatever we want or else we can devastate entire areas of the country, or any other country that pisses me off for that matter."

Ashby was horrified. He'd known there were no bounds to Thantos's ambition, but this went far beyond anything he'd contemplated when he agreed to help Thantos in his schemes. "You mean, you'd actually consider gassing or releasing germ warfare on the people of this country?" Ashby asked, trying to keep his distaste from his voice.

Thantos looked amused. "What? Did you actually think this was going to be a bloodless coup, Johnny?"

"No, not bloodless, but I didn't think we'd be annihilating half the population either."

Thantos waved a dismissive hand. "Oh, I don't think it'll ever come to that. I imagine just the threat of such an action will get me what I want."

"Okay," John said, slightly mollified. "So, suppose you get what you want and suddenly you're in the driver's seat, running the entire country. What then? Once our race is able to come out of hiding and rule the country alongside the Normals, are you going to force all of the Normals to donate blood periodically so we can eat whenever we want?"

Thantos pursed his lips and looked at Christina. "Well, uh, why would you say that, Johnny?"

"I thought the whole purpose of this coup was to make us equal to the Normals and enable us to live openly in society, getting our blood whenever we needed it, without having to kill for it."

"Without having to kill for it?" Thantos asked, with a smirk. "But, Johnny, my dear boy, killing for it is half the fun. Why on earth would any self-respecting Vampyre want to give that up?"

Before John could answer, Christina said, "I told you he didn't have the guts to see this through, sweetheart." She leaned forward, her eyes full of hate. "Hell, I'm surprised the both of them aren't on that vaccine that makes us into nothing more than toothless farm animals."

John ignored Christina's barb, glaring at Thantos. "So, when you're in charge, the Normals will be relegated to something like cattle, to be slaughtered whenever we feel like a little snack?"

Thantos held up a hand. "No, no, nothing like that, John. I'm sure there will be plenty of our race who feel as you do and will be satisfied with drinking *canned* blood. But provisions must be made for those of us who prefer . . . ah . . . a more active role in procuring our blood. So what I propose is to decriminalize killing of Normals for food, that's all. Then it will be every Vampyre's choice on how to get his blood, from a blood bank or from a living donor."

"But," John argued even though he knew in his heart he'd never get Thantos to change his mind, "we've been feeding all the new converts out of stolen blood bank and hospital supplies for the past few weeks, and no one's complained. Why can't we just go on like that?"

Thantos sighed. "The only reason I've been using blood bank blood to feed our growing army is that I don't want dead bodies lying all over the streets to warn the police, and you'll have to admit, it is rather difficult for some of our more famous converts to find the time to hunt down and kill prey with Secret Service agents following them around."

"Come on, baby," Christina said, getting to her feet and rubbing the back of Thantos's neck as she stood behind his chair, staring at Marya with barely concealed hatred. "Don't waste any more time on these two. You're the boss and they'll just have to go along with your orders or else."

"Or else what, bitch?" Marya said, getting to her feet, her hands forming claws as she got ready for combat.

"Are you going to let her talk to me like that, Theo?" Christina whined, suddenly frightened as she crouched down behind Thantos.

He held out his hand as he got slowly to his feet, his lips curled up in a sneer. "Tell your mate to calm down, Johnny, before I have to do something about it."

John had to use all of his self-control not to bound across the table and rip Thantos's throat out as he put his hand on Marya's shoulder. "Let's go, sweetheart. Now is not the time nor the place to have this discussion."

As they walked off, Thantos watched with narrowed eyes. "I'm afraid we may have to do something . . . uh . . . more permanent about John and Marya's attitude, dear," he said to Christina, who smiled evilly at the suggestion. She couldn't wait for Marya to get what was coming to her.

"When the time comes to do that bitch, sweetie," she said, caressing his arm, "let me be the one to do it."

He turned to her. "Okay. Now, do you have the crates of blood packages ready for the cell leaders to take back to their members?"

"Uh-huh."

"Good, 'cause I wouldn't want any of them getting so hungry they act out and do something stupid to draw the attention of the authorities to us." He grinned as they moved toward the door. "In a few days, we'll be so far advanced in my plan that it won't matter, and that's when we'll get rid of Johnny and Marya."

As John and Marya walked toward their car, he shook his head. "This is not good, babe."

"Why don't we just pack up and leave, Johnny?" she asked. "We could go off together and forget about all this and just lead our lives someplace else."

He stopped and turned to her. "I can't do that, darling, no matter how good it sounds right now. When I agreed to go along with Thantos's scheme, I thought we were going to be working toward a country where Vampyres and Normals could stand side by side, sharing the country without animosity."

"Poor Johnny," Marya said, caressing his cheek with her hand. "You are *so* idealistic."

"But that's the way it should be, Marya. There should be no masters and no slaves, just two different species each living their own lives without harming the other."

"But Thantos is right about one thing, John," Marya said, glancing back over her shoulder at the couple behind them.

"What's that?"

"There is a definite percentage of our race who still prefer the hunt and the kill, rather than being spoon fed blood from a plastic bag. So, what would you do about that?"

"I'd handle it the same way I handle it personally, darling, I'd make sure that anyone killed for food deserved to die—it could be part of the prison system or capital punishment, or something like that."

"That'd be tricky," she said. "A lot of bleeding hearts would say it was cruel and unusual punishment."

He grinned and put his arm around her shoulders and led her toward their car. "And they'd be the first people I targeted for food," he said, only half-joking.

Chapter 33

As Elijah came to the freeway loop surrounding Washington, Ed leaned forward from his position in the backseat and pointed to the left. "Take that exit ramp there and go east, Elijah."

"So you still refuse to tell us where you're taking us, huh?" Elijah grumbled.

TJ, who was riding in the right front passenger seat, reached across and punched him in the shoulder. "Oh quit being such a grumpus, Elijah, lighten up a little for Christ's sake. We'll all find out soon enough what Ed's got planned for us."

Elijah sighed the deep sigh of the perennially harassed male faced with unarguable logic from a female in his life.

He cut his eyes toward her. "I should have ripped your throat out when I had the chance, girl," he teased.

She laughed. "Just think of all the fun you'd have missed by not getting to know me," she retorted.

"Yeah, and just imagine how horny I'd be if you'd done that, Elijah," Shooter added from the seat directly behind TJ, "although, now, you can all see what I have to put up with on a daily basis."

She glanced back at him and went, "Pooh, Shooter. If I

wasn't here you'd still be going after anything in a skirt like you did for the twenty or so years before you met me."

"Yeah, you're probably right. But no matter how many I chased or how many I caught, I'd never find someone as great in bed as you are, dear," he said, mock contritely.

Elijah, Matt, and Ed all said, simultaneously as if planned, "Amen."

TJ sniffed. "Well, I'm glad to know I'm appreciated by all the men present."

Sam and Kim laughed, not at all offended by their men's compliments about TJ's prowess in bed. They knew from being able to read their mates' minds that it was all in fun, and besides, they also knew that their own sexual abilities were appreciated just as much, as were the men's by them.

Ed consulted a piece of paper and said, "Okay, Elijah, take the next exit and make a U-turn under the overpass and the place will be about half a block down."

Minutes later, Elijah pulled into a parking lot in front of a large funeral home with a sign that read, ABERNATHY'S FUNERAL PARLOR.

"This is it?" Matt said in a disbelieving tone. "Your great idea is to have some mortician named Abernathy bury all the bodies of the Vampyres we kill?"

Ed laughed, "Not exactly, Matt." He motioned for Elijah to pull up next to the delivery entrance since the place was dark and appeared closed for the night.

Ed jumped out of the car and walked to the door, which had a single lightbulb hanging above it. He rang a bell next to the door and waited. After a couple of minutes, the door opened and a pasty-faced man in pajamas shook Ed's hand and handed him something.

Ed returned to the car and climbed in. "Drive on around the building to the rear entrance, please, Elijah."

Once Elijah had parked next to a set of large double doors, and everyone had gotten out of the SUV, Ed pointed off to one side where three black limousines were parked. One was obviously the type used to transport grieving family members from the funeral home to the gravesite, and the other two were hearses that were used to transport the coffins.

"Those are part of the deal," Ed said proudly, beaming at the group.

"What deal?" Elijah asked, exasperation at being kept in the dark evident in his tone.

"Come on inside," Ed said, "And I'll explain."

Shooter looked over his shoulders at the automobiles as they entered the doorway. "No matter what he says, I ain't gonna wear no chauffeur's uniform."

The group followed Ed down a series of halls and finally gathered in a large, open room with several iron doors in the wall, complete with temperature gauges next to each one.

Ed faced the group. "Now, as Elijah said, one of our major problems is going to be disposing of dead Vampyres after we cut their heads off." He waved his hand at the iron doors. "This is the crematorium part of Abernathy's Funeral Home. It can do three bodies at a time, six if we stack them double."

"How . . . ?" Elijah started to ask.

"Wait, it gets better," Ed said, grinning. "We also have the use of the hearses and the limousine to move around town and to transport bodies." He laughed and spread his arms, "Who's gonna suspect us of riding around town stalking our enemies in a hearse?"

The other members of the group all joined him in laughter and all clapped their hands enthusiastically.

"But, how did you get the owner to agree to letting us use all this?" Elijah asked, still chuckling.

"Remember, when you first asked Kim and I about our psychic abilities, and I told you I was pretty adept at long-distance psychic communication?"

Elijah nodded. "Yeah, you showed me by contacting Sam and having her call me on the phone while she was thousands of miles away."

"Well, since our blood sharing, I've gotten much stronger

and more focused in that ability, so when you outlined our body disposal problem, I called Washington information and got the number of all of the crematoriums in town. After calling a few, I found this one out on the loop near the hotel Sam found for us to stay at, and I told the man I represented several veterinarians in the area. With a little mental push to make him buy the idea, I got his permission to use the crematorium at night to dispose of all the little doggies and cats that our customers were bringing in that didn't survive."

"What about the limos and the hearse?" Matt asked.

"Oh, he agreed to that but he won't remember it," Ed answered. He opened his hand, "See, he gave me the spare keys to all of the vehicles. All we have to do is to make sure we leave them full of gas when we bring them back."

"And they're not used at night?" TJ asked.

"Extremely rarely," Ed said. "And the only drawback is that we'll have to use our regular transportation during the day, since the limos and hearse might be busy."

Shooter snapped his fingers. "I've got an idea, guys. How about we buy or lease an ambulance? We can put some fake name and number on it and it'll make a perfect way to move around during the day, and if we get in a jam and have to move fast," he spread his arms, "then we just turn on the lights and siren and go code three."

"And the neat thing is it'll be big enough inside to carry all of us at once if we need it to," Sam said, getting into the spirit of the idea.

Elijah clapped his hands together. "Excellent, team, you've outdone yourselves. Now I suggest we go check into that hotel Sam found for us and get ready for action."

Shooter moved up behind TJ and pressed himself against her while he circled his arms around her over her breasts. "Great, 'cause I'm definitely ready for action."

TJ grinned and said to the others, "See, Shooter's already getting another idea." She wagged her head. "I don't know if I'm ready for two ideas in the same night."

"Are the rooms you booked connecting?" Matt asked Sam.

"Yes, they are."

He grinned. "Then I don't see why we can't all get in on the action. It's been a couple of days since we shared blood, and I feel about a quart low."

Sam laughed. "Hotels always did make you horny, you dog."

Ed glanced around at the metal tables parked against a side wall. "We could just start right here," he suggested, waggling his eyebrows at Kim.

"No you don't buster," she said, hands on hips. "I am not about to attend any orgy in a crematorium. Don't you have any respect for the dead?"

Ed shook his head. "Nope, but if you're going to be squeamish, let's get going. We're wasting time standing around here talking about it when we could be on our way to doing it."

Elijah pulled the keys to the SUV out and said, "I'm ready."

TJ put one hand through his arm and the other through Shooter's. "Come on, boys, you've got work to do."

Matt yawned. "Now that I think about it, it's been a long trip. I may be too tired to party."

Sam put her arm around his shoulder and leaned her face in close to his. "Want to bet?"

Chapter 34

Theo Thantos was sitting staring out of the window of their suite on the top floor of the Washington Ritz Carlton Hotel when Christina came out of the bathroom. She was naked and was rubbing a towel vigorously through her long, black hair. She was trying to get it dry without using a blow-dryer, which tended to make it look more like an African Bushman's hair than the sleek runway model she aspired to.

She moved over to stand behind Theo. As he continued to stare out of the window without acknowledging her presence, she rubbed her breasts against his back in a suggestive manner before she caught his emotional state—dark and disturbed.

Quickly stopping her flirting, she moved around to kneel in front of him and looked up into his eyes. "What is it, darling? Why are you so upset?"

His eyes looked cold and flat and dangerous. "I've been thinking about our last conversation with John Ashby and Marya Zaleska."

Christina's eyes narrowed at the mention of Marya's name. She hated that bitch and didn't want Theo to ever think about her, no matter the context.

"Oh?" she asked, stroking his thigh with her hand to get him to look down at her body, and hopefully to drive all thoughts of Marya out of his head.

"Yeah," he answered, his eyes finally moving down to glance at her naked breasts. Almost absentmindedly, he reached down and began to slowly stroke her right breast, but it was clear his mind was elsewhere since his eyes didn't soften with lust as they usually did but remained as hard and cold as granite pebbles.

Realizing she was getting nowhere, Christina stood up and draped the towel over her shoulders and put her hands on her hips and spread her legs. "Well, what about it, Theo?" she asked. "What exactly about Marya and John has you so upset and angry?"

He looked at her. "I don't like the way he talked to me, and I especially don't like the way the two of them acted when they started to talk about treating Normals as equals when I finally get control of the country."

Christina noticed Theo's use of the word "I" instead of "we" but decided not to make an issue of it—yet. There would be plenty of time later to remind him that she was an equal partner in this take-over-the-world scheme of his. So, she just nodded her head slowly. "Yeah, they were kind'a wishy-washy about how we needed to take care of the poor Normals and not use them for food, weren't they?" she asked. After a moment, she added, "But, isn't that why you said we'd get rid of them later, when we were further along in our plans?"

He stood up and moved closer to the window, staring down at the people on the street, dozens of stories below. They looked like ants, he thought, realizing that he had about the same amount of feeling for them as if they were insects.

"Yes, but now I don't think we should wait until then. I don't like the way he challenged me about what I intend to do once this is all over. Ashby and Zaleska are not in charge of this coup, I am, and the sooner they find that out, the better!"

"Of course you are, dear," Christina said, sidling over to put her arm around his shoulders. "No one disputes that this takeover was all your idea."

"Damn right they don't, and I intend for everyone to obey my orders once it has been accomplished, without hesitation or second guessing!" he exclaimed. He took a couple of deep breaths and tried to calm himself. "But I think it's time we taught John and Marya it's dangerous to underestimate me, or to try and tell me what to do with my country."

Christina felt elation that Theo was finally going to teach that bitch Marya a lesson, even though she was getting a little tired of his continual use of the singular instead of the plural in discussing who would head the country and make the decisions. "What are you going to do, darling?" she asked, rubbing the back of his neck with her hand.

"I'm going to kill the son of a bitch!"

"What about Marya? Are *we* going to kill her too?" Christina asked, hoping the answer was yes and that he would take note that she was including herself in his murder plans.

"Of course we are. She'd be much too dangerous to leave alive after we kill her mate."

She smiled—he had noticed and he had taken the hint. "How are we going to do it . . . and when?"

He put his arms around her and leaned down to kiss her lightly on the lips. "Very carefully, and right now."

John Ashby was just coming awake when the phone on the bedside table of their hotel room rang. "Hello."

A whispered voice said urgently, "John, it's me, Christina! I need to talk to you right now. It's about something that Theo has planned that I think you need to know."

John came instantly awake. "Sure, Christina, come on down to our room." John and Marya were also staying at the Ritz Carlton, though on a lower floor and in a regular room, not a suite.

"I can't! Theo might find out, and I need to meet you alone, without Marya around."

"Why?"

"Because I can't stand the sight of her, that's why. Now, do you want to hear what I've got to say or not?" Christina said, her voice suddenly hard and harsh instead of soft and sultry.

John grinned. This was more like the bitchy Christina he knew. All the fake sultriness had disappeared from her tone. "Sure. Where do you want to meet?"

"Meet me at cabin number four out at the Rejuvenatrix Spa in two hours. It's the last cabin on the trail down to the river. We can be alone there."

"Okay."

Suddenly, her voice warmed a few degrees and became husky, as if with desire. "And Johnny, I want you to know I'll make it well worth your while to meet me. I'll do things to you that Marya's never even heard of."

"All right, I can hardly wait," John said, trying to keep the sarcasm out of his voice.

After she hung up, he sat there in the bed thinking. Something was wrong. In the first place, Christina had never shown the slightest interest in him sexually, and she was much too shrewd to risk her position with the powerful Theo Thantos to have a fling with someone as low down on the rungs of power as him. Christina was as ambitious and power hungry as she was beautiful—and that was *very*.

The sound of the shower in the bathroom stopped and moments later Marya came out. She was wearing the white cotton robe provided by the hotel and she looked magnificent, with her brilliant red hair glowing and shining as she ran a brush through it.

He patted the bed next to him. "Come here, sweetheart, we need to have a talk."

"What about?" she asked, sitting next to him on the bed, a puzzled frown on her face.

"About a couple of snakes," he answered.

* * *

Precisely two hours after his phone call, John walked down a gravel path to the cabin with the number four on its door and he knocked.

Christina, wearing only the sheerest of nightgowns, answered the door, opening it only an inch or two and elaborately looking around to make sure he was alone before opening it wider.

"Come in, Johnny. Quick before someone sees you," she said, pulling him inside and shutting and locking the door behind him.

Once she'd shut the door she turned and threw herself against him, wrapping her arms around him and pressing her breasts against his chest, grinding urgently against his groin with hers as if she'd been waiting for him all of her life.

He inhaled the musk coming off her body. Damn, she does smell good, he thought. He didn't have to fake the heaviness in his loins her actions were causing.

He took her by the shoulders and held her out away from him. He was having trouble thinking with her attacking his groin and he needed some space between them. He tried to look into her eyes but his gaze kept straying south, to the sight of her dark, brown nipples straining against the nightgown.

She smiled when she saw where he was looking. "Hurry, Johnny, get out of your clothes," she said, reaching down to give his erection a quick caress. "I can't wait to have you," she urged, releasing him to pull at his belt.

While she was undoing his pants, he glanced quickly around the cabin. It was one room with a bath off to one side. The only furniture was a bed and night table, and there was no closet, only a small chest against a far wall where clothes could be hung up. There was no place for anyone to hide.

"Okay," he said, feigning excitement. "Just let me go to

the bathroom first, then I'll come out." He leaned down and kissed her, running his hands over her breasts lightly. "Will you be ready for me?"

"Oh, yes, yes I will, Johnny," Christina gushed, though he noticed her lust never made it to her eyes.

He nodded and stepped into the bathroom and closed the door. He carefully took his clothes off and draped them over the shower curtain rod over the bathtub. There was no need to get them stained with blood.

Then he began to change into his Vampyre form, getting ready for what he knew was waiting for him on the other side of the door.

When he was fully ready, he came through the door crouching low and moving fast. The machete that Christina swung whistled inches over his head and embedded itself in the door jam with a loud thunk.

He whirled around to find himself confronted with two people, also already changed into their Vampyre forms.

Sammy Akins was crouched near the front door, a long sword in his hands, drooling and grinning around large fangs as he moved slowly toward John. "Say good-bye to your head," his hoarse voice rumbled as his eyes danced with the desire to kill.

Off to one side, Christina also smiled as she jerked her machete out of the door jam and circled around to try and get behind John.

"Sorry, Johnny," she growled. "I always kind'a liked you, but you had to go and get hooked up with that bitch and then you dared to question our leader. Now, we have no choice but to kill you."

"So that's what this is all about," John said, moving slowly backward, his eyes flicking back and forth, trying to keep the pair in front of him.

"The boss don't like traitors," Sammy Akins growled, waving the tip of his blade back and forth slowly, bloodlust making his eyes look crazy in the low wattage lamplight of the cabin.

"And," Christina said, her eyes full of good humor at the thought of the death of her nemesis, Marya, "he's on his way to point that out to your mate right now."

Christina glanced quickly over her shoulder at the clock on the wall. "In fact, the bitch is probably already dead."

Suddenly, the cabin door splintered and a Vampyre covered with shining red hair crashed into the room, a double-bladed ax in her hands. "Wrong again, asshole!" she screamed at Christina as she swung her ax in a two-handed grip.

Sammy Akins whirled around just in time to open his mouth in fear when he saw the terrible apparition bounding across the room directly at him. In the blink of an eye the razor-sharp ax blade entered Sammy's head just above his bottom jaw and took the top two thirds of his head clean off.

He grunted once and dropped like a stone, his sword clattering to the floor while his head hit, bounced, and came to rest with restless eyes moving back and forth, staring at its body across the room.

Christina screeched in rage and raised her machete over her head and leapt at Marya.

In one fluid motion, John stooped and picked up Akins's sword, whirled balletlike and jammed the point backhanded into Christina's abdomen, driving her back as the blade lodged in the wall, impaling Christina with her feet hanging two feet off the floor.

The machete flew from her hands as she threw back her head and howled in agony. She choked and coughed and began to scream again, until Marya moved up and wrapped her claw around Christina's throat and squeezed off her air supply.

The two females stood there panting and drooling and sweating crimson, their eyes staring bullets at each other as blood pumped from Christina's wound out onto the floor.

Marya held up the ax and slowly drew the blade across Christina's throat, making a shallow cut that oozed a thin trail of blood. "Should I finish her now?" she asked, looking over her shoulder at John.

He considered their options for a moment, and then he wagged his head. "No, let's leave her like this as a message to Thantos." He bent and picked up Christina's machete, casually moved to stand over Akins's body, and lopped off the rest of his head at the neck.

And then, still moving slowly, he stood in front of Christina, who watched him with wide, pain-filled eyes. "Tell your mate that if he ever tries to find us or do us harm again, *ever,* I'll see that he rots in hell!"

With his final word, he jammed the point of the machete into Christina's lower abdomen, six inches below the sword and just above her pubic bone.

When she opened her mouth to scream again, Marya grabbed Akins's shirt that was lying on the floor and stuffed it deep into her mouth.

"That's ought to keep the bitch quiet for a little while," she said with a smile as she let herself change back into human form.

His blood still raging with lust and adrenaline, John grabbed her, pushed her down on her back, and mounted her, still in his Vampyre form.

As he growled and rutted, pumping his erection into her, Marya grinned and looked over his shoulder into Christina's hateful eyes that were staring at them. "Eat your heart out, bitch!" she mouthed, moaning and gasping as her orgasm began to rack her body.

Chapter 35

As they raced away in John's car, Marya sidled over to sit next to him, like a high school girl out on a date with her boyfriend.

She placed her left arm around his shoulders and leaned her head to the side, watching him as he drove. She could see his eyes flicking back and forth, alert for any danger.

"Take it easy, darling," she said, her voice still husky from the excitement of the kill and lovemaking afterward. "We got away clean."

"Yeah," he said, cutting his eyes at her for just a second. "But Thantos is still out there, and he's got lots of new friends like that little worm we snuffed back there. And remember, Christina said he'd gone to our hotel room to try and kill you while she and Akins were killing me."

He shook his head. "Like Yogi Berra once said, 'it ain't over till it's over.' "

Her brows knit together. "You think he'll still come after us, after what we did to Christina and in spite of our warning him not to?"

He shrugged. "Maybe not immediately, but he'll definitely come sooner or later. He's not the kind of man to suffer a failure like this without seeking retribution, especially not while Christina is there at his side to remind him every day that we got the better of them."

She turned to look out the front windshield. "I knew I should've gutted that wench."

"No," he said, taking his hand off the wheel and resting it on her thigh. "You did just right, sweetheart. Now she'll have to live with the fact that you could have killed her but spared her life. I think that'll bother her more than killing her would have."

Marya laughed. "You're probably right, Johnny." She leaned over to kiss his cheek. "What did I ever do to deserve you?"

He glanced at her, his eyes serious. "Soul mates?"

She nodded, one crimson tear forming in her eye. "Soul mates!" she answered.

"For as long as we live?"

"For as long as we live," she answered, snuggling up tight against him.

It was a ritual they'd started soon after becoming mates, and it never failed to fill him with love.

John drove for another hour, heading north and intending to cross the border into Canada and hopefully disappear off Thantos's radar screen forever.

Finally, he took his foot off the accelerator and pulled off the road into the parking lot of a roadside café. "Come on," he said, getting out of the car. "I need some coffee and I need to make a phone call."

It was a testament to their closeness that Marya didn't question him about what he was going to do.

John took a booth near the front window so he could watch the parking lot—years of caution ingrained in his being. Once they had steaming cups of coffee in front of them and the waitress was out of hearing range, he pulled out his cellular phone and dialed a number by memory.

"Are you sure you know what you're doing?" Marya asked, but she didn't try to dissuade him from his course of action. They were so close that their minds were always in tune and she knew what he intended without having to be told.

He nodded and spoke when a voice answered. "Hello, old friend. It's me, John."

Ed Slonaker covered his surprise well. "Hey, Johnny, how're you doing?"

"Not so good, pal. You got a minute to talk?"

"For you, always," Ed replied, becoming more serious at the tone in John's voice.

"You sound like you're out of breath, Ed."

Ed chuckled. "Well, I *was* in the middle of something . . . or rather someone when you called," he said.

"Oh," John said, grinning. "Want me to call back later?"

"No, go ahead. I need to take a break and catch my breath anyway."

After John had told Ed his story, of how he'd joined Thantos only to find he planned on using Normals as a food supply rather than as equals under the law and of how Thantos and Christina had tried to kill them, Ed interrupted to ask a favor.

"Sure, Ed, whatever you want," John replied.

"Open your mind to me and let me have full access," Ed said.

John laughed, until he realized Ed was serious. "But Ed, I don't know where you are, but it's got to be hundreds or thousands of miles away," John protested. "None of us can read over that kind of distance."

"Trust me," Ed said, "and let me read you so I know I can trust you."

John shrugged, though Ed couldn't see over the phone. "Sure, pal, if you think you can do it, go for it. Everything I've told you is the truth and I've got nothing to hide."

Sure enough, seconds later, John felt the familiar feather-tickle of his old friend in his mind. "I'll be damned," he muttered.

Minutes later, he heard Ed sigh. "It's nice to know we can still trust each other," Ed said.

"So, now what?" John asked, taking Marya's hand across the table and staring into her eyes.

"You've got two choices, as I see it," Ed said, automatically easing into the roles he and John had always had: Ed the mentor, John the willing student and protégé. "One, you can do as you are and run away and hide in Canada or wherever it is you think you'll be safe . . ."

"Yeah, and our other choice?"

"You can return to Washington and help my new friends and I take Thantos and his minions out for good."

John laughed. "Don't tell me you've got an army there with you, pal, 'cause that's what it's gonna take to overcome Thantos before it's too late."

John could almost see Ed shrug, "Naw, it's just seven of us, counting Kim and I."

"Seven?" John almost shouted. He got control of himself and lowered his voice. "Do you realize Thantos has a virtual who's who of Washington in his pocket, not to mention high up muckity mucks in both the police department and Secret Service?" John asked. "Hell, he's probably got over a hundred followers lined up and ready to follow his lead."

"Yep, but it doesn't matter how many followers he has, Johnny. We're going to take the bastard down or die trying, 'cause we don't particularly want to live in the kind of world he's trying to create."

John glanced at Marya and said, "Let me get back to you, Ed. There's someone I have to check with first . . ."

He stopped when Marya shook her head and then smiled across the table at him. "No, we go with them darling."

"Uh, never mind holding, Ed. Just tell me where you are and we'll come join you guys. You're now officially an army of nine."

* * *

It was just after eight the next morning when John woke up to find Ed holding a steaming cup of coffee under his nose. John groggily shook his head and set up in the bed, gratefully taking the coffee and draining half the cup before he came up for air.

He and Marya had arrived back in Washington at almost four in the morning and had gone straight to the room Ed and his friends had procured for them. They'd been too tired to undress and had just flopped down on the bed and gone immediately to sleep.

When Marya raised her head, Ed pointed over his shoulder to a room service cart at the foot of the bed that was covered with plates of scrambled eggs and bacon and sausage and more coffee and orange juice.

Marya bounded out of bed and attacked the food. Around a mouthful of eggs, she winked at Ed. "I can see why Johnny loves you, Eddy."

Ed winced at the nickname. "Okay, okay, it's just some eggs for Christ's sake. Don't go all gooey on me."

"Man, it was lucky the room next to you guys was vacant," John said.

Ed smiled. "Not lucky at all. The man and woman staying there had a sudden urge to return home in the middle of the night, so we took the room for you as soon as they left."

John's eyes narrowed. "More of your psychic magic, old friend?"

Ed patted his leg and got up from the edge of the bed. "We've got lots to tell you and Marya, John, and you've got lots of catching up to do if we're going to have a chance to whip Thantos."

"Catching up?" Marya asked from her place at the table.

Ed smiled. "I'll let Elijah explain it to you, but you're not going to believe the world that is about to open up for you two."

Chapter 36

It took John and Marya almost a week working with Elijah and his friends to list all of the members of Thantos's followers that they knew about, a week that was also used to good advantage by having the group all share blood with the new members of *Elijah's Army* as they called themselves.

One good effect of having so many extra sources of blood to partake of was that the process of improvement in John and Marya's DNA and hence their Vampyre abilities progressed much faster than it had for the original experimenters. A drawback was that for much of the week they were sick as dogs, with high fevers, nausea, and muscle and bone aches that were so bad that on one occasion John asked for a sword so that he could cut his own head off to end the misery.

By the ninth day, however, both John and Marya began to feel almost back to normal. Their physical strength as well as their psychic abilities were much enhanced, and all were surprised to find that Marya had picked up almost all of Ed's ability at long-range psychic readings—a fact that was to prove very useful in the upcoming war.

Elijah, due to the frequency and loudness of their nightly parties, had slowly taken over all of the rooms on their floor of the hotel, telling the proprietor that they were having a large family reunion and needed the extra rooms.

Maids and housekeepers were gently "pushed" mentally to not come on the floor until they were called for, which allowed the group to have their blood-sharing parties at all hours of the days and nights without fear of being overheard.

In fact, it was so private on their hotel floor that when the group came together for their brainstorming sessions, most of them decided to forgo dressing and just paraded around in nude or near-nude states. One drawback of this arrangement was that more than one such session degenerated into wild orgies when couples were aroused by the sight of their new lovers' naked bodies and took the appropriate action. This made for a happy, but somewhat disorganized "army."

Elijah was amazed to find that the constant blood-sharing and the sexual activities that were a natural side-effect of this was causing the members of the group to interrelate almost as if they were all full-fledged mates. The bond between Vampyre mates was extremely strong and intimate, and in all of his two hundred years of dealing with members of his race, Elijah had never seen the mate-to-mate bonding occur between nonmates before.

He was delighted at the happening, for it caused the group to act and interact almost as if it were one giant organism instead of nine separate beings.

On the first morning of the second week after John and Marya's arrival, Elijah called a breakfast meeting in his suite. Once everyone was seated and had plates of food on their laps, he addressed the group.

"Team, it's time we decided on a plan of attack. Do we start at the top with the most important members of Thantos's group and try to eliminate as many of them as we can before they realize they are under attack, or do we start at the bottom and work our way up the chain of command?"

"Both plans have their advantages and their disadvantages," Ed said, slipping into the conversation smoothly. "If we start at the top, there are a lot of very important people in Washington who are suddenly going to be AWOL. It will be hard to keep this quiet for any length of time, since the press keeps a close eye on the comings and goings of Washington royalty and will surely notice if any of the major players suddenly disappears."

"But, if we start at the bottom, the higher ups who wield the most power and are the most dangerous to us will be forewarned of our intentions and will be able to counterattack before we're ready for them," Shooter said, playing the devil's advocate.

Marya cleared her throat, "Uh, may a relative newcomer to this army be allowed to speak?"

Elijah grinned and waved his hand. "Newcomer or not, you've got an equal vote and an equal voice in this man's army, Marya. Go ahead."

"Well, I've been trying out this new long-distance psychic stuff that I must have gotten from Ed, and I've found something strange that I think we should talk about."

"What's that, sweetie?" Sam asked. She and TJ and Kim had taken Marya into their hearts like a long-lost sister and the women were remarkably close friends.

"I think there's a lot more division in the ranks than Thantos suspects. I've found several minds that are actively opposed to what's going on, but that are too afraid to act on their own to do anything about it, and even more who really don't give much of a shit one way or the other—who're just going along with the flow, so to speak."

"Actually, that's not all that surprising, Marya dear," Elijah said. "Even among Vampyres that have been members of our race for many years there is a sharp divergence of opinion about not only taking over control from the Normals but even about the use of a vaccine to stop the hunger. I'm not at all surprised to learn that of the newcomers to our race, many don't want to see the end of our world as we know it."

"But, Elijah, the bigger point you're missing is that this is very good news for us," Sam said, a thoughtful expression on her face.

"How so, Sam?" he asked.

"A real lack of conviction among Thantos's converts means that we don't have to kill everyone in his group. All we have to do is ferret out the true believers and fanatics and make sure we get them first." She shrugged her shoulders. "Once Thantos is no longer around to foment hate and discontent with their status as Vampyres, the fellow-travelers so to speak will just go on about their business and forget all about this revolution stuff."

"Sure," Matt said in agreement, "And once we cut off the head of this beast, the body will die a natural death."

"But we'll still be faced with a whole bunch of new Vampyres who are suddenly without any leadership whatsoever," Kim said. "Suppose they start running amok in Washington, killing and slaughtering Normals once the hunger hits and bring the authorities' or media's attention to the presence of our race."

"That's right, Elijah," John said. "Up until now, Thantos and his cell leaders have been keeping the new converts placated by plying them with blood bank blood. Once he's gone and they start having to fend for themselves, there's no telling how much damage they could do."

Elijah nodded slowly. "Good point, Kim and Johnny. I can see that we'll definitely need to do some remedial education on the newcomers to our race once we've eliminated Thantos and his lieutenants. In fact, one of our first priorities will be to try and get them onto our new vaccine."

"Have you been able to identify any of these doubting Thomas's?" John asked Marya.

"Only one. She has a remarkable psychic power, especially for one so young. The others' psychic abilities are weak and too vague for me to recognize their identities for sure."

"Who's the one you recognize?" Elijah asked.

"Allison Burton, the daughter of the vice president of the United States."

"The daughter of the VP is always guarded by secret service agents isn't she?" Matt asked.

Shooter nodded. "Yep, and that's gonna make her real hard to get close to."

TJ laughed and draped her arm around Marya's shoulders. "With Marya's new abilities, maybe we won't have to get too close after all."

"Wait a minute," Matt said, "If Marya can get these readings, why didn't Ed pick up on them?"

" 'Cause he never met any of the subjects, Matt," Sam said, patting him on the shoulder like he was mentally incompetent. "It's only because Marya and John were members of the group that she's able to track their thoughts from a distance."

"Oh, yeah, I forgot," he said, blushing.

"Don't worry about it, Matt," Ed said, grinning. "Most of us are having trouble keeping track of our new abilities and just what we're capable of, let alone keeping track of what the others in our group can do."

"So, what now?" Shooter asked. He turned to look at Marya. "Do you think you can get into this girl's mind and influence it from a distance as well as you can read it?"

"I think I'll do better if I isolate myself and get as far away from all of your psychic influences as I can." She glanced at John, who was sitting naked next to her and grinned. "Those thoughts and the physical presence of some of us tend to be distracting." As the group all laughed, she continued, "I'll get as close to Allison's school as possible and try to get into her mind when they pick her up this afternoon. Then, if I'm successful, I'll follow at a distance until she and I can figure out how to meet in person."

"That's a good plan," Elijah said, "but please be careful,

Marya. Security is bound to be tight around her and we can't afford to lose you."

"That's right, dear," John said. "And remember, Thantos has already converted some of the Secret Service agents so they may be able to pick up your thoughts if you're not very, very careful."

Marya nodded and squeezed his hand. "Don't worry, sweetheart. I'll be as quiet as a mouse on cotton when I slip into her mind."

"So, there's nothing we can do until this afternoon, then?" Shooter asked.

"No, Shooter," Elijah answered. "Why?"

Shooter shrugged. "I thought as long as there's nothing else to do, we might as well all go back to bed for a while."

"Go back to whose bed, dear?" TJ asked, smiling at him.

"We could always draw straws," he answered, getting a laugh from everyone.

It was a little after three-thirty that afternoon when the private school Allison Burton attended let out for the day. Marya had thought it would be easy to find the young woman, just go to the biggest limo around and get close to it. Problem was, there were dozens of large, black limos lining the street in front of the school, what with it being the toniest private school in the area.

Another problem was that she'd met Allison in some of the meetings, or at least had attended the same meetings, but she couldn't for the life of her remember what the young person looked like. In fact, to one of Marya's age, just about all teenagers looked alike.

She thought about trying to get into the minds of the drivers of the limos that lined the street, but John's warning about the possibly transformed Secret Service agents made her decide to be cautious.

As the crowd of young girls and boys streamed out of the building, Marya decided to take a chance: she beamed out with her mind—Allison Burton!

One girl, wearing a short skirt, white shirt, and sweater draped over her shoulders shook her head and stopped, her hand to her ear as she glanced around the street in front of the school.

"Gotcha," Marya thought to herself, finally recognizing the girl from when she'd met her before. She now directed a more subtle thought directly at the young woman: *Allison, we have to meet. Is it safe for me to approach you?*

Allison's reply was suspicious as the young woman looked back and forth, trying to see who was invading her mind. *Why, what do you want with me?*

Marya got the distinct impression that Allison was afraid she was being targeted by one of Thantos's goons because of her doubts about his plan. Marya immediately began to reassure her mentally: *Relax, young one, I'm on your side, and so are some others you need to know about. Let us meet and I'll open my mind to you so you can tell I'm telling the truth.*

Marya could see Allison visibly relax at her reassuring mental images. *Okay, follow me to my limo and get in after me.*

What about your Secret Service driver?

Marya sensed a chuckle. *Don't worry. If you're not one of them, you have nothing to fear.*

Gutsy girl, Marya thought. She moved out of the shadow of an oak tree she'd been hiding behind and fell into step behind Allison. About half a block down the street, Allison got into the right rear seat of a black limousine, and Marya walked around and entered the left rear door.

She found herself staring down the barrel of a .38 snub-nosed revolver, pointed at her over the seat by a very tough looking female agent.

"Who the fuck are you?" Michelle asked.

"Yes," Allison echoed, "who exactly are you?"

Marya grinned. "You should know that pistols are of no use against one like us," she said, deliberately including the agent and Allison in her comment, since she realized immediately that the agent was also of the Vampyre race.

She turned to Allison and let her mind open completely to the young woman.

Allison's eyes narrowed as she concentrated and entered Marya's mind, exploring every part of it. After a couple of moments, Allison leaned back in her seat and grinned. "It's all right, Michelle. We've finally found the allies we've been looking for."

Chapter 37

Since Russell Cain had other agents loyal to him watching Allison and Jonathon Burton's house, it was decided that it would be too risky for Marya to go to Allison's house, so Michelle called her watch commander and told him that Allison wanted to go shopping and that they would be late getting home.

"Oh, and we need to go by and pick up Bitsy McCormack," Allison said, pulling out her cell phone and dialing without waiting for Marya's okay.

Marya, who with her new expanded mental abilities had no need for cell phones, just beamed a thought at John that she was bringing home company to their hotel and for everyone to get dressed lest they shock the young women.

When they were all finally together in Elijah's suite, extra chairs having been brought in, Michelle sat stiffly on the edge of the group, her hand resting on her purse near her .38 out of habit more than with the thought that it would do her any good if her hosts became hostile.

Sam leaned over and whispered, "You have no need to fear us. We really are on your side."

Michelle was startled that she'd been so easy to read, but did her best not to show it. She was still getting used to this psychic stuff and so didn't realize how strange it was that another could read her mind without her permission so easily.

Elijah had been elected to act as their spokesperson and he stood in front of the group and said, "Hello Allison, Bitsy, and Michelle." He grinned when they nodded their hellos.

He spread his arms, "Here you see before you what is euphemistically called, 'Elijah's army,' and we are here with one purpose in mind and only one—to defeat Theo Thantos and his minions in their attempt to take over the government of our country."

Michelle glanced around at the rather ordinary appearing group and couldn't help snorting a short laugh.

"Ah, I see we have a disbeliever in our midst," Elijah said, though not unkindly.

Michelle shrugged. "I guess so. You see, guys, I know for a fact that Thantos has dozens of new converts, if not hundreds by now. And you're going to go after him with . . . what . . . ten or twelve people?"

"Oh, but you see, Michelle," Elijah said, still with a kind smile on his face, "we are not just people. In fact, we are not even just Vampyres like yourself and your young friends here—we are something new in the universe . . . something special."

"Oh, well pardon me, mister, but you don't look all that special to me," Michelle said, her voice heavy with sarcasm and disbelief.

Elijah waved a dismissive hand. "Oh, I have no doubt that we'll be able to prove it to you shortly, but for now we need to know just how many are there like you in Thantos's group? How many of his followers actively oppose his plans?"

Allison spoke up, "Not enough to do us any good, Elijah.

For the past couple of weeks we've been actively reading everyone we come in contact with to see where their feelings lie." She shrugged. "Most of the ones who are not fanatical about the idea are just . . . ambivalent is the best word I can come up with. They just don't seem to care a whole lot one way or the other, and they certainly aren't against the plan enough to put their lives in danger to help us stop it."

Michelle nodded. "Yeah, but you have to remember, a lot of these people have just been converted against their wills so they have a lot to deal with just being what we've all just become." Crimson tears formed in her eyes and she angrily wiped them away. "Some of us are having a little more trouble dealing with the . . . changes than others are," she finished.

She glanced around at the group. "No offense, you guys, but I so hate what they've made of me and what I'm going to have to do to survive, that I've been thinking of trying to find some way to kill myself rather than have to survive by killing innocent people."

TJ moved to sit next to her and put her arm around Michelle's shoulders. "I know, dear," she whispered, "I felt the same way at first. But, I promise you, it does get easier with time, especially if you go on the vaccine Elijah invented."

"Hey," Bitsy chimed in, "I don't know about all that killing other people to survive shit—as for me, I think it's kind'a cool. But my old man, who wasn't all that good to begin with, has turned into a real bastard since his transformation. He's always hitting on me and my friends, and all he can think about is the power he's gonna have once Thantos has taken over the government." She shook her head. "If you think he's gonna be easy to get rid of, then you don't know old Black Jack," she said morosely.

"And your father would be General McCormack, the chairman of the Joint Chiefs of Staff?" Elijah asked.

"Yeah."

Elijah nodded, thinking hard. "Who else among the followers do you think are the most committed to seeing Thantos succeed?" he asked the trio in front of him.

After a few moments of whispered consultation, Allison spoke up. "There are several, but the ones with the most power and ability to help him are General Blackmon Taylor of US-AMRIID; Brendan Fraser, head of the National Security Council and right hand man to the president; Russell Cain, head of the capitol Secret Service detail; and, of course Bitsy's father, General McCormack."

"Those are the heavy hitters in government," Michelle added, "but there's also his core group of supporters from various business and media interests that helped get him started. He's made them what he calls his cell leaders, and I can give you a list of their names and the businesses they control." She took a clipboard from Shooter and began to write on it.

"What about your father, Allison?" Elijah asked. "Is he committed to this scheme?"

She shook her head. "No. He's as much against it as we are," she said, glancing at Bitsy and Michelle. "It's just that it's harder for him to act since Russell Cain has him watched at all times by some agents loyal to Cain."

Michelle looked up and handed the clipboard to Elijah. He read it briefly and then he looked around. "From what I can see, we've got about"—he glanced down again and then back up—"ten or fifteen heavy players at the most."

Allison nodded. "That's about right, if you mean the most fanatical of his followers. There are others, but if Thantos is eliminated, they'll probably just go away." She snorted. "None of the others will have the balls to try and do anything on their own, especially if they see us take Thantos down."

"So," Elijah said, thoughtfully, "if we could manage to get these people all together at one time and we hit them with everything we have, we might be able to stop this with one decisive action."

Michelle chuckled grimly. "If you manage to kill them before they kill us, you mean."

Allison held up her hand, like a student asking a teacher's permission to speak. "Yes, Allison?" Elijah said.

"I think I know a way to get them all together in one place."

"Oh?"

"Yeah."

"Well, tell us, girl," Shooter said impatiently.

"Just listen to this," Allison said, and she began to outline her plan.

When she finished, Elijah shook his head and grinned. "Out of the mouths of babes . . ." he quoted, causing Allison to blush a deep crimson.

Theo Thantos put down his wineglass and rolled on his side, his hand moving to caress Christina's breast while he moved his head down to nuzzle her neck.

When the phone rang, he cursed and raised his head up. Christina tried to pull it back down. "Just ignore it, darling, don't stop now," she said, her voice husky with desire.

He lowered his head, but the phone kept up its insistent ringing.

"Damn! I can't concentrate with that racket going on," he said. "I'll get rid of whoever it is and then we can begin where we left off."

He angrily snatched up the phone and barked, "This had better be important!"

Jonathon Burton was on the line. "Theo, this is Jonathon. We have to talk."

"Can't it wait?" Thantos replied, smiling at the thought that here he was with the vice president of the United States begging for his attention. He glanced at Christina lying next to him as she began to start without him, easing her hand down between her legs and licking her lips as she stared at him. "I'm right in the middle of something," Thantos added, his eyes on Christina's busy hand.

"No, it can't wait, Theo, not unless you want to see all we've worked for go down the drain."

That got Thantos's attention. He sat up in bed and gave the vice president his full attention. "What do you mean, Jonathon?"

"I have just learned that there's been a major leak of our plans," Burton said. "I have a source at the *New York Times* that informed me he knew all about our plan of a government coup. He wanted to get a quote from me before they went to press with the accusations."

"What?" Thantos exploded. "Are you sure? Maybe this reporter was just guessing, maybe taking some rumors and running a bluff on you with them?"

"Yeah, I'm sure. The son of a bitch named names and places and dates—way too precise to be just rumors. Hell, the bastard knows almost as much as I do, and he's planning to go to press with it in the morning unless we do something to stop him."

Thantos thought rapidly. "How much time can you get me—can you get him to wait by promising to give him an exclusive or something?"

"I can maybe get him to wait one more day if I promise to confirm the details of his story, but I think we need to have an emergency meeting of all of the cell leaders to decide how to carry on from here."

"No, we don't need to get them involved, Jonathon," Thantos said, scarlet beads of sweat forming on his forehead. He was afraid some of the cell leaders would bail if they thought they were about to be put on the front page of the fucking *New York Times!* "All we need to do is send someone to take care of this reporter before he can spoil our plans," he said, wanting to rip the bastard's throat out himself.

"It's not that simple, Theo," Burton said, his voice edgy and seemingly on the verge of panic. "For one thing, I don't know who's been giving him his information, so I don't know how many others are involved, but from the details he knows, it's got to be one of the inner circle who's turned traitor. We also don't know who he's shared his facts with, so killing him might give them the proof they need that he was on to something. I suggest we get everyone together and find out just who the traitor is before it's too late, that way we can possibly force them to retract their story and tell the reporter they were mistaken. If his principal informer backs down, it might make him pull the story for good."

"You might be right," Thantos said, mentally going over in his mind who the weak link might be.

"I'll tell you what," Burton said, "You call every one of the cell leaders and tell them there is an emergency meeting of our task force tonight at the Rejuvenatrix Spa, but don't tell them why. When we've got them all together, you should be able to use your psychic abilities to ferret out the informer and find out who else might know about us. When we know that, it'll be a simple matter to find all of them and eliminate them before they can betray us."

"You're right, Jonathon," Thantos said, thinking the man knew his way around a conspiracy. Guess that's how he got to be vice president in the first place. "I'll get right on it and we'll plan to meet at the spa at midnight in the main auditorium. Once I've got everyone together, I'll go person to person and have them open their minds to me. If anyone refuses, it'll be a confession of guilt."

"That's a great idea," Jonathon said, as if the entire plan had been Thantos's from the start. After a short pause, he added, "Oh, and Theo."

"Yeah?"

"No one but the major hitters need to be called. We don't want the underlings to think we can't control things, do we?" He gave a low chuckle, "Or someone else might get the idea he could cross you and get away with it."

"No, of course not. You're right, only the original task

force members and the important government players will be summoned."

"Good, and Theo, let me know if anyone in the government gives you any static about attending tonight and I'll lower the hammer on them."

"Thanks, Jonathon, and thanks for calling," Theo said and he hung up.

"What is it, baby," Christina said, reaching up to try and pull him back down onto her.

He snarled and grabbed her wrist. "Go wash your hand and get dressed. We've got work to do."

Chapter 38

It was half an hour past midnight before Theo Thantos had everyone gathered together in the main auditorium of the Rejuvenatrix Spa.

He jumped up on the stage at the front of the hall and began to pace back and forth as he talked. "I've called you all here because we have an emergency." He stopped and stared out over the audience. "There is a traitor among us!" he shouted, glaring out at the people sitting in front of him. He raised his hand and pointed at the audience. "And tonight we're going to find out who it is and make him or her wish they'd never been born!"

Before anyone could respond, a voice called from the side of the stage, "I'm afraid that's not exactly true," John Ashby said as he strolled onto the stage, a long *katana* resting on his shoulder. He smiled at Thantos's openmouthed amazement and he looked out at the people sitting there, watching the drama unfold as if it were a play staged for their amusement. "There is not a traitor among you," Ashby called, his voice rising and his face becoming flushed with emotion. "You are *all* traitors," he finished.

As the people in the audience stirred and looked from one

to another, some with embarrassment, others with anger, he gave a slight shrug, "And for that crime against your country, you all must die!"

"Bastard!" Thantos screamed and he started to change into his Vampyre form even as he leapt across the stage at John with his arms extended and his fingers drawn into claws.

John didn't even bother to change; he just whirled around, swinging the *katana* with both his hands on the hilt like a baseball bat. The razor sharp blade sliced through Thantos's midsection while he was still in midair, cutting him almost in half.

He screamed as he fell to the floor of the stage, his entrails steaming in the cool night air as they exploded from his body to writhe and coil on the floor like a nest of snakes that had been disturbed.

John ignored the shouts and screams from the people in the auditorium as he strolled over to where Thantos lay with his arms trying to hold his guts in his body. Thantos was whimpering and groaning in pain as he futilely tried to stuff his intestines back into his abdomen.

John stared down at him without pity and shook his head. He looked up and glanced at the audience, where the people were scrambling and stumbling and fighting as they clawed at each other trying to get to the exits and escape this madman up on the stage.

"So goes all traitors," John yelled, and he knelt and grabbed Thantos's hair in his left hand and pulled his head up. With one quick motion, he cut the monster's head off and held it aloft. Thantos's eyes moved back and forth over the crowd and his mouth opened and closed, but no sound escaped from his lips.

At this signal, Elijah's Army streamed in from the side doors, *katanas,* pistols, and shotguns in their hands. The members of the crowd who'd managed to get out of their seats drew back in the face of this group of Vampyres, whose shotguns and pistols exploded again and again in a cacophony of sound as they proceeded to cut the audience members to shreds.

Brahma Parvsh grabbed his mate, Christabel Chordewa, and held her in front of him as he tried to change into his Vampyre form. TJ cut Christabel almost in half with a point-blank shot from her shotgun. When her body hit the floor, TJ dropped the shotgun and whirled around and swung her *katana* in a whistling arc through Brahma's neck. His head toppled off his body and landed on Christabel's lap, where the blood from her wounds slowly covered it.

Augustine Calmet pushed Gabrielle de Lavnay out of his way when she moved too slowly up the aisle, trampling her underfoot as he scrambled toward the stage, hoping to jump up there and exit the back door.

Shooter leveled his Desert Eagle 50 caliber pistol and squeezed the trigger. The Glaser Safety Slug entered the base of Augustine's skull and exploded, turning his head into a fine, red mist that hovered foglike over the stump of his neck for a few seconds before the body collapsed into a dead heap.

Russell Cain jerked out his Glock 9 mm and managed to get several shots off as he changed into his Vampyre body. The 9 mm slugs hit Sam in the gut and doubled her over, clouding her eyes with pain.

Cain, his change complete now, rushed over to her and grabbed her head in both his claws and strained, trying to tear it off her neck.

Sam straightened and grinned at his feeble efforts. She grabbed his wrists in her hands and with her new strength, bent them back until they snapped like dry twigs under a boot. Cain screamed in pain and dropped to his knees. Sam then took her short sword and lopped his head off with one short stroke.

Christina, who'd been sitting in the front row, leapt up on stage and tried to run out the back door, jumping over her mate's dead body without a backward look. As she loped past John, already changing into her Vampyre form, she came upon a female Vampyre with brilliant red hair waiting in front of the exit as if she knew Christina would try and run away.

Marya stood with her *katana* in her hands, grinning around long, dripping fangs as Christina slid to a stop in front of her.

"Let me go, Marya, and you'll never see or hear from me again . . . please don't kill me," Christina begged. "It was all Theo's idea to kill you. I had nothing to do with it."

Marya laughed low in her throat. "You're not only a coward, but you're a lying coward," she said mockingly.

She took her time and moved the sword up and back as she readied it for the killing blow. She wanted Christina to see it coming.

"Bitch!" Christina screamed as Marya's blade whistled toward her in the semidarkness. Her scream was cut short by the cold steel of Marya's *katana* slicing through her neck.

Marya knelt and picked up Christina's head while there was still the light of consciousness in her eyes. "You should be more careful who you call bitch, dear," she said sweetly.

As the eyes dulled in death, Marya sat the head on its body's chest and sighed. She was going to miss Christina, but not much.

She straightened up and wrinkled her nose at the smell of cordite and gunpowder and the sound of screaming coming from the auditorium, wondering if they were doing the right thing. Did so many of her race have to die this night?

Then, she saw John approaching her with a smile on his face and she knew they were doing exactly the right thing, for both the Vampyre race and for the Normals.

Maybe someday, as more and more of the Vampyre race began to use Elijah's vaccine, the two races could come together and live in harmony, one with the other.

But for now, she thought as John put his arms around her and walked her out into the crisp, clear night air away from the smell of blood and death, this would have to do.

Epilogue

It was almost dawn before Elijah and his friends were done carrying bodies from the spa to the crematorium. Dark black smoke billowed from the ovens and their doors were red hot and glowing from the unaccustomed business of the night.

The spa had been torched to conceal evidence of the massive amount of blood spilled there, but no bodies were left inside to raise questions about why their heads were missing.

Elijah and his friends, aided a great deal by the redoubtable Allison, began a clinic working with the recently converted Vampyres who were left behind after Thantos was killed.

They were all trained in the use of Elijah's vaccine so they wouldn't be at the mercy of their hunger, and they were given instruction in the history of their new race. Most accepted the vaccine gratefully, but those who elected to continue to hunt for their prey, as was their right, were instructed in the necessity of hiding their kills and keeping the existence of the Vampyre race a secret from the Normals.

Two weeks after the slaughter at the spa, Elijah and his friends met for the last time in Washington.

"There was surprisingly little speculation in the Washington press about the disappearance of so many of its more prominent citizens," Vice President Burton said. "I would have expected more coverage."

Elijah grinned. "Psychic ability has its uses, Jonathon," he said, "not the least of which is erasing curiosity before it becomes bothersome."

Burton laughed and put his arms about Allison and Bitsy. Allison's friend was living with them now that her dad was gone.

Bitsy smiled, most of the bitterness that had characterized her personality gone, as if it had left with her dad, never to return.

Matt held up a thick sheaf of papers. "Orders for the vaccine are pouring in faster than we can process them, Elijah. I think this is going to have a major impact on our race."

Elijah nodded. "Vampyres are not all that different from Normals, in some ways," he said. "Given a choice, both races will usually do the right thing."

He looked around at the group of people that over the past months had become as close to him as family and he held a glass of white wine aloft. "To Elijah's Army, a job well done, teammates!"

The group all drank to the toast.

And then, Shooter asked a question. "Elijah, now that we know your theory about blood sharing is correct and that it does vastly improve our abilities, are you going to share the secret with the rest of the Vampyre race?"

Elijah pursed his lips. "Let me ask you a question, Shooter."

"Okay."

"Would you put a loaded pistol in the hands of an infant?"

Shooter looked offended. "Of course not."

Elijah shrugged. "Neither would I, Shooter, neither would I."